DEALING WITH THE VISCOUNT

IMPROPER WIVES FOR PROPER LORDS #1

CLAIR BRETT

This is a work of fiction. Names, characters, places and incidents are products of the author's imagination or are used fictitiously and are not to be construed as real. Any resemblance to actual events, locales, organizations or persons, living or dead, is entirely coincidental.

CB publications

86 Riverside Ave.

Lisbon, NH 03585

Editor: Frankie Sutton

Cover design: Emma Alisyn, Harpy Edits

Author photo: Susan Ray

ISBN: Ebook: 978-0-9983317-0-6

Print: 978-0-9983317-1-3

www.clairbrett.com

This book is dedicated to my mother, Eleanor Blake and daughters Blake and Casey. Thank you mom for holding me to a higher standard than I ever held myself, and making me believe that with hard work I could do anything I wanted. To Blake and Casey thank you for making me want to be a better person every day of my life and also thank you for allowing me to be your mom it has been a great honor. It hasn't always been easy, but nothing worth obtaining should be.

This book and all of my heroines are dedicated to the strong young women like my daughters, to show them that strength will get them where they are going and also, to show them the kind of hero they should all be striving for!

CHAPTER 1

"**W**hy, might I ask, am I sitting dripping wet in this cavern you call a library, when I should be back in London, rewriting my speech to Parliament about the tax on wheat?" Devon looked, he was sure, as bedraggled as he felt. He did not care to be in Scotland any time during the year, but when Parliament was in session was an especially poor time.

Glaring at his long-time friend, he waited for an answer. "Well?" he demanded. The note Devon, Lord Renwick, received, was cryptic at best, and he had expected to find his oldest friend on his deathbed.

"I was asking myself the same thing," quipped Lord Breakerton. "I should think a proper guest would retire and make themselves more presentable before being availed to their host." God, he's enjoying this, thought Renwick. "As for being here instead of London, I sent you a note." His friend waved a hand toward the desk in a haphazard manner.

"A proper guest would no doubt be pleased about being here all together, so let us just assume I am not a proper guest," Renwick bit out, dripping from the drenching rain of the Scottish night. Devon hated Scotland and all it took from him on a good day, not to mention the memories his trek into the hills conjured. Memories he thought buried. The fire burned, illuminating the hearth. Even in the warmer months, a Scottish castle was cold and drafty. Still in his greatcoat, he turned to warm his thighs and legs, which were as wet as everything else on his person. "Why am I here, and do not refer to the cryptic mess you called a note? It did nothing, but cause me to fear for your sanity."

Clive smiled. The library, if one could call it that, looked at one time to be the great hall. It now stood with shelves from floor to ceiling. Not all the shelves were full, giving it the feel of a work in progress. Overall, the atmosphere was comfortable which strangely enough, fit his libertine, rakehell friend.

"Why don't you take those wet things off? We need to talk."

Devon did as he was bid. All the while, a knot began to tie itself in his stomach. Clive, though perfectly able to have serious discord, avoided it whenever possible. Devon's mind raced, listing all that could be wrong. First in his mind was illness, second, money. The latter was discarded immediately. Clive might play the ne'er-do-well, but Devon knew the head for business this man had, not to mention his feelings of responsibility. No, it must be illness.

Devon sat again, but this time in the opposite chair facing Clive. His friend looked grim as he made his way with a brandy for Devon. This was all Devon had left. This one man. Once he was gone, Devon would truly be alone. The only other one, Flick, he could not claim in society's circles.

"What do you know of your wife's death?" The question, abrupt as cannon fire, took Devon by surprise. A long, dormant pain tightened his chest. Damn, he hated Scotland.

"She died. What more do I need to know?" Devon's answer was clipped and bitter.

"How?" Clive pierced Devon with determined eyes.

"Highwaymen. Why are we having this discussion? You know I prefer--"

"Did you see her body?"

"No!" Devon spat out with disgust "I saw her father's body. Again, tell me why, before I leave the way I came." Devon's voice had risen by degrees to match his anger. Swallowing what was left of his brandy, Devon stalked to the mantel. This fortnight had already been hell and he had no care to continue the descent. He didn't think of Ella at all, because if he did, it would remind him of how close he had come to falling into a trap from which his father never was freed. Devon also didn't care to relive the pain of knowing her light would never shine on the world. When she left, Devon had been furious, but just knowing she was still alive would have been a comfort. Finding out she was dead and there was no going back, well that was almost too much for him to bear at the time.

With a calm that grated on Devon's nerves, Clive went on, breaking the silence. "I was out of town when you finally got married, if you will. I never knew any of the particulars of the agreement the two of you struck, save for your first meeting. I was not even present at the ceremony, though I heard it was an elegant affair."

"Yes, it was," Devon agreed, but grudgingly. He tried every day not to think about the one lapse in his otherwise impeccable judgment. One slip and where did it get a man? One would think one would be allotted one mistake in a lifetime. "It was elegant and refined, just as the Ton expected. It looked like a love match." Devon's voice came out as hollow and emotionless. He spoke as though it were the most recent balloon ascension in the park. As if, he was speaking of leaving his mistress. A business deal done, finished. After all, that was what it was. "The agreement was as you knew. We would marry. I would take from her dowry, what her father owed me. Then after a determined amount of time, she would go to Scotland to visit relatives, and once there, she would send word of her death and be out of my life forever." Now, four years later, the deal seemed very foolish. Fleetingly, Devon wondered if they might have made a go of it had she not left unexpectedly before their agreed upon date.

"How did the two of you get on? Were you amicable?"

"Clive, you are my most trusted friend. Do you not think if I were want of discussing this with someone, I would have come to you before now? You were there from the inception. You know well that it was a business agreement. Her idea. I wanted no wife. It was foisted upon us both. Because of her, I was able to fulfill the strictures of my father's will, marry before I was five and twenty and gain his personal fortune. She was able to get out from under the tyranny of her father and all his gambling debts, not to mention, no longer live under the fear of being thrown into debtor's prison with him, her only guardian." It was true that he had not wanted a wife, not even considering his father's will. That is where his good sense failed him. He, now a widower, was left to deal with the memory of a woman he never wanted to know. He couldn't help but think how his own adult life seemed to be mirroring his father's.

"Well, what I am really asking is-- well, did you actually consummate?" Stunned silence met this question. The two men stared off. Devon refused to give away any sign of the emotion boiling over within him, but at the same time, he let his friend know he had crossed the line.

Devon looked into his empty snifter. "You know, I came all this way because I feared you had taken ill. I never suspected dementia was the illness."

Either Clive did not hear, or he did not care to jump at the barb. Instead, he pressed on mercilessly. "I will take that as a yes. Did you talk about children?"

Devon must have looked befuddled, because his interrogator rephrased the question. As if, it was not bad enough the first time. "Did you and Ella discuss what would happen if she became with child, Devon?"

"I will be in my room. Please have your servants rouse me at first light. I would like to gather my staff at the inn we were forced to take shelter in and have them back on the road to England by noon." He turned, heading for the door. The huge empty room closed in around him. His inner being screamed for fresh air. Colors blurred the light, which seemed to temporarily dim. The door was his beacon. In the din, Devon thought he could hear Clive calling him back. The door was more important. Just as his hand grabbed for the knob, his hearing came rushing back in a relentless roar.

"Your wife is alive and I believe you are a father. Did you hear me, Devon? Your wife is alive. You are a father, old man. I swear it."

For a stunned moment, Devon's feet froze, unable to move. His breath came in grunt-like gasps. Amazed he could find his voice, he muttered, "That's impossible." Then he left.

Once in his room, Devon tugged off the wet clothes and hung them by the fire. On the bed was a robe laid out, waiting, and on the table by the fire was a large decanter of brandy with one glass. Clive must have thought it a kindness. Devon didn't particularly care for his friend's good hospitality at present, but he wasn't about to let the brandy go to waste. Slumping in the chair naked, forgoing the robe for the time being, he grabbed the decanter and poured a generous amount into the glass.

How long he watched the flames dance in the hearth, he wasn't sure, but the candles had burned down quite a bit. Of all the reasons for being called, his wife being alive and he being a father, were not on his list. Looking at the brandy still sitting patiently in the glass, he took a long drink. Was it possible? Could she be alive? His whole body seemed to cry out at the thought. He thought back to the day he got the news of her death.

Upon her departure, Devon had taken to sulking, which was not like him, but he had also decided their arrangement was working out better than he expected and he had been toying with the idea of suggesting that she stay. Unfortunately, she left before he could discuss it with her. Needless to say, his temper was in rare form and well fed by his stewing. When the messenger was announced, he received him, along with a letter from the local magistrate expressing his condolences for the loss of his beloved wife. Devon's temper was pricked even more, knowing that she did follow through with their agreement and obviously had no emotions engaged during their short arrangement. It wasn't, however, enough to prepare him for the courier's next statement.

Looking deeply into the fire, the scene replayed within the dancing flames:

"Thank you, sir. I appreciate your speed in getting word to me. Please, go to the kitchen and they will see that you are fed well and given at least one meal for your travel back." Setting the letter aside, Devon bent to the correspondence he dearly needed to attend to, but knew it was a useless employment. How was she able to leave without having any feelings for him? The courier's voice gave him a start, being that he had been dismissed.

"Pardon, My Lord, but..."

"What man? Spit it out." Devon was in no mood to deal with drivel.

"Well, My Lord, where you be wantin' me to leave the bodies?"

Cold dread seeped into his bones, replacing the petty hurt he had been nursing.

A coal snapped, drawing Devon back to his nearly dark room. He rubbed a hand over his face to dry his cheeks from the emotion of it. Dead, she was actually dead. He remembered that the next several hours went by in a numbness he had never experienced before. That is, until tonight. How could finding out that someone was dead, and then finding out he or she was alive cause a person to feel the same all-consuming numbness? It felt as if he were falling. His head swam with sensations more than memories, each one causing a roaring in his ears. Taking another drink, sniffing the strong crisp aroma of the now warmed brandy made him realize he was not dreaming.

Shivering, Devon remembered he never donned the robe left for him. He rose, adding a few sticks of wood to the now low burning fire and padded to the bed. He knew there was not much darkness left to him, but exhaustion and emotion pulled at his conscious self. Dropping into the huge bed and pulling the covers over his head, he hoped to let oblivion take him. Clive, no doubt, expected him to react badly, so he was not worried about his friend's wounded pride, but the question swirling around his very soul was. If his wife was alive, did she want to be found, and even more importantly, did he want to

6

find her? He let sleep take him, but he knew it would not be restorative, not this night.

Devon woke with a start, drenched in sweat and tangled in a knot of sheet and blanket. Where was he? It took him a long moment before he was able to order his thoughts enough to remember last night. Falling back onto the pillows that had not been thrown on the floor from his thrashing, he let out a frustrated sigh. He was in Scotland. The memory of his conversation with Clive rushed back. What was he to do? Nothing had come to him before he fell asleep early this morning, and unfortunately, he still had no ideas.

One thing he was certain of was the dream that had just awakened him. The same dream had haunted him for the past three years. Ella came to him, as she had that one night. She made love to his body, but the moment he tried to reach out to her, she was gone in a swirl of mist. It was a dream, which always left him aching, painful with physical need for her and another pain he didn't care to put a name to. The dream had been gone for some time. Devon assumed the absence of it proved he was well healed. "Now what, you fool?" he snapped. "Do you grab onto a far-fetched tale from a well-meaning friend and grasp the chance she might be alive? It is more likely Clive has finally fallen to the dregs of his wild life and begun seeing visions." Talking to himself was not proving productive, so Devon untangled the sheets from his long legs and swung them to the floor.

His plan would be simple. He would spend a few days with Clive and play out this fantasy of his. When Ella was nowhere to be found, then he would leave and head back to London. Clive's sister, Margaret, would need to be made aware of her brother's delusions, however. He would make a detour before London and stop at the country home. Margaret and her husband were currently in the country enjoying their newest child, or so the social pages said.

Devon padded across the room, donning the dressing robe left for him last night and pulled the bell. He would have a bath before he met Clive for breakfast, as the road dust from his journey was still evident, but the sooner he got this over with, the better.

The morning rose bright with no signs of rain. Once bathed and dressed, Devon made his way along the winding hallways and narrow staircase typical of ancient castles. Even with his questions about Clive's propensity for drama, he still found the idea of his long-time cohort thriving in such a setting hard to accept. Yet, last evening, Clive looked more content than he had for many years. Devon made his way past the great doors leading into the library and wended his way toward the sound of voices.

Once Devon emerged from the maze of stone, he found himself standing on a long stone terrace. Squinting from the glare of morning sun, Devon was able to see an outstanding garden, where even in spring the riot of color was awe-inspiring. A noise to his left drew his attention. Sitting at a small, but well-set table was Clive.

"Good morning, old chap. I was hoping you would sleep in a trifle more, but Charles informed me that he gave you assistance." Clive attempted to sound genial, but Devon noted the cautious tone in his voice.

"Yes, I hope you don't mind." Devon took the only other place set at the table and allowed a footman to fill his cup. "Since my valet is still holed up at the Inn, I was in need of his services."

"I have taken the liberty of sending a message to the Inn. I am sure the roads will be passable by later today, if the sun shines as bright for the rest of the day." Clive put down his newssheet and sat back watching Devon with concern clear for him to see. "I do want to apologize for last night. I had hoped to break the news in a better manner, but then, well, at any rate, I apologize."

"Thank you."

"For getting your servants or for apologizing?"

"Both, I suppose."

"You still don't believe me." Not a question, Clive sat looking at Devon with a strange mix of humor and sadness.

Just then, two footmen emerged with large trays laden with an assortment of breakfast meats, breads, cheese and fruit. The two men sat in silence drinking their coffee and enjoying the splendor of the gardens. Once the footmen filled both plates, leaving the remainder of the food on a nearby table, they left, and Clive continued.

"Do you think me cruel enough to toy with your obvious pain, or are you erring on the side of madness?"

Devon couldn't help but smile at his friend's close estimation of his thoughts. It spoke volumes about their closeness for so long.

"I had chosen madness. I've never known you to be cruel."

"Ah," Clive smiled and chuckled over his cup, "I can assure you my family has a history of many sins, but madness isn't one of them. With such a sad tendency to having female children, one would assume otherwise, I know," he joked, kidding about his over-abundance of sisters and female relatives. One trait Devon found intriguing since female relations were non-existent in his family.

"Well, you do realize the talk of late, with you fleeing to this barbaric wilderness and all. I have even heard your dear mama mention the term 'mental ailment' more than once when discussing your current state," Devon quipped while partaking in a well-stuffed piece of sausage. One thing was sure, he wouldn't starve while visiting.

"Yes, well any lack of wit can certainly be traced back to my dear mother, but--" Clive's expression turned solemn. "I know what I saw, man. Who could mistake Ella?"

Devon placed his fork on his plate and sat back. Emotions raw and exposed churned. Placing his elbows on the arms of the chair, he steepled his fingers in front of him. Ella, he had not used her name for four years. What he wanted to do was beat his friend bloody for bringing feelings he had well and buried back to the surface. Instead, he searched his friend's face, for what, he wasn't sure. After several tense moments of silence, Devon's heavy sigh broke through.

"Are you that certain? You did not spend so much time in London that year. The two of you met but a handful of times. Her beauty was evident, but no more so than any other English beauty. I am sure there are many women in Scotland who could rival her."

Clive sat with a calm expression on his face, too calm for Devon's liking, and listened to his friend dispute the possibility. "You said yourself you didn't look at her body. Isn't it possible it wasn't her?

Mayhap, they took on a passenger, or even a passerby who witnessed the shooting."

Raking a hand through his hair, Devon fought an uncontrollable urge to flee. Every muscle in his body was prone to take flight. Why was he having to relive this again? Why couldn't he be left alone? Through gritted teeth, Devon measured his words with care. This was his friend after all, and he didn't want to say or do something he would regret later.

"How might, I ask, would Ella have been spared?" He had thought of these things in the early days after the tragedy. The answer to this question was by far the most agonizing of all the possibilities he pondered. "There is only one reason a highwayman would choose not to kill a female hostage, if they have already disposed of all the others. I personally do not care to think on those possibilities."

Clive winced at Devon's implication, but remained still and smug. "I am fairly certain she was not kept as a concubine if that is what you are suggesting. I think the better possibility is that she was away from the carriage when it was taken upon. Is that not a possibility?"

Devon had to admit that scenario was one he preferred to consider during his darker days. He would sit in his warm, almost comforting study, thanks to Ella, drinking large quantities of brandy while thinking of ways she might still be alive. She never felt dead to him. When his father died, he felt a finality, but with Ella, it never came. He suspected it was because their agreement had left many loose ends.

"Fine, let's imagine for the moment that she was in the bushes at the time. How would she have ended up here? Isn't that a bit too much of a coincidence?" Devon surely didn't believe in fate.

"Actually, it is entirely possible. You see, Ella's father and I are connected through the Scottish line. I never mentioned it because it is such a weak connection it hardly garnishes merit, but it does exist. Ella, no doubt, was planning on reuniting with some of our poorer connections here in Scotland."

Devon sat in utter silence. It was true. If one wanted to look back far enough, most English families had familial ties and Devon could well understand why Clive would keep such a connection quiet, considering the Baronet's tendencies to gambling. If word were to have gotten into the rumor mill, Clive would have had every man and moneylender in greater London banging down his doors.

"Why not tell me?"

"I don't know. It never seemed like it needed to be mentioned. I also knew the reason for the marriage and didn't feel you would want the waters muddied with any extraneous information. You two had made it cut and dried." Clive relaxed back into his seat. Taking his cup, he motioned for the footman to refresh it.

"You're serious, aren't you? You truly think she is alive." Devon heard the astonishment in his own voice. Could he believe? Should he believe? Moreover, if it was true, where did that leave him? There was still the agreement. He would be breaking it by seeking her out. The bigger question was whether he wanted to see her again.

CHAPTER 2

The storm was over. Ella took a deep breath, breathing in the clean, crisp morning air, still heavy with the smell of rain. Last night's storm had been the worst since moving to Scotland four years ago, and that was saying something. To her surprise, the morning rose brisk, but not cold. She had the back door open wide due to the large brick ovens of the bakery stifling the room with heat. Ella shivered though for the hundredth time, wishing the air was the cause. She sighed again.

"Blasted storm," cursing, knowing that the storm was not the cause of her unease.

"What's that, missus?" Penny, the apprentice, asked with a grunt while kneading a batch of yeast dough. "Ye like me to close the door? Ye seem ta be chilled."

"Thank you, Penny, but I am fine." She wasn't, but how to explain escaped her. The storm itself had frightened her like no storm since becoming an adult. Her fear doubled due to the fact she had no one to comfort her. She was the one doing the comforting. Shaking her head at what she termed pure stupidity, Ella turned from the bright spring morning back to the dim workroom. Bread needed to be made. There was no time for woolgathering. No time to consider the last storm that scared her so much was a lifetime ago, when she was the one being consoled by her husband.

"Are ye sure you're well? Ye have been sullen all morn?" Penny's lilting voice soothed Ella's nerves, but only just.

"The storm had me up most of the night, until I decided to give in and start the ovens early. I'm tired, that is all." Ella punched a batch of yeast dough back at the large worktable with more force than necessary. The storm hadn't been what drove her from bed. She would have been able to drown it out with a well-placed pillow or two. No, what drove her from bed had followed her to the workroom.

Last night's storm punctuated the fact she was alone — and had wanted it that way, until now. Ella had made the choices that brought her here and was fine with that, even proud. If not for the recent blackmailing threats targeting her business and her family, she would still be content with her choices. She flopped the dough over and gave it another punch. Her recent concerns and the ferocity of last night's storm must have brought on her dreams.

Every attempt she made during the raging storm to calm her soul and sleep, he would be there. With every clap of thunder, she would get a glimpse of sun-kissed flesh. A brush of skin across her nipple. Soft lips on her neck. She had tried to bury her memories deep, her feelings too. If she allowed it, she could remember how it felt to have a champion, someone who cared.

"Oh, damn it all," muttered Ella as she quelled a shiver for the hundredth time. She needed to remind herself, she could count on the caring, which is why she left. She would not allow her own emotion to be engaged if she wasn't certain of his. Now, she wasn't sure which path was quicker to a broken heart.

"Missus," gasped a startled Penny now, standing at the oven turning the many loaves of bread. "Did ye drop it?" Her back was turned. Good thing. Perhaps Penny didn't see the blush rise to Ella's hairline from the sensual memories and remembered sensations flashing through her mind of another time.

"Sorry, I just... ah, banged my finger. I am fine." The answer seemed to be a sensible one. Now, what was a sensible answer to her recent case of nostalgia? Why after four years was she dreaming of her husband? It was not as if she had had extensive experience. If she were dreaming of a naked man, he would be the only one she had ever seen. There were many plausible reasons she decided. The recent rash of burglaries for a start. Or the newest Lord in a string trying to gain her favor. Perhaps, just when the wind started to bite, she was reminded of when she first arrived here and what drove her from London.

The two women worked in companionable silence the remainder of the morning. Ella was thankful. She always felt that a problem had to be dealt with in a practical manner, which meant thinking. After another hour, Penny broke the silence.

"Where is the wee bairn this morn? 'Tis not like her to lie abed?" The whole bakery smelled of sweet yeast. Ella was just finishing with scrubbing the workbench.

"The storm kept her awake as well. You seemed to be the only one sleeping fast last night," Ella pointed out with a smile. "I left the curtain pulled this morning so she might sleep in a bit." As if conjured by their topic, both looked up as Maddie clumsily made her way down the stairs still dressed in her nightdress, dragging a rag doll behind her. Every curl on top of her head seemed to dance with each step. Ella smiled, ruefully knowing that she did not get those curls from her. She had never, even as a child been able to hold a faint wave in her yellow hair. Having a daughter with raven hair as curly as hers was straight naturally caused some looks when they went about the countryside.

"Ah, here is the little lag-about now. Morning, lemon drop, hungry?" Ella grabbed a grumbling Maddie, sweeping her into her arms and nuzzling her neck until Maddie couldn't help but squeal with delight. Her still warm body from sleep felt solid and all that was good in Ella's life. The one thing she never thought she would have and the one thing she would die for was her daughter. She squeezed the child a little harder for good measure.

"Mama, stop. Stop Mama! Not awake," Maddie gurgled through the laughter. Ella allowed her to wiggle out of the hug and scramble into a chair at the end of the workbench. Penny placed a bowl of porridge and a piece of fresh hot bread drizzled with honey in front of her. Meanwhile, Ella ladled a cup of milk.

She managed to get Maddie dressed with only a minimum of difficulty. Her curls were another story, but once done, Maddie settled herself in the front of the bakery at a small table with her doll and some other trinkets. Such a good child, Ella thought as she turned to head back into the kitchen to make some gingerbread. The bread was almost sold out. The remainder of the morning had gone smoothly. No wayward thoughts at all, Ella realized, until now. Another shiver slid down her body. "Stupid woman!" She chastised because even if she wanted to go back, she would be going back on an agreement. One that was made before her feelings were in jeopardy of being engaged. Just then, the bell on the shop door tinkled.

Ella grabbed a tray full of hot scones to offer her new customers. Business was always better when people knew what they were buying. Tray in hand, she put on her brightest smile and made her way into the brightness of the bakery front to greet her customers.

The morning had started out just passably well, Devon thought, as they hitched their horses and made their way around the ruts and puddles to the bakery. The sun shone bright and most of the soreness from the night before had gone with the storm. He had hoped to talk Clive out of this foolhardy attempt to prove himself. He had not wanted to embarrass his best friend. Since this was the hand he was dealt, best to get it over with. He needed to tramp into this bakery and prove once and for all to Breakerton that his wife was dead and that he had no child. The truth of it lay heavily on his chest. He attempted to shake the feeling.

"Now, we are only going to look and see if we can get a glimpse of them, correct old man?" Breakerton asked with a cautious tone.

"Why don't you just relax? I promise I will not embarrass you. I will look, deny your outlandish claim and then be off to pay a visit to your sister and discuss your dementia. With any luck, I will be back in London in four days' time." Devon did not intend to stay any longer than necessary. He needed to get back home and get on with his life. A life without a wife, or child. One where he woke alone every morning and retired alone every night. It is a good life, Devon chastised himself. Just the life a man should want. No woman to muddy the waters.

There was plenty of activity in the village now that the rain had stopped. A group of women gathered down the street admiring the wares in a shop window. The inn also was full of activity, as many of the guests who would have been stranded by the storm made their way to their curricles and carriages lined in front for the trip home. If the road from the castle was any indication, Devon doubted they would get far. The village itself, however, was quite nice. It had an easy disheveled feel to it. He was reminded of the tiny rotting cottage with the bright colored flowers covering the rot, where Ella lived when they met. This town would have suited her. Both the village and his dead wife had an air of unrefined beauty.

Breakerton stopped in the street and jabbed Devon on the shoulder. "Look, there in the window is the child. I told you, didn't I?"

Devon turned to see the child. "My God," he whispered and stood frozen, the air being pulled from his lungs. At a small table in the front window of the town bakery sat a child, a girl with raven hair. Her tresses were barely reined in by a bright red ribbon. As she danced a tattered doll around, Devon was afforded a clear view of her face, which was as light as brushed porcelain, with bright pink cheeks. The child was in good health and well cared for. However, her eyes were what mesmerized him. They were as large as saucers and doe shaped at the corners. The color seemed a striking contrast to the whole. Bright azure blue. Once he remembered wanting to drown in those eyes. The world started to shift, and he felt light-headed. My God, I am going to faint, thought Devon as he felt a hand grasp his upper arm to steady him.

"I say, old man, are you quite all right?" Breakerton held fast.

Pulling away, Devon couldn't answer his friend. Speech was

beyond him. He had a daughter. There was no denying. She looked the perfect mix of the two, with Devon's midnight black, curly locks, and her mother's porcelain skin and huge blue eyes. If that were his daughter, then just beyond the door, he would find... Ella.

His wife.

What would he do when he saw her? He had thought about it many times, but he never gave much credence to the possibility. The village that just a moment ago was quaint began to close in and feel tight. The unrefined beauty was now tarnished and dark.

His legs felt like anvils. His head swam. She's alive! The cry swelled in his chest begging for release. For the briefest of moments, he felt complete. I didn't fail her. She made it unharmed. Having so much to share with her about life at the Tate, Devon took a step forward, then stopped.

"Devon?" He heard his friend quiz, but he could not answer. Never had his body rebelled so to one thing. His chest swelled with complete joy, or was it pain? The heartbeat was loud enough for all those in the village to hear. What would he say to her? What if she didn't want to see him? What if she did?

Like the calm, which came following the night's storm, another question came to Devon. What if, after seeing her, he realized he was never that enthralled after all? Until Breakerton dragged him here, he had believed he was better off without her. What if he were?

Making up his mind, Devon straightened his jacket and hat, and marched with determined steps toward the door of what was in truth, his wife's lair.

"I say, Devon, didn't we agree just to look right now?" Breakerton asked while attempting to keep up. "You don't want to say something without first thinking it through, do you?"

"Clive, I am disappointed. Are you not the one with the attitude of jumping into the game without first knowing the rules or the stakes?" Devon asked with affability.

"Well, yes, but that was for me, not a man like you. And, if you were to partake in that philosophy, let me suggest you start small, like at the whist tables at Whites." However, for Devon, his argument albeit sound, was impossible to accept. Once through the door, he could have used a few moments to compose himself, or time to observe Ella without her being aware. The bell of the front door jingled their arrival and within seconds, there she stood. The store and everything in it fell away in a swirl of memories, or were they dreams? Like the woman standing before him.

He stood silent, not wanting to frighten her. Just as always happened in his dream, she would vanish once he reached for her, and with her, what would he lose this time? She stood frozen as well, but composed herself with haste and made to arrange pastries on a tray, which Devon hadn't noticed until now. With her busying herself, he forced his attention to the shop. Clean. Well appointed. Very much like the bakeries that one would find in London. The smells filling the space brought him back to the kitchen in the Tate. Warm and inviting, tempting the customer to stay and linger. He found himself drawn again to the woman he never thought he would see again. Then, his mind raced back to the beautiful child sitting only yards away.

As he spoke, his voice did not sound his own. It came out gruff and ragged as a man after a long ride in the desert. "What is her name?"

He half-expected Ella to play dumb. She paused in her organizing long enough to flinch as if caught in a lie, then stood tall and looked him in the eye. What he saw made his heart tear open in his chest. Fear. He had seen that look once before, but not as easy to read. She was scared of him. Why?

Replaying in his foggy mind all that had transpired between them until now, he watched as she took the time to cross the room and all but usher the child into the safety of the back room. Once she returned, she answered his question in a tone so quiet he had to bend to hear her.

"Maddie is what I call her and she is none of your worry, my Lord."

"I am not my Lord, I am your husband," Devon stated with a bit more force than was necessary. Was he actually hurt because she

18

wouldn't call him as such? Devon tried to shake his head clear, but it was useless. The closeness of her all but forced any sane thoughts from his mind.

"Hush! Would you like the whole of the village to hear you?" Yes, in fact, I would scream it from the rooftops, was on the tip of his tongue, but Devon wisely held it back.

Ella swept around the counter, closing the distance. She was close enough if Devon wanted to, which he did, he could have reached out and brushed the flour from her cheek. He noted, even in a rage, her features remained very young and vital with only a hint of the four years that had passed. As if to whisper maturity, the corners of her eyes donned fine wisps that would one day be deeper lines from many moments filled with laughter. Until now, none of those moments was with him. Her caustic tone brought him back to her tirade.

"If you'll remember, my Lord," she spat, "we had an agreement. I fulfilled my half and left as was agreed upon. Were you not satisfied with the terms? I followed them to the letter."

Unable to follow the thread of her words, he was still determined to learn as much about his newfound daughter as he could. They could have this argument another time. He wanted to know about –Maddie.

"How old?"

"I beg your pardon?" Ella asked, obviously exasperated at being ignored.

"The child, how old is she?" Devon asked, intent on an answer.

"That's none of your concern," Ella spat back and turned to busy herself with her back to Devon in obvious dismissal. This did not sit well with Devon. He had a child, and by God, he was not going to walk away from that. He knew the receiving end of such a decision was not pleasant. What did Ella think of him if she thought he could be dissuaded?

"It's my concern if she's mine!" Devon, now piqued, just managed to keep a rein on his emotions. He knew she couldn't be older than three, but he needed to hear it. He needed Ella to admit it.

"Quiet! What makes you think that?" Ella shot back, with more confidence in her voice than what was showing in her eyes, still filled with fear and something else. Was it sadness? His heart tugged at the thought.

"You mean you cuckolded me while you were still under my roof?" The question was preposterous. He might not know his wife as some men did, but he knew her sense of honor would not allow such a thing. He knew it was a challenge he just threw down like a gauntlet, but at the same time, the thought of another man touching Ella seized his muscles and raised his ire.

She eyed him for several moments, looking over at Breakerton who was now inspecting a pastry so closely one would think he was counting the seeds in the strawberry filling. She turned back to Devon, giving a heavy sigh. Her eyes were no longer filled with so much fear. However, for the first time, he realized they were filled with an overwhelming sadness and tiredness. Perhaps, she was the one traveling through the parched desert and not him.

"Why are you here?" she asked with no small amount of resignation in her tone. Inside his glove, his hand itched to cradle her face, pull her to him and just hold her. He knew he could take the weight of her burden and shoulder it. He could take her home and they would... They would what? Fall in love?

The bitterness of it all hit him like a blow in the stomach. Before he realized it, he was four again grasping at the hem of his mother's dress wanting something, anything from her. He loved her, after all. A cold wall formed around him. It was something he had not needed for four years. He would not be that pathetic little boy. His whole life had been a testament to the art of indifference. At that moment, he had the consciousness of mind to remember two things. First, she was a woman and women always knew how to play a situation, and secondly, this was Ella. She knew the game and she was making up rules as she went along. She held a full hand and was very good at bluffing. Raising his chin a notch, he made a mental note to be more diligent in his dealings with women, as to remember their true nature. That was to control and drain only what they wanted from any situation and leave.

"I am here because someone brought it to my attention that my Viscountess and daughter were living like lowly bakers. I am not sure at which point your glorious plan went awry, but it will not do if those in London were to become aware." His words came slow and metered with just enough steely edge. It didn't feel as satisfying as he had hoped.

If she could make rules, he could as well. He, unlike her, had the law on his side. Even in Scotland, she would have to follow suit. He was the head of this family; that being the most loosely held adaptation of the word, Devon thought with bitterness.

"You know, I never put any stock in what London thought. They will think as they like. What I do in the wilds of Scotland is of no interest to them. They never noticed me when I walked among them." She stepped back as if he might reach out and grab her. The fear he had seen earlier was back ten-fold. Damn, he felt as if all he knew was twisting and weaving in an ugly knot.

"I am well aware none took notice before. However, you are now the wife of a Viscount and that makes them interested, particularly when you are believed to be dead." Devon hissed in her face. "The only solution is for you to close your shop and get the child's things together. I don't know what I shall do with you, but I will think of something." Devon wasn't sure when he made that decision, but the surprise on Ella's face mirrored his own. Once he got her away from this place, he could work on unraveling his feelings, but right now, he needed to get her alone to either throttle her or tumble her, and he wasn't sure which seemed more tempting at the moment.

"No." That got his attention. Devon straightened the seam in his gloves with care as not to reach out and throw her over his shoulder. A knot began to grow in the pit of his stomach. A warning flashed in his mind not to corner her. This was Ella, wisdom lost out. He was beyond calculating his next move. Caught in the moment and the need to take Ella and possess her, he spoke before he could stop.

"I-I am sorry, I don't believe I heard my wife correctly. Did you just say no?"

"That's right. You might not be aware, but I own this bakery. I am not just a serving girl. If I leave, I will no doubt lose quite a bit in profit while I am playing your little game."

Just then, the bell on the door tinkled and in came a girl no older than ten and six. She was pretty, and oblivious in her innocence of the drama playing out.

"Good day to ye, Mrs. R. Is Maddie ready?" It was on the tip of his tongue to remind the child she was speaking to a Viscountess, but remembered in time that she was nothing more than 'Mrs. R.' here. A pang of something roiled inside him.

"Ah — ah, yes, Rosie, I believe you will find her in the back licking gingerbread batter." Ella stepped out of the way for the younger girl to make her way into the back room, and Devon suspected to put the counter between them. Only moments later, Rosie and Maddie came out, passing by the veritable sea of adults in the storefront. Maddie stretched her arms up for her mother's hug. Ella bent down to the child's height to give her a kiss.

"You behave, understand?" Ella advised. "Not like last time when you wandered off. You scared the Widow Toms to death! Understand? Stay right with Rosie. Hold her hand."

"OK, Mommy. Hug!" Maddie squeezed Ella around the neck, planted a gingerbread kiss on her cheek and trotted off. A well of wanting wound around Devon's heart and lungs, seizing his breath. Would he ever have his daughter beg hugs from him? Would he know how to return them as easily as Ella did now? Then Devon's conscious hit on the one thing it could understand. This was not his world. He did not belong in any part of it. Right now, the idea of ever being part of it was almost an impossibility. The one point that rankled the most, however, was the realization he could not enter her world as readily as she had entered his. Nothing had prepared him for this. Swallowing what he couldn't admit was disappointment, he needed to get the situation back on familiar territory.

"Where is that child taking her? What are her qualifications? My daughter should not be wandering off in a peasant village. She should be in a school room learning things an heiress needs to know." He slammed his white linen clad fist into his palm for emphasis.

"She is my daughter, and I will not have a veritable baby shoved into an attic nursery to be ignored by those who should love her, and never experience life." Ella stepped toward him as a female lioness would to protect her cubs. "You need not worry about my daughter. She will never be a burden you must carry," she said with final certainty.

"I think it is time you left, my Lord. We are about ready to close and I have much work to do. Lord Breakerton, please take some pastries with my compliments. They will just go bad if you don't." Ella turned and bent to retrieve a box to fill. That was when Devon realized Breakerton had come up beside him, waiting to what? Protect Ella from her own husband? A sick feeling began to grow deep within as he realized his fault. Was he the monster he felt like or was he justified?

"Thank you, my Lady, they look delicious." Breakerton bowed like a gentleman as she handed him a box filled with baked goods.

With sadness in her eyes, she looked at Lord Breakerton and in a quiet voice said, "Please don't call me that again. I am simply Mrs. R., my Lord." She turned back to Devon still standing tall and proud. "I will expect you gone when I return." She gave him her back and retreated into the kitchen.

Outside the bakery, the sun now beat down drying the ruts. Life went on as usual for those in the village. Devon felt cold despite the sun's heat.

"Well, old chap, that went well," Clive quipped. "Come, let us go back to our den and lick your wounds, or at the very least have some brandy."

"I am not finished with this discussion yet," Devon demanded and moved to go back inside.

"Oh, my boy, I am afraid you are for now." Clive put a staying hand on Devon's chest. The pressure made Devon look down to register his friend's presence. "You know as well as I, or you would if you were thinking with any logic, that little crumpet that is your wife will only fight harder when pressed. Best to let her sit with this and allow you time to calm down."

Devon wanted nothing more than to go back into the bakery and demand Ella go with him at once. But for what purpose? He didn't know how to take care of a family or if that was what he wanted. Four years ago, it was the last thing he cared about, but now, it would be best to let her be for now. If nothing, else, Devon had to rethink what he wanted out of life, and if it was something that he could even hope for. He allowed Clive to lead him from the bakery, but not before Devon made him promise to have the building watched for fear of Ella taking his daughter and running just like his mother. Well, not quite. Devon's mother did not want any attachments when she left, so he was at least warmed by the idea that Ella could never leave her own child behind.

Continuing past the large workbench and the massive brick oven, Ella all but ran above-stairs. Once in her small living quarters, she went to the only window that looked out on the street. She stood, unable to catch her breath. A voice in her muddled mind warned he could just follow her up. Then what? She would have no means of retreat. She knew, however, he would not follow. Sure enough, within moments, both men emerged on the street below. Without consent, her heart flew to her throat and what little breath she had left, caught.

The two men crossed the street and mounted their horses. Ella remained at the window until they rode out of sight, heading south of town. She hoped they were heading back to London, but from what little she knew of her husband, he was not a man to be brushed aside. Satisfied the two would not return for the moment, Ella allowed her nerves to uncoil a fraction. She needed to think and fast. With Maddie visiting, she had some valuable time alone. Not wanting to let the chance go, she grabbed a worn cape, put Penny in charge of the shop and headed out across the long rolling field heading north.

With well-remembered steps, Ella's feet carried her along as she tried to put today's events into perspective. When Devon first appeared in the bakery, Ella's pulse quickened. Her first thought was that he had come to take her home, but that was quelled once she looked into his eyes. Hard, accusing pools. Knowing his propensity to erect a wall to hide his true self, she would not have let his eyes alone tell her he wanted to remain distant. The other more painful facets of their encounter caused Ella to wrap her cloak around her, hug herself against the pain, and fight back the tears stinging for release. She used to believe her father was the only man who could make her feel less than she was, but in truth, she now knew that to be a lie. If a man could still make her feel such pain and loss, what would he do to the heart of a little girl? No matter what her body wanted, her first responsibility was to protect her daughter from the hurt she knew from a father who didn't want her. In the back of her mind, something whispered. If he didn't want her, why did he make it known he knew of her? Ella pushed it back. In her experience, it was best not to hope for things that never came. Not to mention how much of it was intuition and how much just blind, sad hope? Maddie wasn't worth the risk.

The hem of her skirt dampened from the grass, but she needed the air and openness. When she had seen him in her bakery, he all but filled the space. What his large body and deep accusing eyes did not fill was filled with a humming that vibrated her very skin. A part of her had wanted to run into his arms and bury her face into his waistcoat to hide from the world. The relief hit like a wave on the beach, only to do what waves do and disappear back into the vastness. Once the initial joy faded, her fear rushed in filling her heart with heavy regret. It was apparent why he had come. He was trying to put to rest any possible scandal. That would be fine if it were just her, but Ella needed think about her daughter. Their daughter.

Why he was so interested in her, she could only fear the worst. Had she given birth to an heir that would have been different. A son would be of prime interest. A daughter, however, was considered a burden, a worthless waste of porridge to be exact. Once her mother was dead, Ella's father had wasted no time in reminding her of the fact almost daily. Anger, old and well fed from that time, reared its head. The chill of the wet field was replaced with a warmth fueled by her anger. Her breathing picked up as she remembered her life with such a man. She embraced the feel of it. Men of power or the illusion of power like her father, would never abide weakness. Therefore, she spent her life proving a female could be as strong as any man. In the end, what did it matter? Standing in the field, still damp from rain, Ella stood tall. Raising her face toward the sky, breathing deeply the smell of damp earth mixed with wildflowers. Her anger subsided, but not her resolve.

Despite her alarm and possible fear that her husband had just blown in with the recent storm, there were more pressing matters to attend to. For instance, the latest letter from the blackmailers that appeared two days ago, not to mention the robberies of late on the road to Edinburgh. She had to decide what to do. If she didn't pay the amount stated in the note, she knew something would happen. Yet, if she did pay, again she would be losing money, money she could not afford to lose. If only she could be certain she was not the only one receiving the notes. She had only one secret that she knew of, and that one had just left her bakery.

The other shopkeepers were all male, save one. Mrs. Farlane, the owner of the modiste and milliner would not even discuss the possibility. If Ella could not get the other shopkeepers to rally with her, or worse, if they were not being blackmailed as well, she was on her own, which was more dangerous, because that meant it was personal.

She still had a few days before payment was due. She needed to find out as much as she could about new people to town, or even those who were more unseemly than she might have guessed. In order to do that, she would need to go where all the gossip was passed about, the Buckshead Inn. It was time to talk with Mr. Bryant about needing some extra money. She hated to have people in town thinking she needed wages, but it would give her a chance to listen to talk as the ale flowed. Truth be told, in her practical way, she might find out information to aid her in ferreting out this wastrel and gain more funds to pay the blackguard's money to ensure her safety. She would continue to turn over her husband's sudden appearance in her mind, but his Lordship would just have to wait.

As Ella made her way back to the bakery, she couldn't help but smile at the thought of his reaction if he knew she was putting him on the back burner. She always tried to enjoy the little pleasures in life.

CHAPTER 3

*H*aving shaken the initial shock, Devon wasted no time in calling for his staff, still holed-up a village away. He dispatched a missive to his steward concerning several business dealings, one to parliament sending his regrets about missing session, and another more personal one, which he put the most importance on.

The rich brandy tasted almost sweet, as the sounds of his people settling in permeated the thick doors of Clive's library. However, Clive did not appear to be enjoying the deep flavor. Devon enjoyed the look of suspicion on his face.

"May I inquire, as to your current brooding? I thought I was the one to brood while you, the one to celebrate."

"Yes, well, I am just confused is all," Clive stated.

"And your confusion is caused by what?" Devon asked, trying to stay with the thread of the conversation. His mind kept wandering to Ella.

"Were you not in the same establishment I was?" Clive responded with annoyance. "Was I the only one to notice you were discharged? She wouldn't even credit you with the child. Doesn't that rankle a bit?"

Devon thought about their meeting. True, it had not gone the way he would have liked. What he would have liked was for Ella to see him enter the shop and run into his arms, but this was Ella. She wouldn't be glad to see him. He knew from the beginning her goal had been to be a free and independent woman. He symbolized all she fought to be free of.

Until the very moment he saw her and his daughter, he never wanted a family of his own. He knew he didn't deserve the chance, not after being the loudest proponent against the indifference of women. Devon was grasping for a prize he might never win, but in a moment of calm realization, he knew he had to take the chance. Nothing would give them the sort of life Clive grew up in, but he would give Ella a safe place and Maddie...well, he would give Maddie what she needed. What that would be was irrelevant at this time.

He couldn't place it, but he felt a measure of relief almost radiating from Ella when they spoke. Her words spoke of betrayal and un-kept promises. Her eyes showed the fear of seeing him in her domain. She was making a life for herself and his daughter, but something caused her relief at the sight of him. It was so potent to him he could have almost claimed it had a scent. It was a heady feeling to have such a reaction from Ella, even if she meant to hide it. The why of it was more troublesome.

Was she in some kind of trouble? Ella would never admit so, but something was afoot. For the brief time spent in the shop, it seemed well... A sharp whistle brought him back to Clive.

"I am sorry to interrupt your woolgathering. However, I was beginning to feel neglected."

"Sorry, I was just considering our little reunion. I don't believe it went as poorly as all that." Devon, allowing Clive the chance to shake the almost comical gape of his jaw, rose to refill his glass and stretch his impatient muscles. He craved action. For the first time in years, he felt a purpose and wanted to act, but couldn't, not yet.

"I was right. You obviously were not in the same shop as I, because I saw a woman all but run my best friend out of town with a hot iron in her hand. She even attempted to convince you that her daughter wasn't yours. Not exactly my notion of a loving reunion." Clive snorted and downed his drink, extending the empty glass to Devon, which he refilled.

"On the contrary, what you saw was a woman trying to protect what she sees as her independent state. What you didn't seem to notice was an underlying air of relief about her."

"I think you should sit down and give over that glass. Spirits don't always sit well with everyone. It seems to be making you have visions." Clive gestured to the full glass in Devon's hand. Devon answered with a mock toast and a long draw off the amber liquid.

The afternoon sun had waned and the crisp evening air seemed to swell and glide into the room carrying the cool smells of late spring. A fire gave the room a warm welcoming glow. Devon had no doubts about what he was about, and once he explained his plan, Clive would see it had merit.

"Regardless of whether you believe me or not, I know what I saw or felt. She was on some level relieved to see me." Devon made his way back to the chair, stretching his long legs and resting one booted foot on his ankle.

"I knew it! Only a man in love could fabricate such a romantic tale," toyed Clive.

"Ha, you of all people know me better than that. I will never fall in love. It is a useless emotion, at least for a man. There is nothing wrong with a woman being in love with her husband however. In fact, in this case, I think it will be the only thing to bind said wife to her husband." His feelings toward Ella would work themselves out once he had things well in hand. He would not let a woman tear his heart to shreds as his mother did to his father. Until Ella was bound to him by her own love, would he take the time to consider his own attachment to her.

As light dawned in Clive's eyes, Devon could see him weighing their options. "You plan on seducing her and making her fall in love with you. A bit underhanded, even for a cynic like you, but how do you plan on succeeding without falling into your own trap?"

The humor and excitement lightening Devon's mood slipped for a moment as he leveled a deadly serious expression on his friend. "I can, without a doubt, guarantee I will be in no such danger as falling into my own trap. For if I did, wouldn't I be the biggest of fools?"

"Well, I can see your point. After all, who would want to fall in love with a beautiful, smart, strong, articulate woman who has proven she can give you heirs and will hold to a bargain struck? It is preposterous really."

Devon hid the urge to remind Clive that of all people, Devon was unable to love and gain love in return. He was hoping if he had no expectations of being loved other than to bind Ella to him, he might...

He dared not think what he might want. Best to keep it simple. He wanted Ella. Simply Ella.

Three nights passed without a word from Devon. Ella's nerves began to fray. Every time the bell rang heralding a customer, she all but dropped whatever it was she had. Part of her feared it was another blackmail letter, and part feared it was Devon again. More unsettling was the part, still small but gaining strength, of her disappointment each time it was not Devon. She was almost ready to commit herself into Bedlam. She would be surprised if she had the concentration to work on her books at the moment.

Weakness.

She had no time for such foolhardy ideas as passion. And, what did she know of passion? One night in the bed of her husband would not constitute any sort of expertise in the realm of the bedroom. She knew what was expected of a wife of the Ton. As a Viscountess, she would be expected to comport herself in a certain way. Her life was just the way she wanted it.

Well, not exactly. If it were exactly as she wanted, she would not be in the middle of The Buckshead Tavern pouring ale, and listening to a group of men talk about everything from their crops and livestock, to their wives and others' wives. Men, no matter their station, seemed to speak the same language.

Mr. Bryant had been more than happy to give her work. A very nice, almost fatherly man, he happened to be in need of more help since his daughter had taken ill, so the arrangement worked well. Ella even heard Mr. Bryant telling one of the men that she was helping out until his daughter was back on her feet, which meant Ella no longer needed to come up with a reason for being there.

That was the good news. The bad news was that she had yet to hear anything she thought would aid her. At the very least, she was hoping in conversation to find out if The Buckshead was being black-mailed as well, but either Mr. Bryant was being very close-lipped, or he had not received any threats.

Tonight, the patrons were many of the same as the previous night. Men coming in to drink ale and visit. There were, however, a few men from farther afield on this night. The roads were repaired and the busy route had picked back up.

Scottish men, Ella decided, were much larger than English men were, for she had yet to be able to see anything but barrel chests and large elbows. Her petite stature made traversing the tight taproom difficult empty handed, but with tankards and pitchers full of ale, she smelled more like the tankards she carried than a gently bred woman.

"Here, lass, ye take much longer and weel be dyin' o' thirst!" A large man hollered from the corner near the fire, which on this night was unlit to Ella's relief. Several of the men with him chuckled and nodded in agreement. They were not men she recognized, but their demeanor had been nothing, if not jovial all night.

"Sorry, sir, it's difficult finding one's way through so many. I did bring two pitchers in case I am unable to get back as you might like," she said as she set out the pitchers with a kind smile, hoping the bribe of an extra pitcher would hold them off.

"Hey, Ian, I think she likes ye'," a young redhead joked while elbowing the larger man to whom Ella was speaking.

"I thinks ye might have the right of it," the larger man barked. Without any warning, his large meaty arm snaked around her waist and dragged her down upon his lap.

Quelling the fear rising in her, Ella surveyed the area. She had no way of getting the attention of Mr. Bryant on the other side of the room; that was certain. Even if she were able, this man could be outside with her before Mr. Bryant could come to the rescue. None of the other men seemed to notice. She decided talking was her only choice.

"Well, sir, that is very flattering, but I must get back to my duties. There are many men here tonight and I believe they are all just as thirsty..." She patted his arm and made to rise. It didn't work.

"Well, mayhap just as thirsty, but I doubt any are as hungry." She turned to see his eyes sparkle. She didn't think it was with humor. The other men with him roared with laughter at his comment. Not sure what he meant, she was certain she would not like it.

"Now, sir, I am trying to be civil. However, I must insist you release me this instant." She started wriggling and prying at his hand trying to loosen his grip. The man's response was to chuckle and nuzzle her neck, at which, she yelped with surprise.

"Sit still, lass, ye are makin' me spill me ale."

"If you will just let me go–"

"I don't think so, I think I like ye where ye are."

Ella opened her mouth with a smart retort, but it was not her voice that was heard over the crowd.

"I believe the lady has asked to be released," a deep voice came from behind her captor.

No, no, no, no. She would have taken ten smelly, grabby, men to the one man with that voice.

"Ye be on your way, Brit. I don't think tis any of your concern." The man didn't even turn to see the hard plains of Devon's face. Ella turned away from the scene and squeezed her eyes shut as tightly as possible. This couldn't end any other way but badly for her, no matter how it ended.

"I will ask one more time for you to unhand the wench. I am sure you are a reasonable man and will understand that there is but one serving woman, and many men who are waiting for their drink. I am not one to get in the way of two lovers, but could you possibly do your fondling after we have been served."

The man holding Ella threw back his head and laughed, at the same time releasing her, but not without slapping her on the backside hard enough to knock her into several men on the other side of the fireplace. Gaining her composure, she smoothed her dress and wended her way through the crowd to the bar with as much haste as the crowd allowed. Wench? Wench? Lovers? The irony of it might have struck her as funny had she not been the one the men were discussing. She had just allowed Devon to call her a wench and she could do nothing about it.

The deep breathing she did only helped her gain her composure a smidge, but she was able to grab two more pitchers of ale and again attempt to squeeze her way through the crowd. This time, she was attempting to avoid Devon. He had better luck finding the only serving 'wench' in the crowd, however, than she did avoiding one of many men in the group. About halfway through the room, she was stopped short by a broad, well-tailored chest.

"Good eve, Ella." She could all but feel her name vibrate from his body.

"I am terribly busy, as I am sure you can see, my Lord. I am sure if you ask Mr. Bryant, he can arrange a private parlor for you." She stepped to the side knowing she would not be allowed to pass.

"I think we need to talk." His voice was calm. Too calm. She looked up into his face. His eyes were not as hard as she expected, which caused her pause. "I realize this is not the place for such a conversation. However, we will talk soon."

"Fine, but please, don't ruin this." With pleading eyes, she willed him to play along. He studied her face until she thought he might pick her up and carry her out over his shoulder.

"My friend and I are in need of a private room and do not care to wait for the owner to pry himself free," he said in true aristocratic form for all to hear.

She bobbed a curtsy. "Yes, my Lord, if you will just make your way toward the stairs, I will be along in a moment." Without hesitation, she took the opportunity of his glancing toward the stairway to skirt around him and disappearing in the crowd. All of a sudden, she didn't mind being so small.

From the other side of the room, she could see Devon standing on the rise of the stairs searching the crowd, with Breakerton at his side. As if he could feel her gaze on him, he turned his head in her direction and their eyes locked. Again, what she saw was not what she expected. What she expected was censure and anger, not the humor and twinkle she was met with.

He even dropped his head as a gesture of defeat. Her toes tingled and heat rose up her body causing her to slosh more ale down her arm as she turned from his stare.

He would leave her alone for now, but she knew her time was short and she almost wished she were back on the other man's lap. It felt to be the safer place at the moment.

The remainder of the evening went without incident until very late. Many of the men had given into the need to find their own homes, because of wont to settle in or for lack of remaining funds. The ones still milling about were younger and most without families that Ella knew of. She was tired and bone weary, thinking ahead to her own duties in the bakery on the morrow, only hours away. Mr. Bryant broke down and lit the fire, sending wood smoke into the mix of ale, cigars, and the smells of hardworking farm men. The smell was sure to remain in one's nostrils for at least a fortnight. She busied herself with wiping down the empty tables. She wasn't even sure if Devon and Clive were still above-stairs. She hoped not.

At a table in the back of the taproom, one of the few round ones, most were long benches with nothing more than shorter benches for sitting on, two men sat with their heads bent together in conversation. Earlier, she noticed them watching her, but as the events of the evening turned, she realized many of the men watched her. She went to the bar for another pitcher of ale and headed toward the group.

"I thought you gentlemen would like one last pitcher before we close." She set the pitcher on the table, looking to make sure Mr. Bryant was close by, which he was. He had paid very close attention to her the second half of the evening. She figured Devon had spoken to him at some point.

"Ah, thank ye, lass," the oldest looking of the two acknowledged her.

"Just traveling through?" she asked moving to wipe down the table next to theirs.

"Naw, we live in the next village over, Cornick," the man answered. The younger man seemed to find that amusing as he tipped his tankard to his lips.

"Isn't that almost a day's ride? Whatever would you be doing here this late?" Ella questioned. It was a reasonable question considering the late hour and these men were not guests of The Buckshead; that much she knew.

"Well, lass, we's just here checkin' on–" the younger man started to explain, but stopped when the older man gave him a forbidding glance.

In the silence, the older man explained, "We are looking into a business venture we are undertaking. This seems a very busy village, and we were checking out our prospects, as they were." His words rang true, but something in his voice and eyes spoke a different story.

"Sorry, lads, but we are closing for the night. Thanks for the business." Mr. Bryant walked up behind Ella and put a hand on her shoulder. "Why don't you dump the water and settle your things whilst I finish with these young ones."

Ella saw the warning in Mr. Bryant's eyes. She also noted the fact he did not mention she would be going back to her own home alone.

"Thank you. I cannot wait to find my pillow. That is for sure," she answered grabbing her cloak and heading out the back door. She knew those men were up to something. The hairs on the back of her neck prickled in awareness. They spoke of the town where they were from as if she should know it. She had made it to the edge of the road when a deep voice came out of the shadows.

"It is not safe for serving wenches to be walking alone so late." With no little emphasis on the word wench, his voice was stern, but not threatening. Ella jumped at the breach in the silence, but calmed.

That is until a large hand reached out and wove around her elbow. The contact in the darkness of the night was electric. Her arm filled with warmth, sending the heat along to her shoulder and lower to her chest and stomach.

In an attempt to gain her composure, she allowed him to guide her onto the street heading toward her bakery. After a few minutes of silence, she broke in with, "Which part of this little scene are you enjoying more?"

"What scene would you be referring?" Devon asked with practiced innocence, she was sure.

"I am referring to the one where you see me having to make a wage at the local tavern to be able to carry on without your assistance, or where you must come to my rescue in the taproom and save me from some drunken farmer. Perhaps the scene where you can go around calling me wench and I cannot but smile meekly and allow it," she retorted, allowing her exasperation to show, but fighting to hold back a smile.

"Well, I cannot say the first makes me particularly happy, but being your rescuer and having leave to call you wench are both quite tolerable experiences, I have to say."

"I will have you know, the reason I was at the Tavern was not for the reason you think," she said, defending herself. She had worked damn hard to gain a life and good living for her and her daughter, and didn't want him thinking she hadn't. Why it rankled her so, Ella would think on later.

"Oh, what then were you doing at the tavern serving ale to the local men?" he asked with a bit more annoyance and less humor.

"Mr. Bryant's daughter has fallen ill and he needed the help. His daughter helped in my shop last year when Penny fell ill. I am just returning the favor."

"Oh, I see." The remainder of the walk they completed in silence. At the back door leading to her kitchen, Ella turned, looking into the dark shadow that was Devon.

"Thank you for rescuing me from that man, and for walking me home. I am safe now, so you may leave."

"I may leave here tonight or here forever?" he asked. She wished she could see his face. His voice sounded civil enough, but she knew his eyes would tell. Not knowing why, she didn't want to give him his leave just yet. She thought he was giving her that opportunity, but couldn't be sure.

"I am not sure what it is you want, but I assure you, I am doing fine and you need not feel any misplaced responsibility to me." Ella knew what a feeling of unwanted responsibility could do to the way a person felt about another and she didn't want Devon, of all people, to see her that way. So much so, her throat tightened at the thought of him seeing her as a burden. Her eyes burned and her heart felt heavy. Could there ever be a time when she wasn't a burden? She doubted it. Her sadness at the thought made her grateful for the shadows hiding the single tear she was unable to hold back.

"I will be truthful with you. I am not yet sure what I plan to do with the information of you being alive and of my daughter, but I will not leave until I have made my decision." Again, his voice was calm, but this time, it carried a deadly serious edge that vibrated along her spine, prickling every nerve.

Her voice all but squeaked in a raspy tone as she asked, "What decision is that?"

"You will know when the time comes, but until that time, you may plan on seeing me often."

The world shifted under her feet. If she had only run for her door and shut him out as soon as she saw the bakery, she would be inside and he would be out. It wouldn't change anything, but she wouldn't be wiser to it. "No, you cannot be lingering about. The others will know something is not right. I will be found out a fraud. You must leave!" A knot formed deep in her stomach just thinking about spending time with Devon again. She left last time for fear of being seduced by her own fanciful dreams. The knot grew bigger as her panic rose. She opened her mouth to argue more, but was thwarted.

Devon made shushing sounds and placed a feather light finger on her lips to quiet her. The contact had the desired effect. She was sure. She froze, immobile. He moved his finger from her lips up her cheek and back down tracing the line of her jaw. His wayward finger stilled under her chin where he tipped her face up. He couldn't know how the touch of one of his fingers could befuddle her senses, or could he?

"I promise I will not be overly attentive to you, unless you give me leave. I will be staying close by doing some seasonal sport. I will, however, require some of your time to get to know my daughter and the kind of life you are offering her here in a bakery. I think every other evening will do for a start."

"Wait," the spell, which seemed to encase her with his quiet, deep voice, broke at his dictate. How was she to deal with the blackmail letters and threat, run her bakery, and give Devon every other evening? She would get no sleep whatsoever. She had to do something. "There is no way I can commit to every other evening. I am going to be helping Mr. Bryant for at least a sennight every other evening, and on those evenings I am not, I have to spend time with Maddie and sleep. You do not understand how early one who runs a bakery must rise each morning."

Devon studied her until she all but squirmed. She didn't think he could see her features. She couldn't see his. She, however, had all but memorized his face from her dreams. What was he considering?

"Very well, we will start with a meeting two nights from now. It will be Saturday night. I trust your shop is not open Sundays, is it?"

Her exhaustion pulled on her and dragged her down. She tried to think what Sunday was holding for her, but couldn't. "I– I don't think I have anything, other than the Sunday service." Something was needling in her mind, but wouldn't shake clear. "Fine, Sunday evening then after eight o'clock. I will meet you here at the back door. Now, I must go. I only have time to bathe and change, before I must start the fires for the day's baking."

Again, he studied her, still holding her chin. Quietly and gently, Devon released her and stepped back from the door. "Until Sunday then," and he turned and headed out into the darkness of the field.

Senses reeling, she made her way to her living quarters. A low fire still burned. The upstairs room was warm and cozy, and Ella made a point of closing the heavy door at the top of the stairs to keep out the early morning chill. First, she checked that Maddie was well. As expected, she was curled up in the middle of the bed they shared, deep in the blankets with her doll. Penny lay asleep on her pallet near the fire. Neither stirred as Ella washed as much of her body as possible to clean it of the smells of the tavern. The blasted cat Maddie had befriended was downstairs making havoc by the sounds. If he could be caught, he would find himself outside for the day if there were a mess. She changed and made her way downstairs to coax the large ovens into service.

As soon as she reached the middle stair, she smelled the familiar scent of wood smoke. Once down the stairs, she saw for sure both large fires blazed and crackled ready for use. On the large workbench lay a bunch of spring wildflowers.

Devon. Perhaps the cat was not to blame this time. Ella sensed she was in more danger than she first thought. Her heart beat harder in agreement and she could still feel the sensation of his finger on her lips. She pulled the flowers to her nose with a shaking hand and decided she might not be as prepared for this as she hoped.

CHAPTER 4

"You sir, need to sit. It will be of great expense to you of course, if I am in need of a new floor once you have finished grinding a ditch in the middle," Clive drawled at Devon while sitting at his desk working through correspondence. Devon, however, paced with barely restrained frustration.

It wasn't so much what Clive said, but as usual, how he said it with an irritating air of humor. It wasn't as though any of the mail received by him this morning held a note canceling his evening engagements.

"What would you have me do?" Devon snapped.

"Well, I would suggest questioning Ella as to why she needs to cancel. Perhaps, she does have a valid reason. And, might I suggest using parchment and ink, for I am sure she can't hear you rant from this distance. If she could, I would hope she would have been here hours ago to save me the pleasure of listening to you."

"Tell me again why I haven't called you out yet?"

"Because, my besotted friend, I am the one voice of reason you actually listen to."

"Lord, help me," Devon quipped as he sprawled into the chair in front of the desk. He wanted nothing more than to march down the hill and demand she give him a valid reason for keeping him at bay.

The missive was short but polite. It said she had not remembered an errand she had to attend to and would not be back until late Tuesday. It wasn't bad enough he was going against everything— everything he knew about women by choosing to expose himself to Ella again, but now she was dismissing him. This should be a sign to run. Logic would dictate as such, but he couldn't. Now that he had discovered she was alive, he couldn't turn his back. He should. It couldn't end well for him, he knew from watching his father, but for some reason, he didn't care.

"You received this note, what two hours ago? Whatever she was going to do, I am sure she wouldn't have left before luncheon. I would suggest you send another missive asking, not demanding," Clive added with a knowing look, which grated on Devon's already threadbare nerves.

"What errand is going to take her away overnight?"

He doubted Ella would tell him the truth, considering she hadn't offered the information in her first note, but that would at least keep the conversation alive. He rose from the chair and made his way to the bell pull. Clive rose as well, giving Devon the use of his desk. He poured two generous drinks and settled in the chair with his footstool.

Devon got the missive composed, blotted the ink and Clive gave the note to the youngest, and most reliable of his servants to deliver, with an order for him to wait for a reply. With Clive's servants, the term 'reliable' was tenuous at best, but he took the drink offered to him and began a slow turn about the large room to wait.

An hour later, Devon had his answer, but the response was one that he did not relish. His pacing once again took on that of a caged animal. The once obscenely large great hall, come library, became stifling within its confines.

"Are you sure?"

"Aye Milord," the young boy stammered. "Miss Penny herself told me."

"When?"

"She left at sunrise. Miss Penny also said she doesn't make the whole trip in one day. She will make it just outside the city tonight."

Devon's head swam. "Does the bloody woman know the potential dangers facing anyone on the road to Edinburgh? Has she lost all sense?" He glared at the messenger waiting for an answer.

"Miss Penny told me Mrs. R makes this trip four times a year during good weather," the young servant answered. "That way, she can fill her larder for the winter months."

What Devon wouldn't do to have his pretty wife's neck to wring right now. Instead, he had a very young, very nervous servant. Devon knew how intimidating he could be and even though he would like nothing more than to take his frustrations out, tearing the young servant limb from limb would not resolve anything. The one person, along with her pretty neck, responsible for his current state of hysterics was at this moment traveling north to purchase supplies for a bakery Devon planned would not be her responsibility in a very short time.

"Thank you, Brian, you may leave. If you stop by the kitchen, I am sure cook will give you something to eat before you go back to your duties." Clive filled the silence. Brian bowed and hurried away. "Now what?" He asked turning back toward Devon. "And before you answer, ask yourself what prize you are aiming for."

Devon all but growled his frustration. His instincts screamed for action. Riding one of Clive's prize stallions, he could catch up with her at the posting inn outside the city. But, then what? She would never agree to leave without her supplies and he couldn't very well carry her kicking and screaming out of the inn. He could go into the city and collect the supplies needed without her, but her appeasement again would not be gained.

Clive was correct, however. He had to remember his goal. He was seducing her, right? In order to do that, he needed her content and pliable. Ella with a bee in her bonnet would not be easy to seduce. In addition, he had to admit he was more than a little curious as to how she dealt with her new life. If he did follow her, but stayed to the shadows, he would be available in case of an emergency. He would also be able to get to know the inner workings of his wife's mind, a pastime he was quickly beginning to enjoy.

"Can you show me the route she would likely have taken and a quicker route so I might make up time?" Devon asked his friend. Clive stood in the center of the room, arms crossed, eying Devon. "Oh, blast it, man, I am only going to play look out. What did you think? I was going to run into her rooms and carry her squealing and thrashing out the door?"

After a moment's pause, Clive quipped, "No, but you considered it. Of that I am sure."

Noise met Devon as he entered the taproom of the posting inn. He hoped this was the inn in question. Making his way to the back of the large busy tavern, he got his answer. An older couple, the owners, he assumed, were standing at the bar quarreling. Devon took a seat near the stairs to the guest rooms within hearing distance.

"Will ye calm yerself? The lass is fine. She's just late in comin' is all. I won't send Timothy out. Tis not safe."

With an exasperated tsking sound, the woman replied, "That's whot I've been tryin' to tell ye. Tis not safe for a lady such as Mrs. R to be on the road after dark. Timothy knows his way."

"Listen woman," filling a tray with tankards of ale, the innkeeper spat back, "she pays weel, I'll give her that, but not weel enough for me to send a boy a huntin'. If she doesn't—"

Just then, a young gangly redheaded boy came from the way of the stairwell, very out of breath. "She's 'ere. Just arrived."

"Heavens be!" The older woman sighed, looking to the ceiling. "Timothy, go to the front guest room and start the fire. The poor thing must be exhausted."

Devon moved with haste, as to beat the young man up the stairs. Making his way to the guest rooms above stairs, he noted the quality of the wood and the cleanliness. This was where those with money would choose to stay. Not having time to wonder as to Ella's monetary needs, he filed the information away.

The front guest room, the largest and most extravagant room available, stood as the first door in the hallway. In the daylight, the large windows banking one wall would flood the room with light. The floor was polished to a shine with small rugs covering it to keep cold feet at bay. The bed was large, with what looked to be expensive linens. Again, the question of Ella being able to afford such luxury came to mind.

Footsteps coming down the hall brought him back to his purpose. He needed to hide. He took two steps toward the dressing screen. Ella would use the screen even though she was alone. The only other available hiding place was the wardrobe set against the wall just opposite the fire. With no time left to contemplate, Devon surged for the wardrobe, just getting the door closed, save for a crack, before the Young Timothy emerged into his line of sight.

As expected, the young man laid and lit the fire, tending it to a warm glow throughout the room. Not quite as expected, Devon heard more footsteps, and then watched Timothy rise from his endeavors with the fire.

"Put that down right here close to the fire. Ma wants her not to get a chill."

Damn!

Devon decided he should have waited to hear the remainder of the conversation in the taproom between the innkeeper's wife and Timothy. Had he been prudent, he wouldn't be in the tenuous position of hiding in a wardrobe knowing he would have to stay and watch his wife take a bath, for the object two other men were setting close to the fire was a bathtub. This was very bad.

"Good, go down and tell Sarah she can start filling the buckets. I need to wait until the fire takes before I help."

The other two men grumbled about Timothy not helping, but

didn't dare argue outright. They left moments later. Those leaving, however, did not help Devon one bit. If Timothy left as well, he might be able to get out and make his way down the back staircase he had seen on his way up.

But, no, as his luck so often ran, Devon was stuck. He had meant only to stay long enough to dissuade his concern. On the trip, once Devon caught up with his wife and her guardian, if one could call the lad that, Ella appeared fine. As the day wore on, she stopped more often and became much less animated-- unlike her usual self. The last glimpse he managed to steal before they were plunged into darkness, she looked dreadfully pale. Had he not heard the young man with her mention how close they were, he would have emerged from the shadows to end the trip. Just then, Devon got a sinking idea. What if he was the cause of her countenance? What if his very existence in her life was putting such a strain on her? The thought made him feel small, smaller than he had ever felt. As a child, he had felt as small when one of his father's lovers had claimed having a child underfoot drove her to her bedchamber with palpations and nerves. He had wanted to be invisible. He had wanted to be anywhere but home. That was how he felt now.

He had ridden hard through the brush and forest to beat her, and find a way to hide in her room just to make sure she was well. However, he did not want to sit and watch her bathe. Well, on more consideration, he couldn't think of anything else he would rather do, but being trapped in a wardrobe as a thief stealing her privacy was not the way he wanted to do it.

Instead, he would have preferred sitting at the tub's edge watching the water lap over her shimmering body. He could imagine her full breasts floating to the surface, exposing one rosy nipple to the cool air. *This is the reason I can't sit here. I'll die of an apoplectic fit before she finishes.* He thought as he attempted to shift, making room for his growing erection. Shifting was impossible in the small space without bringing notice to his hiding place.

The buckets of hot water came one after the other, until the tub was full. Just as Devon had given up hope, Timothy turned to leave with the last empty bucket swinging from his hand. Devon's view of the door was blocked so he waited, listening for the door to shut. Perhaps fate was smiling down on him, just this once.

"Ah, Timothy, are ye finished?"

"Aye, mum. Mrs. R, good evenin'," Timothy answered and greeted the illustrious guest.

Fate wasn't smiling, it was laughing– heartily.

"Good evening, Timothy. It is nice to see you again." His wife's rich voice filled the room.

"Ye may go. See that yer father doesn't need anythin' before ye go help in the stables."

A pause indicated to Devon the young man would have liked nothing more than to bypass one of the two chores, but decided not to argue. "Yes, Mum. Have a good evenin' Mrs. R."

"You as well, Timothy," Ella replied with a smile in her voice. Devon could still hear in her voice the fatigue pulling on her.

"Such a good boy, that one. All right, here ye be. I was dreadfully worried ye had come to a bad end this evening, gel." The older woman said as she came into sight. He still couldn't see Ella. "I know ye didn't request it, but I had the lads bring in the tub and fill it with good hot water. There's nothing like a good soak to cure travel weary bones."

"Oh, Mrs. Borrik, you shouldn't have gone to any trouble. But, I have to confess, it looks rather inviting. Thank you."

"Don't even think on it, gel, you just get yourself into that hot water and rest. I'll send one of the gels to tend you in the morning. The usual time?"

"Yes, that would be fine." Ella stepped into his view as she walked past the tub and placed a small traveling bag on the stool next to the dressing screen. "I would inquire as to the letting of this room for tomorrow as well. I know I only wrote ahead about tonight, but I do not wish to be in the dark on my return trip. I have to admit to you I have been awfully busy as of late, and I fear it is catching me. I do not believe I can make this trip again on the morrow."

"It is yours, gel. Now, hop into that bath, use some of those scented oils on the table, and just let your body rest." The woman took Ella's hand and gave it a motherly pat, then turned to go, closing the door behind her.

Ella picked up her bag, turned and made her way out of Devon's sight to the bed. Straining to listen, he heard the linen shift as she sat to take off her traveling boots. Devon heard each in turn hit the floor. His mouth went dry. He had assumed Ella would be too virtuous not to use a screen when one was in place, but then none of his mistresses ever had second thoughts about undressing out in the open. This was not his mistress; it was Ella. An Ella he didn't know existed, but one he would like to be introduced to.

With no warning, a very naked Ella walked into view. His gut clenched sending white-hot desire to his groin. She had a bottle of scented oil and poured it into the steaming water. The smell of lavender assailed his senses. His vision on the other hand was filled with Ella.

God, she was beautiful. Had he ever seen a more petite fragile looking woman? Bending to test the water, she gave him a perfect view of her arse and hips. His hands tingled in remembered caresses. He noticed the swell of her hips was more rounded. Not overly so by any means, but enough so he noticed. She turned to pluck a piece of linen from the nearby stool placing it closer. This view was just as delectable. Her stomach where once it had been flat, gave way to a softness accentuating her rounded hips. Again, he approved. She was too thin by far four years ago.

Now, after giving birth, her body had blossomed into a siren's. Her breasts, still pert but a bit larger and fuller rounded out the image of his perfect wife, the mother of his child. The thought of Ella giving him a child seized his lungs and tightened around his heart. *His child.* He was brought back the sound of water lapping the edge of the tub. At that moment, Devon could have expired from the lust boiling through his veins. The urge to touch her was so strong he caught himself just before he pushed the door open, almost giving away his hiding place. So drawn was he to her sensual form that his heart beat so loud in his ears he was sure she would hear.

Ella graceful as ever stepped into the tub and slid under the still steaming water. Damn her. To add to the effect she let out a hearty sigh of pleasure as she let her head fall back against the tub. Devon could almost taste the steam in the air. His chosen hideout closed in around him. He wanted to move. Muscles were beginning to react in grievance to his current position. At that moment, she slid her way down until her head was under water. Taking the opportunity, he stretched as best he could and shifted so his legs were more comfortable.

In agony, Devon watched his wife, unaware of her audience as she went about the business of removing the road grime which comes with travel. He was like a child watching someone eating a cake he could not indulge in. As Ella ran the soap over her long leg, he had to swallow a groan. For the one hundredth time in the last ten minutes, he waged a war within. What would she do if he were to show himself? Would she ask him to join her?

He would rip his clothes from his body, and hurt himself getting into the tub. Another groan rose to his throat, but again he forced it down.

What had happened? He was the one always in control. He never had times when he couldn't control himself, or his thoughts.

Ella was the problem.

For some reason, when she was involved, his steely control vacated his being. Left behind was a beast living off his senses. If he didn't gain control, he might ruin his chances right now. Not to mention prove Clive correct in his estimations. Devon closed his eyes, taking deep breaths until his feeling of control returned, if not in full force, at least in part. Opening his eyes, he spied Ella still lounging in the tub, now with her head against the high back, her hair falling off the edge in silken shimmering stands. Droplets of water rolled along the slippery tresses falling to the floor. Her eyes were closed. She looked almost content. He watched for what seemed like an eternity without as much as a movement. She was asleep.

Blasted wonderful.

Now he was stuck until she woke. What if she didn't wake until morning?

Devon had to do something. If she spent the night in a cold bath, since the water would have cooled by now, she might very well catch a chill, or at the very least be sore tomorrow. Then a worse thought sprang to mind. If she stayed asleep, she might slip under the water and drown. He had a vague memory of trying to wake when she first moved to the Tate. He could have shot a pistol in the room, and he was sure she would have slept through it. Very cautiously, he swung the door of the wardrobe open enough to step out. As he did, every muscle in his body protested. Wardrobes were not made to be hiding places for fully-grown men.

Ella never moved. She slept like the dead.

Now what?

If he woke her, she would thrash him within an inch of his life. He already knew he couldn't leave her, so his only option, *wasn't this wonderful*, was to try to move her without waking her.

Sighing, Devon stepped over to the stool and stripped off his waistcoat, cravat, and shirt. He would no doubt be as wet as she was when he finished. Cool air abraded his already sensitive skin. First order of business was to stoke the fire back to a comforting blaze. Then standing over his sleeping wife, he knew this would no doubt be the hardest thing he had ever done. Was this how knights of old felt? *Unlucky blighters!* He was about to take his clean smelling, wet, not to mention naked wife out of the bath, dry her body with his own hands and not be able to do more than kiss her on the cheek and leave. What crime would a man have to do to endure such torture?

He watched her sleeping for a moment longer. Not two weeks ago, he thought her dead. The power of it hit him like an anvil to his chest. His throat caught and he felt the distinct sting of what would not become tears abrade his eyes. It was almost more than he could bear. He never let himself mourn her. Never.

He had convinced himself it was her choice to leave, as it is every woman's, and he would not mourn someone he had never loved. The ignorance of his words then, stung today. The emotion hammered to come forth. If he allowed it, he knew the sob that would be wrenched from his soul would wake her and scare him to his core. Devon swallowed his pent up emotions and ignored the one lone tear that meandered down his cheek while he bent to tend to his very much alive wife.

Hands shaking, Devon reached into the tub and under Ella's back and legs. Her soft body molded to his embrace. He closed his eyes praying for some of that control. In one smooth motion, he straightened with his still sleeping wife in his arms. The water sloshed and splashed covering him. She nuzzled closer, cradling her head in the crook of his neck. The water clinging to her was cool, but her body was warm and lush. The softness of her skin against his own, like satin against wool warmed him, and made him aware of just how delicate she was, regardless of what she would say to the contrary. He made his way with ease to the bench in front of the hearth close to the fire. He set to drying her, starting with her shoulders and arms, making his way down her body.

He understood her weariness. Only a person with true exhaustion would sleep through such an intimate encounter. It scared him a little to think she could sleep through this onslaught. Once done, he could only reach his shirt to cover her now dried body. He ran his hand down her dripping hair to take some of the water out of it. The tenderness of the moment rocked him. It was the most innocent touch he had given, but it was the one that rocked him. Never had he put himself in the position to care for another with so much thoroughness.

Devon sat holding Ella to him. He rubbed his hand along the soft skin of her arm. How had he survived four years without her in his life? Had he actually told everyone who would listen, he was better off? At this moment, he knew he would never be able to let her go. In this moment, he understood his father.

Shaken by what he could only call an addiction to this woman sleeping in his arms, he decided he needed a better plan. He couldn't depend on the hope of her falling in love with him because, it was too risky. He had to think of a way to convince her, without appearing the lovesick pup that, she would be better off in London with him.

A shiver slid through her translucent skin before she snuggled closer to his bare chest.

"Mmm, Devon," she mumbled in her sleep. To hear his name slip from her lips while she dreamed was almost his undoing. At the same time, the fear of her waking and finding him with her in his arms seized his lungs. He froze, not breathing until she settled back down and began to snore softly in his lap.

He reached into her bag and came up with her nightdress, deciding time was at a premium if he wanted to get her to bed without her knowing. Devon managed to slide it over her head and around her shoulders covering her perfect body. Once home in London, he would make sure he had every night rail she owned burned. He wanted her naked in his bed. No barriers.

His current plan was to get her settled in bed, fix the fire again, and slip out the way he came. Devon needed time away to think and contemplate his next step. Standing with her in his arms and noting that she weighed no more than a feather, he walked to the bed. Ella snuggled into the depths of the fresh linens and pillows. Leaving was imperative, but not just yet. He took the chair and sat, not ready to break the spell.

Lying in the darkness, covered by the voluminous blankets, his wife looked frail and innocent, not to mention delectable. Since their reunion, Devon had not had the opportunity just to watch Ella until tonight. In fact, he could only recall a few times he indulged in the sport of watching the whirlwind that was his wife. This— this was a novelty. She lay sideways facing him. Only moments ago, she had been sprawled on her back with one delicate arm raised over her head, resting on a pillow of pale hair. Now, both hands were tucked together under one rosy cheek. A perfect complexion, save the dark circles ringing large doe eyes. Even the long, thick lashes kissing her cheeks were not enough to hide the signs of fatigue. His hands lay palms down on his thighs. The need to touch the fine skin made them tingle. Fix the fire and leave, he reminded himself.

Devon leaned over the bed as he began to rise out of the chair. At the same moment, Ella moaned, reaching for the blankets that she pulled into a bundle near her body, cradling it in her arms. Sighing with contentment, she settled back in but Devon noticed, a wrinkle of worry furrowing her brow. Her thoughts, it would appear, were not as slumberous as he thought. Sighing, he was lost to more than just this one night. He settled back into the very straight, very uncomfortable chair to deal with his stiff joints, and his growing desire. He was beginning to understand how a man like his father would suffer all those years alone with just the slimmest hope his love would return. For this woman's love, Devon would spend an eternity in hell if she asked.

It was going to be a long night.

CHAPTER 5

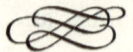

*G*ulls squawked overhead, dropping from the air, plucking a nice, fat fish from the barrels lining the docks. The briny scent of the sea mingled with the exotic spices and warmth of the sunshine to add color and texture to the normal dankness of the harbor. No matter how many times Ella came to shop here on the docks, she never got used to the contrast.

It would probably be easier, not to mention safer, for a woman to shop at the local merchants. She always used the practical reasoning that she needn't pay the exorbitant amount the merchants charged, when she could shop right off the ships just like those very shop owners. The prices were exceptional and she could compare the quality as well.

Her true motive was much less practical. Growing up in London, Ella loved the diversity she could witness. Not as sheltered as her more affluent counterparts, she had more freedom. She staunchly maintained that she disliked everything about the Ton to anyone who might ask, but as a girl and later as the wife of a Viscount, she dreamed of being welcomed into the world she was never quite allowed. She would spend her time instead, wandering around the different parts of London experiencing as much life as she could.

Now, holed up in a tiny Scottish village, she missed it. She loved the bakery and all the people who accepted her without question when she needed it most, but this was her time. She was a million miles away from her daily drudgery, her responsibilities of a mother. The other thing her trip this time took her from was Devon. Was it a good happenstance or not? That remained to be seen.

The one smirch on her otherwise welcome diversion was her two o'clock meeting to exchange what the blackmailers called a 'partial payment' for more instructions. She likened it to a twisted game of treasure hunt, where the player had to pay for the next clue. The problem was this particular player didn't care to find the end. Ella was getting a sinking feeling it would not be a fortuitous last hand.

Two o'clock was still many hours away and there was shopping to be done. From inside her satchel she extracted a small, well-worn notepad and a small pencil. Glancing at the entries from her last trip, she added a new date and column to record all the ships and their current prices. As she made her way down the long dock, her mind drifted to the events of the previous day.

Her trip yesterday was by far the most difficult she had ever taken. When she reached the safety of the inn, she all but cried. She never would have asked for a bath at such a late hour, but reminded herself to leave a very generous amount on top of her normal payment. She had not slept so well in a very long time. It still niggled, however, as to how she managed to get from the bath to her bed with no memory of it. True, there were many nights when she first took over the bakery that she didn't remember crawling into bed from exhaustion. That could explain last night's events. She had a memory of Devon as well, but since her dreams had been tormented by the blasted man, and his strong body and compelling stare since he had stepped back into her life, she was certain it was just more of the same, school girl wishes.

Ella would have dismissed her unease had it not been for the chair placed next to her bed when she woke. She wasn't sure what woke her, but something had. When she jolted awake, she noted the chair. When she rose from the bed, she had to move the chair to get around it. The embroidered seat and back were still warm as if someone had just vacated it. Had she slept so soundly that, one of her unknown enemies had entered her room and sat watching her undeterred? *Not behavior an independent woman would want to admit.*

"Here, Miss, I av' the best exotics on the wharf," shouted one scraggly looking man.

"Naw, all 'e's got is moldy bread. Now, if ye want quality, ye trot right over 'ere."

"Thank you, gentlemen," Ella said with a genuine smile. "I make it a point to check all that is available to make certain I am getting the best price. I will keep you both in mind." She moved with confident strides. Eric would be no more than twenty yards away when she looked back. Before, she had tried to convince him she did not need him following her. Today, however, she was thankful for his presence.

"How are you, miss?" The next captain asked in a respectful tone. As Ella reached him, the baskets and barrels spoke to her of far off places and adventure. Each had been ordered with care and was overflowing with abundance. She looked to her pad to check the name of the boat. Finding it, she turned to the captain.

"I am fine, Captain, thank you. I see your travels have been successful," she answered while mingling around the many items for sale. Even though her journey had been for her usual spices and other ingredients, she couldn't help when a beautiful silk wrap caught her eye. It was an explosion of colors, and giving over to the urge, she let it slip through her fingers. It was warm from the sun and felt like water caressing her palm.

"It would look magnificent on you, miss. Go ahead, try it," the older man urged, hoping to add the expensive shawl to his sale.

Ella laughed, "I am afraid, sir, trying it on would be all I would be able to do. I do not have the funds to own something so decadent." As the last word slipped from her lips, she spied something else. "Oh, this is simply adorable! Where did it come from?" The wooden elephant was heavy in her hand when she picked it up, with shimmering sapphire eyes, and ivory tusks, complete with a woven basket ready for a child's doll to take a grand safari.

"India, miss. I had gotten it for my niece, but I am afraid I will not be seeing her until she is much too old for it."

Closing her eyes, Ella could see Maddie's face light up with excitement. "How much?" She asked before she thought better of it.

"Five pounds."

"Oh," she gasped. "Well, I am sure the child who it goes to will love it." She turned, putting the toy to her back, thus out of her mind, replacing it with a pang of frustration at the amount she would be parting with later. "So, what have you this trip?" Getting right back to business. Better not to dwell on what she couldn't have because that would lead to self-pity, and that was something Ella couldn't afford.

"Ah, well if you look over here," he moved on, no doubt unhappy of losing such a sale. "I was a lucky bloke this time round. I have for you the world's finest cinnamon and anise from the orient. I also have lemons and limes. What else are you looking for, Miss?"

"Well, shall we start with the anise? What have you for a price?" When he rattled off the price, Ella felt the world shift.

"Sir, do you realize that price is double from what you quoted me last year past?" Hoping to barter, knowing there were other ships with much better prices down the line.

"It was a mighty hard sail this time round. I lost a good lot of my first cargo," he interjected with quiet, but painful misery. This, by looking at his inventory, was not accurate.

"I am dreadfully sorry, sir, but if I were to pay such a price, I would be running myself out of business."

The captain turned a rather unmanly shade of pink, as he began to mutter. Before he had a chance to counter her much less than desired offer, she smiled and pushed ahead to the next item.

"What of the cinnamon?" she asked, bending to the barrel, inhaling deeply the rich scent. She loved the smell. The added benefit that it could be stored for an extended period made it a staple to flavor everything from tarts to meat pies.

Again, the price was too high. Ella recorded the prices he offered and moved on. Not the vendor for her. She still had many ships to visit before her scheduled meeting, but she did need to go to the bank beforehand to acquire the amount the blackmailers demanded. There had to be a way to ferret them out and end this. However, what was it? Moving to the next ship, she focused on her notebook once again.

Devon watched as Ella haggled with the most unsavory of men. Then she would jot prices, he assumed, into her little notebook. He wasn't sure what annoyed him more, the fact she felt this was required of her, or the fact that she was good at it. There was no doubt he would grind his teeth to dust before this day ended.

He was beginning to understand just a small part of how Ella could have been so exhausted last night. A good sentnight in a hot bath would suit him just fine. Yesterday's ride had been hard physically and emotionally. Riding to catch up, then being filled with concern for Ella's health as he watched her become frail in front of his eyes, had not been a benefit.

Had that been the end of it until this morning, it would have sufficed, but no such luck.

It was a good thing he didn't gamble much anymore.

He then spent a fitful and uncomfortable night sitting vigil over her as she slept. He only just made his escape this morning before the maids started their work. Acquiring a room of his own, he changed into a clean shirt with haste. Devon washed the road dirt from his face, scrubbing the now visible stubble. With no shaving tools, it would only add to his already haggard appearance.

As a vendor strolled by selling meat pies, Devon's stomach groaned from hunger. He stopped the boy and purchased three. The young entrepreneur trotted off with three times what he expected, as Devon didn't bother to get change. The cold pie tasted good which surprised him. He had never before bought any fare from a street vendor. He chuckled that by default, it was Ella who introduced him to such a novelty.

Looking up from his feast, he found her. His eyes were drawn to her. So petite and delicate, yet she handled herself with efficiency and a regal air. Just then, she stopped to admire something other than blasted food stores. Devon walked closer to see what would catch his frugal wife's attention.

Hanging on a peg, Ella was admiring a silken shawl. Bright red with embroidered flowers of every conceivable color. It was bold, but at the same time, wholly feminine. It was Ella. He knew without a doubt, if she bought something frivolous, it would be the elephant for Maddie and not the shawl. Devon was not close enough to hear what was said, but he saw her shoulders rise and fall with a sigh before turning from both items as if to forget their existence. She went to work marking down prices. She didn't look happy in response to something the weathered braggart said. Having promised himself he would just watch her, Devon all but crawled in his skin with the need to put the man in his place. He was talking to an English Viscountess after all. He should show some respect.

But here, she wasn't a Viscountess. She wasn't his Viscountess. All of a sudden, his three meat pies didn't settle so well with the knot forming in his gut. She didn't want to be his anything. Well, that was going to change. It had to.

As Ella moved on, Devon moved too, careful not to be noticed by her escort. If he were Ella's first defense against attack, they were all in trouble. The man, well boy, Devon concluded, couldn't keep track of Ella and all the other people in the crowd at the same time. Devon had been following them since they left the inn and not once did the young man take notice of him. He would make sure Ella was aware of his shortcomings, or at the very least, give the blighter a lesson or two of his own. If his plan didn't work... *it had to work.* Hhe would not leave Ella unprotected.

One hour later, Ella had finished calculating in her notebook and made her way from the docks to the center of town. This time, her escort walked with her side by side. The trip would have been much more comfortable by hack, but perhaps she couldn't afford such a luxury. In the crowded city, Devon was forced to get closer to the couple as not to lose them. In doing so, he was also able to hear their topic of conversation.

"Well, I think I did very well today. Prices are going up, but I won't have to raise the price of bread just yet, which is fortunate, because with all the rain, I am not sure the villagers would be able to afford it," Ella said.

"As my Penny has said time and again, you give half your loaves away anyway."

Ella chuckled, but not of humor. Devon thought it was more from embarrassment.

Changing the subject, Ella went on, "I will not be long in the bank because I sent a letter ahead so they would be expecting me. Give me half an hour, then flag down a hack. I don't care to make this same trip back to the docks alone with that amount of money."

Trip back? To the docks? Alone? Alone, being without the younger man? What money?

Devon's head swam. If she hopped in a hack in the center of the city, how in bloody hell would he be able to protect her. A chill ran down his spine with droplets of sweat.

"I still don't like the idea of you alone. Why can't I ride in the hack and just stay out of sight?"

Alleluia, the boy had some intelligence and he was using it! Good chap!

Ella sighed, exasperation clear in her tone. *Not good.* "Eric, I have told you already they said bring no one. They will know you. They obviously have been watching me for some time if they know so much about me. I can't risk it."

"But–"

"No, they aren't going to harm me. I have something they want and they have all but informed me they are not finished draining my accounts yet, so just go back to the inn and wait. I will come to the stables the moment I return to assure you of my safety."

"All right," the young man gave in. *Coward!* "If you are not back by three o'clock, I will be returning to the docks after you."

"Fair enough." Ella put her hand on his arm as they reached the steps to the large bank building. "And Eric, thank you."

"Now, you know after what you've done for my Penny I would do anything for you."

"Well, thank you anyway." She turned heading up the marble steps "Remember, give me one half hour."

The young man smiled and waved before she disappeared inside the bank.

Ella was in trouble. The fear fell heavy in his chest, almost making it impossible to breathe. She was in trouble and didn't tell him. That part of the truth stung, but to her way of thinking, he knew it made sense. First, he was a man. He knew from experience the men Ella had dealt with, her father in particular, were not the kind to fix problems, but rather to cause them. Secondly, they had a deal, and to Ella that deal was binding. She had promised not to be a burden and ever come to him for assistance. She might still think the stipulation about going to debtor's prison was still an option. Lastly, she was trying to be independent. If she asked for help, she would be failing in her estimation.

Yes, he knew her motives too well. They would be his if he were in the same situation. He knew none of her reasons were valid, but he could see the logic. Trust no one, keep your promises, and prove to the masses you can handle anything. It had served him well in business, though not so well in his personal life.

Devon reached the top of the stairs before realizing he had been climbing them. More information was needed in order to be of any help. The bank was a good starting point. If he could see whom she was talking with, he could use his title and his money as a bribe, even in Scotland, to find out everything about his wife's financial well-being. Beating her back to the docks would not be an issue, as moving on foot was much quicker than a hack maneuvering through traffic.

Inside the bank, it was cool. As his eyes adjusted, it was easy to find his wife. She was the only female. Banks were not a place women frequented with regularity, so he was not the only one who took notice. She was sitting with a very young, green-looking bank clerk discussing paperwork. The clerk rose and made his hurried way across the bank, disappearing in the back. The interior was resplendent with large marble pillars and floor, making Ella's serviceable travel gown look dingy set off by the white of the marble. She looked so small sitting under the vaulted, cathedral style dome with large windows running the length of one wall. Though they flooded the expanse with light, they looked as though they might gobble her small form up.

The young man came back with as much purpose as when he left. Ella, who had been sitting straight, perched on the edge of her chair sat straighter, if it was possible. The man took the bank notes and counted them out for her. Devon couldn't hear the man count, but the amount was large, that was obvious. A shot of renewed fear lanced through him. Whatever trouble she was in, it was not to trifle with.

Ella put the notes into her satchel, thanked the clerk, and made haste out into the sunlight. He watched through the window, as she was handed into the hack by the boy and was whisked away toward the docks.

Devon turned, directing all of his attentions to the young clerk. No one else as of yet had grabbed the empty chair, so Devon made determined strides across the room to extract all the information he needed.

Ten minutes later, Devon was back out on the street making his way through the maze of people and buildings that was greater Edinburgh. The information he garnered spun in his brain. He made his way back from where he came, and sure enough, reached the docks in time to see a swish of gray skirt round the corner by the wharf. He made haste and turned the same corner, stopping dead. She was back at one of the ships. It wasn't a ship she had visited in the morning. This one had the look and feel of a smuggler's ship, dirty and sinister.

The captain was more than weathered and scraggly. This man was dangerous, and his wife was speaking to him. In fact, she was close enough so he could grab her if he so chose.

Blasted!

Devon walked past and made his way to another ship selling its wares. He couldn't hear a word being said, but Ella's posture was stiff and skittish. She reached into the satchel pulling out the folded pile of bank notes.

She might have been scared, but Devon noticed she was using her head. She held the notes close to her chest with her hand extended palm up waiting for something. After what Devon was sure was a moment to try to intimidate, the ugly man placed an envelope in her hand and reached for the notes. Ella grabbed them back from him to examine the letter.

Devon was just about to intervene when the man chuckled and stepped back, arms crossed waiting for her to decide. She made up her mind and handed the notes over. She turned and all but ran from the wharf. Remembering her comment to Eric about being watched, Devon took another route between two buildings to the other side of the docks and reached them in time to see Ella re-enter the hack and turn toward the inn.

He had two choices. He could hope that Ella confide in him and ask for his help, or he could go into her room and read what was in that letter for himself.

The first choice would show him in a better light, but if his wife and daughter were in danger, he would be happy to have his wife mad at him. After all, if she were mad at him that meant she was alive. Alive was more important now. He would see that letter tonight.

CHAPTER 6

*N*ever having stayed more than one night at the inn, Ella was unprepared for the evening bustle when she returned from the docks. Her nerves, worn and tattered from the afternoon meeting, only acted to pique her current level of anxiety. All the way back in the hack, she had been trying to name her unknown blackmailers. She had hoped to arrive early to order a tray in her room, and take a quiet evening to regain some control.

Head bent, she jostled her way through the throng, attempting to make it to her room. It was not to be. As she would have placed her slipper on the first stair, the innkeeper intercepted her. Ella gave as kind a smile as she was able and waited while the man caught his breath.

"Ah, Madame, ye almost got passed, dinnae ye?" he said with a jovial smile.

"Yes, sir. Having had such a full afternoon, I am looking forward to finding my bed."

The man's unease was apparent as he glanced behind him at a closed door and shifted his feet, making the skin on Ella's arms prickle. What would it matter if she were hoping to take to her bed?

"Well, not just yet as ye have a visitor, and from his speech, direct from London. Says he has some business with ye."

Devon.

Well, so much for a quiet evening to gain control over her once ordered life. She should have expected he would follow her. Didn't he once say he always got what he wanted?

"Where is the gentleman?"

"Oh, he's in the private parlor; ordered a meal for himself and you. About every half hour, he comes out asking if you've returned. Shall I announce you?"

"No, thank you. I must at least tidy my person. I won't be more than a few moments. Please don't announce me."

The innkeeper gave her a dubious look, but nodded and left. No doubt if Devon had arrived earlier today, the poor innkeeper had been hounded to death. Her husband did not like to wait. It was, of course, more likely that he had arrived yesterday, and the mystery of how she made it to her bed, and the empty chair was solved. She should be horrified and angry at his presumptuous behavior, but instead, a shiver ran along her spine, and her heart swelled at his care.

Her husband.

The thought brought her up short and she almost tripped going up the steps. She couldn't decide if the butterflies wreaking havoc in her stomach were anticipation or warning. She knew it would be prudent to assume the latter, but the thought of Devon sitting in dinner attire sent little chills through her body. No, she couldn't keep thinking of him that way. When she thought of them being man and wife, her mind would drift to their one night together, and... well, that wouldn't do at all. Since his return to her life, every time they inter-acted, she felt more anticipation than trepidation. If this continued, she would be lost again. Racing up the stairs to her room, she cleaned her face, tidied her hair, and donned the best of the gowns she had brought with her. When dealing with Devon one must be at her best. With any hope, her appearance would give her strength.

The back parlor was attached to the main room by a thick oak door. Ella swung it open hoping to gain a glimpse before he saw her. Where the door was silent, the noise of the taproom was not, and Devon turned from the fire to catch her in his gaze.

Her breath caught. His eyes held such intense emotion that she all but turned and ran from the room. The fire cast shadows over every rigid angle of his face. Feeling the urge to apologize for keeping him waiting rose in her throat, Ella instead, cleared it away and broke eye contact. Not sure why he had followed her, Ella decided to play the game.

"Good evening, my Lord. I wasn't aware you intended to take in the local fare on your visit. How are you liking your trip thus far?" Careful to keep a good distance between them, she moved around the large round table set for two and made her way to the dark window, but it was of no use. His presence made the room small and she could feel all around her.

Devon made a show of bowing before answering. "I am finding Edinburgh as I find the rest of Scotland, damp, cold, and wholly not to my liking, my lady." He added her title with a tone that spoke more of possession, than social rank.

"I am sorry you are more inclined to the more genteel clime of London. I trust you will be in a hurry to return soon then?" The energy between them crackled around the room. Devon prowled around the room to her side. The hairs on her arms buzzed with the energy surging from him.

"I must stay until my business is complete."

Before Ella could comment on what business he meant, either to steal her daughter away, or to force her to give up everything and live a loveless life in London with him, the innkeeper's wife appeared with a tray carrying lamb stew and fresh biscuits with poached buttered potatoes. The smell made Ella's mouth water.

"Shall we?" Devon's husky tone and proximity made her jump. Looking up into his eyes, they were no less intense, but not as hard. If she were to guess, amusement danced in their depths. Was he enjoying their verbal sparring? She doubted it. Her father always said that was her greatest fault. Well, there were many faults he called her greatest, but he mentioned her propensity to argue more than others. She also remembered the time spent in Devon's company. He had enjoyed a good discussion and they had more than once exchanged verbal banter. She had to remind herself he wasn't her father, or perhaps she should make an attempt not to remember it. Thinking he was like her father would help keep him at arm's length, but it would be a lie, and her sense of fairness would not allow it.

"Yes, thank you." She allowed him to lead her to the table and help her take a seat. Once the innkeeper's wife had finished setting out the dishes, she left, closing the door. Silence filled the room again. For several minutes, they sat enjoying the exceptional meal, not needing to talk. Secretly, Ella was thankful for at least this change in her plans. She hadn't realized how hungry she was. It also gave her a reason not to look at her companion.

She dared a glimpse only to find him sitting back in his chair, elbows resting on the arms with hands clasped on his stomach.

"Is something wrong with your meal, my Lord?"

"Well, now that you asked, the conversation is a trifle dull. I was hoping for more in the way of entertainment."

She couldn't help a slight curve of her lip as she smartly replied, "Well, I am sure if you asked the innkeeper, he would be able to lead you in a more apt direction for entertainment. I am certain you could find a gentleman's club with cards to your liking." She knew the barb would sting, or more than that, hoped that it would. She wanted him to know she knew the kind of man he was.

"I have not played for four years. I was taught how unsavory and all consuming such a habit could be if one wasn't careful. As I remember, you are more than able to entertain me in any way I may wish, which dulls the allure of the tables any day." The devil danced across his face, while hers burned with the heat of scarlet flames. She had hoped to avoid an outright discussion of her one indiscretion. He was no gentleman to throw it in her face. Her temper rose higher than the blush, but the admission of the fact he no longer gambled warmed her heart. *Oh, Lord help her.*

"I would be grateful if you would leave that particular topic off our list of conversations, please," she said tartly, but wouldn't look at him.

"As you wish. I didn't intend to unnerve you. I apologize."

His words shocked her, not so much that he apologized, but that they sounded sincere. She sat moving her mutton around the plate with her fork without speaking.

"Why did you leave?"

"Four years ago or Sunday?" she asked, hoping it was the latter.

"Both, but let us start with this little venture. Why the quick exit? Are you that scared to talk with me?"

Now, he was trying to goad her into a temper. "I am not scared to talk with you. I forgot I had planned my trip is all. It's not every day your husband, who doesn't exist, appears in your store wanting to meet his daughter. I have told so many that you were an officer and died in the war that I almost began to believe it as well." Her honesty surprised them both.

Devon chuckled, but he noted a hint of what he would call sadness in her voice. "Well, I think I understand that. It is almost as disquieting as finding out a woman you buried four years ago is alive and wandering the Scottish hills with a daughter. I am thinking we are even," he said with a more casual air than he felt. Since she brought up four years ago, he took the chance to find out whom he buried. "Perhaps you can clear something up for me."

"I would be happy to if I am able." She looked dubious in her belief of being able to do as he requested.

"When you left," Devon took a moment to steel his emotions. It was imperative he not give away too much, "I knew you considered our agreement fulfilled, but then when two coffins appeared on my door step..." Emotion choked his throat.

"I am truly sorry for that. I had no idea they would bother to bring the bodies back to you. I never knew," she said with genuine compassion.

"Who did I bury?"

"A passenger we were giving a ride to. We were three days into the trip and I became ill. I couldn't keep much food down, and the motion of the carriage made it worse." She retold the story with a look as if she were reliving it. "Father was very put out about the whole ordeal. We had stopped on the road so that I could be sick, but father had complained the previous time that he did not care to witness such and that I needed to take myself away from the carriage, so I went into the woods out of sight and hearing. As I was retching, I heard the horses and the first gun shot. I should have attempted to stop them, but I was so very frightened."

"Had you been that foolish, I would have buried three coffins." A hard, raw edge in his voice surprised him. He cleared his throat to be rid of it.

"I know. I think I also suspected at that point that I was with child, even though I was trying to deny it. I crouched in the thick brush and became as small as I could. They killed Father and the young woman almost immediately, then spent the better part of an hour going through our belongings." She was speaking at almost a whisper. Devon had to lean forward to catch every word. "Once they left, I remained in the bushes until dark and then ran through the woods until I came to a farm house. I made up a story about being the widow of an officer who was killed. I said I was just trying to get to my family up north so the gentleman took me, but once I was there, I discovered that my great aunt had passed and there were no other relatives in the area. That is when the baker and his wife took me in."

"So, the braggarts didn't find you? You were able to escape with, if no money and belongings, at least your life," Devon said more to himself to come to grips with the truth of it all.

"Oh, I didn't lose my money. Before the trip I had sewn pockets inside my traveling dress to hide the funds from Father, so I had the money with me. All they stole was some of my mother's jewels, and what my father had of value."

"I thought the worst. I assumed when I saw your father in the first coffin..." He had to stop talking to keep the memories at bay. If he kept going, she would see that which he could not allow her to see. He knew better than to show such emotion to a woman, because they would use it against you, just as his mother had done to his father.

"Again, I am sorry if I inconvenienced you by--"

"Inconvenienced me? Is that what you think I went through? An inconvenience?" Devon interrupted her mid-sentence. He must have reacted with more emotion than he meant, because she sat back with a look of unease. "Look, Ella," Devon went on, taking a hefty drink from the balloon glass in his hand. "I only want to talk. You keep looking at me as if I am a rabid dog about to attack."

"You'll excuse me if I am cautious. If you recall, I have made bargains with you in the past."

Devon nodded and raised his glass in a mock toast. "As well you have, Madame."

"What is it you want of me? What do I have to do to expedite your return to London?" She had changed the subject and he allowed it. Her history wasn't going to advance his purpose right now.

Devon sat and tried not to wince as her words hit him. It was on the tip of his tongue to tell her. *Fall desperately in love with me and give me your soul.* He didn't deserve her love, he knew. It would be too much to ask for, and before he could consider wooing his damnable wife, he had to protect her from an unknown evil. That only made him feel a fraction less contrite for spiking her wine with laudanum. Never had he felt it necessary to drug a woman to get what he wanted, but knowing his wife as he did, this would move things along. He got the feeling time was of the essence in this matter.

Still, it seemed a cowardly, not heroic deed.

Her change of dress usurped his chance to nick the note from the pocket in her gown. He had to get into that room, but in her current state of pique, there was no way he would be able to persuade his way into her bed and by default, her room. To make matters more dire, she wasn't drinking her wine. It seemed she wanted to keep her wits about her. Devon smiled to himself. She was a force to reckon with.

Now, his challenge began unnerving her enough to persuade her to take a long calming drink of wine. It came to him like a lightning bolt. So swift was the thought, he almost caught himself grinning like a child with a new toy.

Clearing his throat, he sat up a bit straighter, reaching to pluck a grape from the fruits left on the platter. After enjoying the cool tart fruit for only a moment, he continued.

"I propose another deal. A wager really, not dissimilar to the way you introduced yourself to me. Are you still a gambling woman?"

He congratulated himself, for the instant the words slipped from his lips, her color piqued and her eyes widened. It only took her a moment however to compose herself into the proper widow she had convinced herself she was. Before he could stop himself, visions slipped into his memory of a hot summer night, the smell of honeysuckle and her soft skin gliding all around him. It was a memory he had relived many nights, the first and only time they made love. He would have that passionate, wholly feminine woman in his arms again.

Remembering where he was, he shifted in his seat. Now was not the time to let desire overshadow his objective. Devon could see her studying the wine, debating if it would help. Once she consumed the drug, his desire would be cooled. He would not take her to his bed unless there were no questions about her true desire as well.

Before she could calm her nerves, he continued, "My deal, love, is simply this. You agree to let me spend time with Maddie and get to know her," putting up a staying hand when Ella would have argued, "I am not finished, hear me out."

She made a very unladylike snort, but waved him on with her hand and sat back with her arms crossed.

"Thank you, I will agree not to mention I am her father. I would like to add that I do legally have every right to see my daughter. Also, while I am becoming acquainted with Lady Maddie, I would require the right to spend time away from Maddie, with you."

One soft, beautiful brow rose to a perfect arc, but Ella sat silently, waiting for the rest.

"While I am playing pretty to you ladies, I will endeavor to persuade you that I am a man cut of a different cloth than your father. If, after my stay, you agree I am as I say, I would ask that you move closer to London, as I am want to see my child as she grows."

"That's it? You want to get to know Maddie and if you can

convince me that you are a suitable parent, I will move closer to London? What if I decide you are not what I would expect a perfect parent to be?"

Devon had to smile. She was already scheming a way out, but to his relief, as she attempted to act in control, she drew the wine glass to her lips and took a long sip.

"Well, that is the part concerning Maddie. There are two parts to this deal." He saw her grow stiff, wary, and just a little confused, as the bitter taste of the drug hit her tongue. "You will allow me complete access to you."

"What does complete access–? Oh!" When she realized he was demanding the right to warm her bed, she turned blaze red. That struck him as telling, since any widow he had ever engaged with was beyond the blush when the conversation turned to talk of the bedchamber. True, the only widows he had contact with were those of the Demimonde who Clive was acquainted. Still, he felt it a very good sign.

"Our original agreement was only one night, and that was your stipulation, not mine. I gave you that. This wager is nothing like the one we struck four years ago. I simply proposed a logical solution to our similar dilemmas. You had to up the ante," she argued, starting to look a bit confused. "I only wanted to get married so I could access my dowry to pay you my father's gambling debt and have enough to flee to Scotland. We would not be sitting here had we gone with my plan without alteration," she pointed out. "I would have fled and faked my death, end of story."

"You did follow through with your part of the bargain, complete with coffins, which I was not expecting. You, however, were the one to act. You came into my bedchamber in the dead of the night taking advantage of the fact I was only partially awake. You can't expect me to count that." He was holding onto the hope she was less experienced than she was letting on. He gave her a hard, grave look across the table, trying not to spoil the look with a smile.

"I, well– I thought that would suffice, yes. You mean to tell me that we were able to create a child, but you don't want me to count that as an intimate coupling?"

Perhaps, he hadn't put enough laudanum in her wine. "Well, yes, it was as you say, but for my part, I was not able to enjoy it as I would have liked. I propose we have another go. It couldn't have been that undesirable, could it? If it was, I feel I cheated you. You deserve my best efforts, and by waking me as you did, well, I can hardly say if I was able to achieve that for you." Devon leaned forward capturing Ella in his heated stare.

The fire popped, breaking the awkward silence. Ella jumped at the sound and realized the room had begun to spin. Was he suggesting what they shared was not adequate with his usual ability? She must have misunderstood what he was saying. By the gods, if he could set her afire as he did that one night without trying, she would surely die if she allowed him to give his best go. "I, sir, think you did a fine job on your first endeavor."

It would be kind of him to stop jumping around so. He was making her dizzy from his movements. His voice washed over her like a warm blanket. What was he saying? Next thing she knew, his hands were rubbing up and down her bare arms. Flames rose inside her. It was as if her senses were on alert. His breath was at her nape now, and he smelled of fruit and wine, and something that was Devon. She wanted to go back and ask him why he would want to spend time with Maddie. She couldn't inherit. She wasn't a son. What could he possibly— the thread of her thoughts danced just out of reach. Why was she so confused?

"I know I can do better, sweeting, I just needs try. Do we have a deal?"

After a breathless moment, Ella heard herself answer, "Yes." She'd done it again. She had given herself to the devil. Nevertheless, as her mind shifted from one thought to another, she wanted to be with him; wanted to feel his hands and mouth on her. Hadn't she dreamt it night after lonely night? She felt herself cheer at the idea. Having her Devon to herself at least one more time. Into her thoughts, his husky voice swelled, mixing with her scandalous images. Somewhere in her mind, she heard herself say no, but it was so faint and she couldn't remember why she would want to refuse him, the man she could not refuse anything.

Oh, she shouldn't say that. He shouldn't know that, should he?

"Let's get you upstairs, shall we love?"

"Yes." She couldn't believe she was going to go through with this.

A sturdy arm wrapped around her waist, guiding her out the door and behind the bar as to avoid the crowd. The taproom was full. That much she could tell, but the noise and colors seemed to swell like the waves at sea. Before she knew it, she was at her door, propped up by Devon who juggled her in his arms while opening it.

"While I get things ready, why don't you rest on the bed? You seem to have had a tiring day."

As he placed her on the bed, careful to put a soft pillow under her head, her last thought was that it was nice to be taken care of by the ones she loved. Then the darkness and warmth took over.

Devon managed to get the snug boots off her small feet, and then he turned Ella over in order to have better access to the buttons. He pulled the dress over her head, balancing a dozing Ella with his free arm. Then came the stays and he dropped the bundle to the floor. Once finished, he sat in the chair he had occupied the night before and watched, as his laudanum drunk wife lay silent and vulnerable on the bed. She had actually agreed to sleep with him again. His desire rose just thinking about wrapping those lithe legs around him again. He would have her, but not tonight. She would need to be awake and an equal partner. He rose from the chair and made his way to the reticule on the small dressing table to find out what danger he had to deal with before he could begin to seduce his wife.

Inside, he was surprised to find a small lady's pistol. It was of good quality with engravings of flowers and vines around the barrel. He would have to remember she had a weapon before he tried to woo her too much. Sliding the pistol back, his hand brushed against what he was looking for. A letter.

Removing the paper, he noted the quality was very poor, not the paper that anyone of importance would use. The penmanship was poor at best, but good enough to make out.

"Ye know what we want. We know what ye are. A bastard in lady's clothes. If ye knows what's good ye, wait fer another note to pay double the sum ye jus did. It costs pounds to keep us quiet and ye and yer bairn safe. Meet at the ruins in Finees in a sennight. You'd do weel to remember the child always pays for the sins of the parents."

Devon cursed at the cryptic note. What was it with Scots? Couldn't they just say what they meant? Someone was blackmailing her, but why? Did they know who she really was? Was his being there putting her in danger? His instincts said no. If they knew about him, they might have tried to contact him and gain even more funds. No, there was something else here, but the question was, did Ella know? Her note mentioned *sins of the parents*. Was this about her father? Did he owe money to men in Scotland? Devon didn't doubt it, but that didn't feel right either, and if this was about her parents, Ella might not know anything. Just then, she moaned and tried to roll in the bed.

While she was drugged, he could ask her questions and she would have no way of knowing what went on. He used to go to one of his father's mistresses when she was laudanum drunk and ask her all sorts of questions. If she had remembered, he would have been lashed for it. He was sure he could find out something.

Reaching the bed, he pulled the chair closer and turned it so he could straddle the seat, making a small barrier of the chair back between them, and brushed an errant wisp of hair from her face. Close to her ear, he whispered, "Darling? Darling, can you hear me?"

"Mmm, you sound far away," she replied groggily furrowing her brow in confusion.

"No, sweeting, I'm here with you." To prove his point, he took her hand in his and rolled his thumb over her knuckles in a gentle rhythm. She relaxed her scowl and sighed. "Darling, I am going to ask you some questions. You need to answer me."

"Yes, just don't stop rubbing my hand. Feels good."

Devon smiled knowing it was a good thing on many levels that she would not remember this night. "Who is blackmailing you, love?"

Again, she frowned and turned her head back and forth. "Don't know."

"Why are they blackmailing you?"

"Not sure," she answered after a moment's pause. "Bad men."

"Have they hurt you or Maddie?" Devon held his breath waiting for what he feared to hear.

"No, letters get worse each time. Trying to find them. Find why."

"Could it be they know about you and me?"

"No, they know about my mother. Mention her often. Didn't like her."

Her movements became far more uneasy and her expression was one of confusion. Devon sat in the silence stroking her hand in slow rhythmic circles until she stilled and her face was clear of any worry lines. She looked angelic lying on the bed with her long blonde hair. She also looked helpless and vulnerable. He would find the fiends who were terrorizing his wife, and put an end to their scheming.

Clive would know whom to contact to learn of Ella's family. He would sit down with the man and find out all he could. Devon would also get to the task of searching out the blackmailers. He would start by finding out if there was anyone in the surrounding villages who all of a sudden seemed to have come into some wealth. The threat didn't seem immediate, so he would also make sure he planned time to woo his wife and get to know his daughter, and by default, protect them.

"Devon?" Her voice was but a rasp.

"I'm here, love," Devon said as he leaned in. "What is it?"

"Kiss me." She turned, without opening her eyes, her full lips parting, so he could just see the tip of her tongue. His own mouth went dry.

Devon drugged her only to get information he knew she wouldn't give otherwise. He would not take advantage. However, since he had lost her four years ago, hadn't he dreamt about covering her mouth with his? It's not as if he was going to ravish her.

What could it hurt?

He leaned in inhaling her. She was a mix of honeysuckle with the remnants of the exotic spices on the docks. It was intoxicating. The first contact was a slight brush of his lips on hers. He didn't want to start and find she didn't mean her invitation. At the deep moan of approval, his touch became more firm.

Her lips were better than any dream. Warm, lush, and full of life; life he never thought he would taste again. Emotion, strong and sharp, drove into his chest and throat, paralyzing him. If he lost control now, he would regret it. When he would have pulled away, Ella picked up her head following him and tasted his lips with her sweet, honeyed tongue. It was almost his undoing.

Devon wrapped his arms around her lithe body, pulling her into him. He was thankful for putting the chair back in his way or he might have given in and crawled into the embrace of her arms. Desire shot through him with a hot intensity he had never experienced. He had to keep some control. He would take his time kissing her, tasting her, but he couldn't let it go further, not yet.

When he returned his lips to hers, he took charge, delving with his tongue into her sweet mouth. She tasted of wine and the faint bitter bite of the drug reminding him of his limits. She was a wonder, giving and taking all he offered. When her hands wound around his neck to bury into his hair, he moaned deeply in his throat. Their kisses became hungrier, more demanding. He ripped himself free.

She breathed heavy, chest rising and falling. Her lips were swollen and a slight rash around her mouth and cheek gave away his need for a shave. Ella's skin was flushed and hair was mussed. She looked as if she had been thoroughly tumbled.

Devon couldn't resist the need to lie next to her. He came out of the chair and stretched out on the bed on top of the covers. She mewed, turning into his chest. Her hand wound its way up his shirt and into the hair at the nape of his neck. Once she snuggled into the hollow of his arm, he knew he was finished. The chance to spend the whole night with Ella in his arms was more than any man could overcome. Devon slid from the bed only long enough to undress and slip under the covers, taking a pliable Ella with him.

It would be so easy to take her body, but it wasn't just her body he wanted. It was her soul. The warmth radiating from her washed over him. This time, it was his turn to snuggle into her softness, wrapping his arm around her waist, pulling her to him protectively. His body reacted, but tonight was about feeding his inner desire not his physical one.

Her warmth filled him. Knowing he didn't deserve to feel so cherished, when she rolled and nuzzled his neck, gave him a pang of guilt. He was stealing what most men saw as their right. He shouldn't want this so bad, but that wouldn't stop him now. He half expected her to vanish in a swirl of mist like in his dreams. It would serve him right if this were a dream. If it was, he hoped he never woke. Devon drifted off to sleep on a cloud of honeysuckle and satin skin.

Ella couldn't remember being so cozy. She had the covers pulled up to her neck and they were warm and soft and cradling her in the most incredible warmth. She hadn't opened her eyes. It was like a dream she didn't want to end. If she could just stay here a few minutes more. As if to entrench herself deeper, she burrowed into the bed.

She wasn't alone.

Once Ella moved, the film of sleep lifted and the hard truth pressed against her back with only her shift to shield her. A decidedly male, hard truth. In a wave, the previous night, or part of it, came rushing back. They had dinner, talked, and then she lost the thread. What had she done? What had she said? Still not opening her eyes, she tried to determine if he was still asleep.

Being early, the inn had not come to life yet. The birds were already busy outside the window singing their songs. Her breaths came stiff and quick. Devon's breathing, on the other hand, was soft and steady. His arm draped over her waist, holding tight but not in a threatening manner. She thought of Maddie with her favorite doll. She would hold it tight enough to know if it was taken, but not tight enough to break it. His chest covered her back with strong, solid flesh. With every breath from his mouth, the hair around her ear fluttered and tickled. With caution, she moved her leg back until it came into contact with his. Long and covered in soft hair, her toes didn't reach his feet, even stretched out to their full length.

Her head began to hurt, not a full-blown headache, but a throbbing, slow and persistent. That wine must have been stronger than she realized. She had a choice to make. Did she jump out of bed and demand him to leave or remain where she was and absorb the feel of being held? It was a feeling she realized she missed even though she had never experienced it. How many nights had she dreamt about being in his arms, with his strength surrounding her and protecting her from the world? Was this what women who found love had to look forward to? If so, she didn't understand the women of the Ton choosing to wed for gain instead. She felt safe. The storm could rage outside, but in his arms, she would feel calm.

Mind made up, Ella sighed and tried to commit every point of contact with this man to memory, but it seemed her body remembered without any aid. There was not a tender spot. He was all hard plains and firm muscle. Where she was rounded, he was not, but she seemed to be made to fit in the crux of his body to perfection. She wiggled to go deeper into the valley that was his embrace. Just as she was beginning to feel relaxed about sharing her bed with a man, the man in question roused. Devon's hand slid from her waist to her hip. Electric shocks trailed along her skin where he touched. She came alive, like she had been asleep these four years waiting. Waiting for him to wake her from her sleep.

Her skin prickled as his feather light touch ran along her hip and down her thigh. His large hand was soft unlike her calloused ones.

"Devon?" she whispered.

"Yes, love?" He answered, a tentative note in his voice.

"I like that," she admitted shyly after gaining a bit more confidence.

After two heartbeats, when she thought he might decide her too forward, he made a noise low in his throat that vibrated in his chest and against her back. His hand followed its path back, but instead of stopping at her hip, it wound its way up, over her belly and rested on her breast. The heat from his hand spread from its point of contact down to her belly, causing it to clench and flutter. His breath was warm on her neck before the soft sweep of his lips, and then the heat of his tongue sent chills to meet the heat from his hand. It tickled, but in a wholly sensual way, she wanted to feel again and again. If she was going to let this happen, she needed to take in every sensation and put it to memory. Many nights she would relive her one and only time with Devon to get her through. She would need to have this time to get her through when he was gone again. For a moment, the loneliness that had engulfed her when she left the first time tightened her chest, making her never to want to go back there, but her desire pushed it back down where she had closed it away for so long. She would no doubt have to wrestle it again, but not this moment. She was in the arms of the only man that had ever treated her well. She could still feel his detachment, the same that had prompted her to flee before, for fear her feelings would not be met in turn. She could not allow the hope that this was different. She just needed to allow herself the moment. She gave herself up to the sensation.

CHAPTER 7

*I*t was time for Devon to show Ella what she would be missing. He knew his love would never be enough to keep her. His love had not been enough to keep his mother from leaving them, so no matter the extent of his love, he knew it was lacking and that he didn't deserve her love either. However, if he could bind her to him physically, he might have a chance to keep her in his life. If she felt the pleasure they could have, perhaps it would be enough. He knew if he fell into his own trap, he would be lost. If he loved like his father, he would never be over her, so keeping it to the physical nature was best. His desire was nearly out of control after spending the night inhaling her intoxicating scent and feeling her warm body next to his. If he thought on it too much, he might consider that he might already have lost his heart. Devon would not think on it then, instead, he would feel... and smell... and taste, until Ella was part of him and his memories for eternity. He gently cupped her bosom in his palm where he noted it was heavier now that Ella had carried his child, but that only made her perfect. Her nipple was already swollen; hard, and it peaked and rubbed against the center of his hand. She had matured in four years. Tentatively, Devon fondled one tight globe. Her soft moan was encouraging, sending heat through his already throbbing body. He needed to have her naked.

"Darling," his voice was husky with his controlled desire. "I want to feel you without all this fabric."

The silence was deafening and Devon had to rest his forehead in her hair to quell the need to roll her to him before she consented.

"All right."

Before she could change her mind, Devon pushed up on one elbow to rise above her and rid them of the offending material. Looking down froze him. His wife looked up into his eyes with wide unsure depths. Her hair was down and hanging around her like golden silk. Her lips were full and red.

God, she was beautiful. His heart slammed against his chest taking his air.

Finding his voice, he continued. "I am going to slide it up over your head, all right?"

"Yes."

She remained still, but very pliable as he lifted her shoulders and slid the shift over her head, sending it to the floor next to the bed on top of her other forgotten clothing. Once he reclined her back onto the pillows, he took the opportunity of his position and remained above her. He placed an elbow on either side of her and began stroking her long hair with his hands.

Her breasts pushed against his chest and he could feel her deep breaths.

"Relax, sweeting. If you want to stop, we will. I want you, but not until you want me as well." He might well expire if he didn't have her now, but he would never force her.

"I... I don't want you to stop," she said in a small voice.

"Good," Devon said with a nonchalance he didn't feel. "I don't want to stop either, love." He continued just to lie there feeling her under him, when she reached up and started rubbing his back. His muscles tensed under her attention. Damn, her touch was like fire.

Before Devon could bend to cover her mouth, she took the lead and rose to brush her plump lips against his. The contact ignited the slow burn and before he realized, they devoured each other. The frenzy began to build and build until Devon thought he would catch fire. Her scent and hair entrapped him. Her touch was as hungry and needy as his own. The feel of her in his arms filled his chest with emotion he couldn't examine yet.

Turning back onto his side next to Ella, he attempted to pull back enough not to consume her. This was about her, not him. He had to get control. The one thing he was unable to do last time was something he would not miss this time, however. Gingerly, he pulled the blanket from her body. His breath slammed into his rib cage. Her skin was milky white with proud ruby nipples. Her stomach was not quite flat, but the gentle roundness gave her the look of the mature woman she was. Her long legs spread toward the bottom of the bed shifted under his scrutiny, causing the sheets to shush in the silence. At the apex of her legs, he saw the patch of golden hair hiding her feminine core.

"God, Ella, you're beautiful," he said reverently. If Ella answered, he didn't hear her. His heart roared in his ears, which he couldn't ignore. With slow movements, as if she would disappear if he were to move any other way, he reached out and spread his hand on her stomach. The place where she had cradled and protected his child. Where part of him had grown. It amazed him more than he realized. The fact he could cover her stomach with his hand amazed him. He had missed so much. She had been alone and scared, not knowing what to do, while he had sulked about like an angry child who had a toy taken from him. Looking down at his dark tanned hand only made her pale skin shimmer in the morning light.

He glided his hand down to the place he wanted to be. Her heat on his hand was almost his undoing. She was ready for him. He parted her legs and ran his hand up her milky thigh. She was soft and hot. He opened her and slid one finger inside. On her moan, he began a slow rhythm to bring her to a peak. Her movements, slow and slight at first, became more demanding as he built her passion. He couldn't wait much longer. He had to be inside her; had to feel her heat. Just as he thought he might have to take the lead, she spoke.

"Devon," she said with a gasp, "I want to feel you inside me, now. Please." Her hips rose, lifting his hand and her off the bed.

Devon removed his hand and rose to cover her. Her scent warm and musky filled the air, making him dizzy. Her heavily lidded eyes were wild with desire-- her skin flushed and ablaze with passion. He positioned himself to enter her, but held back searching her face for second thoughts.

"Now, Devon! I'm going to explode," she demanded.

It was all the encouragement he needed, so he slid into her to the hilt. Her muscles tensed around him. Her eyes were wide at first, but softened before fluttering shut. He held himself still to let her become accustomed to the feel. Before he would have, Ella began to respond under him in tantalizing movements. Devon read her unspoken plea and helped her set a pace that would not allow any extended play, not this time. He was in heaven and wanted to stay there, but his wife had other ideas. She took the lead and set a pace, Devon knew he would be wont to keep considering how close he was to climax. She wrapped her arms around his neck and her legs around his hips pulling him into her more deeply.

Their release exploded around them with a force Devon wasn't prepared for. He swallowed her screams with a deep kiss. He collapsed, shifting only enough to keep his weight off her. Both lay exhausted and spent. He reached around, drew the blanket over their sweat soaked bodies, and drifted off with the feel of Ella gliding her hand up and down his back. At last, he was home.

Wrapped in Devon's embrace, Ella listened to him breathe. She often would lie next to Maddie and revel in hearing her steady breathing, but the feeling she had now was different. It warmed her in a way she had run from four years ago. He had been the one to place the wager this time. The one damnable thing she could remember from last night, was agreeing to yet another wager, but could he live up to his claims? Could she dare to take such a risk with not only her life, but with her daughter's? Last time, when she thought she had control of the situation, she left with her heart in tatters. How would she survive this?

Devon must have sensed the unease, because he moaned and pulled her closer. She loved the feel of his body next to hers. She felt protected and— loved. A lump formed in her throat. She would never allow Maddie to go through what she had to endure. It was hard to believe the man who had just brought so much pleasure, would be cruel, but she thought of her own mother. She couldn't believe the woman would have cleaved to a man such as Ella's father had she known what he would be. Devon had never been cruel, as she had seen her father be, but the fear was that he would change once the responsibility of raising a child set in.

If it was just Ella, she could easily be lost in the fantasy of this moment. That was the main reason she fled before, because she could have stayed if only he had asked. Her greater fear was that he wouldn't ask. Without a doubt, if she spent the time he asked, she could fall in love with him and again deal with heartbreak worse than when she left for fear of falling in love before. The question was whether the pain she knew she would eventually face, be worth the short time she could have with him. The answer would not spare her misery. She knew that.

Devon grumbled in his sleep and rolled away. She took the space and the opportunity to think about their lovemaking. The first time, she hadn't known what to expect, but she hadn't expected the uprising of feelings she experienced, not to mention the physical pleasure. It had blown her away. She almost decided to stay a bit longer, but instead, chose to run for fear of being hurt worse. This time was eerily similar in that respect. If she allowed herself to admit she enjoyed the encounter, which she had without measure, she would have to give him a feather in his cap toward their wager. Ella sighed heavily, knowing she would not be able to deny the utter pleasure he could bring to her. No other man could set her ablaze as Devon could. Even just thinking about it, she could feel the heat starting to build inside. It had been four years since the last time, so it was possible she didn't quite have the memory of last time to compare the two. However, since that was all she had, she would have to agree Devon put forth his best effort both times she had made love with him.

If she was going to be fair, she needed to give him access not only to Maddie, but also to her. If Ella did what he wanted, she would be lost. Perhaps she already was. Just then, she was reminded by her logical side that Devon would want nothing to do with her once he found out she was being blackmailed. Most men cared little of the issues of women, and it would be inconvenient when the woman you are spending time with has to give away a small fortune to unknown braggarts. With no title, save the one he gave her when they wed, Ella had no known connections and once the Ton learned of how she had been living these past years, well, she would be more of a pariah than she was her first go around. No, Devon would be wiser to tuck tail.

Ella slid from the bed taking care to be as quiet as possible. Her weight barely made any change in the mattress, so Devon slept on. Her responsibility was to the bakery and Maddie. She couldn't be concerned about Devon. He would realize he still detested Scotland and that this foolhardy venture was not worth his time. If she could keep their contact to a minimum until then, she might be able to get free with only minor heartbreak.

Ella plucked her gown and boots from around the bed. The gown was hopelessly crumpled and would need a great deal of work to bring it back to its beauty. She laid it out on the small table in the center of the room and folded it as best she could. She went behind the dressing screen to don her traveling clothes. By the layer of frost along the edge of the window, it was a crisp Scottish spring morning. She made sure to put on an extra pair of stockings. Once dressed and packed, she decided to let him sleep. He looked horrible in the light of day, as if he hadn't slept in days. Ella knew that feeling and wished she was still abed with him, but it would do no good for either of them to wake in each other's arms again today.

Taking a piece of paper from the small desk in the corner, she sat to compose a note. It had to be dismissive, but not insulting. It also needed not to let him know she had already made up her mind, because until he realized she was not what he desired, he would see her as a conquest. She thanked him for his concern, and said she would be seeing him later, hoping he would get bored long before that. Right now, she needed space— as much space as possible. If she could keep him at bay long enough, she could build her reserves to protect her heart. That is what she told herself, but that logical being inside her told her it was already too late because that had been taken four years ago.

On soft tread, Ella left the room with her belongings and made her way to the taproom. Once there, she asked Timothy to fetch Eric and get the gig ready for the trip back. She also ordered a basket of food for the trip. She was famished, but did not dare take a meal at a table. The basket would be plenty to keep Eric and her full and satisfied on the trip home. It was also important to settle her bill. That would be something Devon would try to do and she wanted none of his heavy-handed handouts. She was still an independent woman, and while the money was sorely needed to pay toward the next black-mailers' payment, Ella refused to become indebted to him again. Mayhap, Devon would wake before anyone thought to go and tidy the room, but there was not she could do if otherwise.

As the gig rambled out of the Inn lot, Ella sat with her back straight and eyes forward, not looking back. For if she did, there was a chance to decide it a better choice to return to his arms and that warm bed. No, there was nothing there for her, and she would do well to remember that. That was the only thing that saved her last time, remembering she was not a Viscountess or his lover. To let her resolve falter now would only mean more pain later. Instead, she watched the sun's rays begin to melt the frost on the grass and warm the world.

Her belly growled and reminded her of the basket. "Well, Eric, are you ready for a feast? What would you like first?" she asked, putting the morning's events from her mind, at least for the time being.

"No, you eat first, Mrs. R. I will have what is left," Eric declined.

"Nonsense, I had them put a basket together that would feed us both. Here, have some bread and a piece of cold chicken." She handed him the food, then dug in to find a juicy piece of hen for herself. The food took her mind off other parts of her body that would have argued. The last thought she allowed herself on the subject was why men could so prance into one's orderly life and muck it up with a caress or a kiss.

Devon stood in the window overlooking the Inn yard and watched as his wife's gig rambled down the road and out of sight. His body ached from... well... the list was long. It ached from the journey he took to get here, the fear that he held at bay when he followed his wife to the docks, and anger he controlled when he would have chosen to throttle the man Ella was forced to interact with. It also ached from a night spent holding the woman who was his wife, but not allowing himself to take advantage, but at this moment, it hurt most of all, because he spent too much damn time this morning holding himself still as not to scare her. When she had first awoken, he was already awake and enjoying her warmth next to him, but once she roused, he held himself silent allowing her to come to terms with him in her bed. Just when he thought she would send him out with a boot to the head, she had opened to him. His body reacted at the memory, but it was something else that had him more concerned. It was as if a huge weight had been lifted from his chest.

Once sated, they lay tangled together, but he did not sleep as she assumed. He waited, wondering about her next move. He would have hoped for a repeat, but instead, in true Ella fashion, she ran. He had expected it however, so it had no bearing on his plans.

As the gig vanished over the hillside, he turned from the window and gathered his clothing. While dressing, Devon decided to give her time. Right now, he thought as he tied his cravat into a simple coun-tryman's knot, she thinks she has the upper hand. If Devon let her alone for a while, she would be lulled into thinking his interest was waning. Besides, he would not know until he returned to Clive's if his secret weapons were en route yet. She could hold her own against a man. She just considered them all like her father, but she would not have so much luck with the two women whom she was closest to. It would also give him time to do some digging into the blackguards who were blackmailing her.

Again, he was sure Clive would see her leaving without so much as a thank you as a loss, but Devon was beginning to believe that when Ella ran, it was because she was afraid of her own feelings. Their lovemaking was amazing. He had relived their one night together more times than he could count, and today's exercise only solidified the fact that they fit as if they were made one for the other. The way her body responded to his touch told of the connection. There was not one thing about her that didn't call to him: her scent, her taste, her curves and softness, her longer than imagined legs wrapped around his hips. Damn, he needed to get on the road and let the cool morning air have its way with his ardor. When he got his wife back in his bed where she belonged, he might not let her out for a month.

Devon quit the room and made his way to the stables. He didn't even bother stopping to settle the bill, because Ella no doubt, already took care of it. She wouldn't want the owners knowing he had spent the night. He would not have to take such an unpleasant route back, so Devon let the mount saunter along at its own pace as he gave himself time to rest. He would need to be rested up to take on the blackmailers and to deal with Ella in the process. Clive would have resources and would aid Devon however he needed. For now, he wouldn't be bogged down by the details, those would come in due time. Presently, he gave himself leave to wonder what the Tate would be like filled with the laughter of Maddie and Ella. What would a family dinner be like? He was never allowed to eat with his father, but Maddie would be refused nothing. No hapless nannies or boarding schools. She would have the best of the best, but she would never be absent in the Tate. Ella had put her mark on the house before she left and he hoped she would transform it when she was back. The house, like him, mourned her for far too long. Now that she was back, everything would go back as it should. The thought brought him up short.

The horse must have felt his reaction because he shook his mane and nickered in complaint. Blast, Clive may have been more on point than even his friend knew. Devon had spent four years convincing himself he was better off and that he was incapable of loving a woman, because when he did, they left. What if his father's legacy wasn't that of never being able to love, but instead, one of loving so much that you would rather leave the world without the object? His father had tried to fight it by loving every woman he could get his hands on, but Devon fought it by forgoing love all together. As the horse followed in his wife's path, he mused that both were just as destructive and painful, but perhaps it was not the time to make this a family legacy. Ella was not his mother and he was not his father after all. Sitting a bit higher in the saddle, Devon edged the beast along. Giving Ella space didn't mean he was without purpose for the next day or so. Following the sun, he began to order the tasks and the details fell into place. First being another intimate encounter with his wife. The love making this morning had proven she was affected, and before she was able to find a way to justify that, he would need to build on it. This time, however, it would be a place she couldn't help but be reminded every time she went there. He smiled to himself as he let the horse take him back to Aires Meade.

The larder smelled of the new spices that Ella had yet to square away. The bakery had been busy since her return and she and Penny were out straight. She had managed to get at least a small amount of rest when she got back a day ago, but her dreams were troubled by visions of her wretched husband. Her Wonderfully talented, skillful, wretched husband and she felt lighter just thinking on him. She still wasn't sure how he found her or what he knew of her situation.

"Mrs. R?" Called Penny from the outer room. "We are ready to leave, but the princess wants a hug before we go."

"Be right there," Ella answered, tying the last bundle of sage to hang for the winter months.

Penny and Ella were going down by the river to spend the night with Penny's grandmother who was feeling out of sorts and wanted company. "Do you have the dinner I packed?" Ella asked Penny as she scooped up Maddie in a big hug filled with kisses. "You need to be a very good girl. Penny's grandmother is under the weather."

"I know, but she says I make her feel young," Maddie chirped in her mother's arms.

"We will be home by sunrise in the morn," Penny assured her.

"That is fine. Since you made a batch of bread this afternoon, there will only be one for me to deal with on the morrow. Tell your grandmother to feel better."

"Bye Mommy," Maddie called as they left by way of the kitchen door. Ella would need to take at least another hour to get the larder in order, and then she planned on eating some stew and heading to bed early.

The larder was dark, but Ella had put a candle in the small window to give her enough light to work from. After only a few minutes, she was interrupted by a knock at the door. When she opened it, thinking that Eric was looking for Penny, she was set off balance by Devon.

"Good evening." His deep voice washed over her, setting every nerve on fire. Drat him. She needed to be able to show him she was not affected. It would help if she wasn't reliving their most recent activities at the Inn, or if she wasn't lost swimming in his liquid eyes, or perhaps if his deep baritone wasn't in her ear, and his hands, well everywhere. *Oh, Lord.*

"Hello, I wasn't expecting to see you tonight." She faked her indifferent tone. Her breasts tightened in her dress, rubbing along the seam of her chemise to show her charade. She would consider her traitorous reaction later, when she was alone. The sooner she could get rid of him, the sooner she would be alone and able to school her emotions. Tears burned behind her eyes. If only she could trust enough, she would launch herself into his protective embrace... but her father had taught her any sign of weakness was an opportunity to hurt, and oh did she feel weak at the moment. If she allowed it, she could start to consider a life beyond her current state. That would not do.

"May I come in? I know you were not expecting me, but I thought we could spend some time together."

"Well, you are welcome to come in, but Maddie is gone with Penny for the night and I am busy organizing the larder, so I am afraid I do not have time to tarry." She turned and walked away from the open door. She needed distance, because her heart was beating too hard and she was too happy he wanted to spend time with her. This would not do.

"I would like to help if I can. Perhaps, if we work together to get your work finished, you will have time to sit down and discuss things."

"An English Lord, organizing food stores? I am sure you are not serious," Ella scoffed, surprised by his offer.

"Are you insinuating that an English Lord is too stupid, or too lazy to do any task?" he asked with a smile, sending shivers and heat low in her belly.

"Fine, you may help." If she began to quarrel with him, they might begin to enjoy it as they used to when she lived with him. "If you are tall enough, I won't have to worry about the step stool."

"Perfect. I am glad I came when I did then." He followed her dutifully into the small room that had gotten smaller since he entered. There was no room for her to turn around by herself, but with his large form in the middle of the room, she was forced to be in contact with him as she sidled past. "What first?" he asked.

"I need to hang these sage bundles on those pegs above the top shelf. Can you reach if I hand them to you?"

"I think I can handle that," he replied, his warm breath brushing over her neck and shoulder, sending shivers along her skin.

It took a moment before Ella came to her senses and began handing him the bundles. They worked for several minutes in companionable silence, which was just as disconcerting for Ella than if they were talking. Two people should not be comfortable in silence together. They just shouldn't.

"Done, now I need to put the cinnamon in the box up there." She reached around him to the wooden box on the top shelf. She had to use her hand to steady herself on his back as she leaned. His back muscles rippled as he turned, raising his arm up and over her head, until they were facing each other. Ella gasped at the contact and in doing so, inhaled his scent. Her head filled with the cleanness of his saving salve, then the smell of leather, and a cool spring night in the moors. Together with the spice smells, it was intoxicating.

"I think the cinnamon can wait," looking down at her. His body blocked the one candle in the dark room, but she felt his eyes boring into her soul.

"Why can the cinnamon wait?" she asked on a wisp of a breath, because he was taking all the air from her lungs.

"For this," he said bringing his hand to her shoulder, sliding it up to her neck in such a soft caress, Ella thought she might be dreaming. Devon guided her head toward him. He put his other hand against the wall, above her head and leaned into her. Devon engulfed Ella until it was only him. Everything else fell away.

He surrounded her and filled all her senses. She couldn't escape, not that she wanted to. She wanted this, oh God did she want this. She knew there would be a price to pay for indulging, but that would come on the morrow, right now, right here, it was Devon. She let her eyes flutter shut.

His lips lowered onto hers, his breath heating her face as he closed in. His hand, now cradling her head and cheek smelled of the sage leaves he had been stocking for her. The scent of brandy and apple danced on the whoosh of breath leaving that beautiful mouth, and the taste like a decadent dessert. His touch was as smooth as the brandy he tasted of. Devon's lips were full and soft, but with a firmness that would brook no argument. The kiss wasn't cruel, but it was demanding, leaving no question in Ella's mind what was about to happen in the larder. They could have kissed for only moments, or for hours, but the haze didn't lift when Devon pulled back and leaned his forehead on hers.

"Damn, Ella," he said with heavy breath, "if you want me to stop and not go further, you need to speak now. I don't know that I will be able to walk away if I continue." The tension in his body rolled off him swirling through the small room, making the space even smaller. He rested his head on hers while she contemplated her answer.

Beyond speech, Ella reached up on tiptoes bending his head to meet her lips as she kissed him. She felt the low, deep moan from Devon as he wound his arm around her waist, never breaking their kiss, and backed her up against the cold wall of the larder. She was being devoured like one of her pastries as Devon's mouth moved from her lips to her jaw, then her ear. He plucked her earlobe with his teeth, using just enough pressure, sending shivers down to her stomach. From there, his expert mouth moved down her neck, which was decidedly more sensitive than Ella had given it credit. A soft moan escaped when he made his way to the sensitive skin just above the bodice of her dress.

With his free arm, Devon pushed the bodice from her shoulder until he had released her bare chest. The cool air mixed with his warm breath was a heady combination and her nipples hardened. His hand covered her small breast. His touch was soft, almost timid as he took his time driving her to insanity. She laid her head back and let the sensations take her; so much so that, when Devon spoke, the noise jumped her.

"I need you to sit back on that barrel, love," he rasped out. "Can you do that?" When he had taken off his waistcoat, Ella wasn't sure, but she held onto his shirtsleeve clad arms as he guided her to the assortment of barrels. He laid his jacket and waistcoat on top to make them more comfortable. "Lie back," Devon instructed. Ella did as she was bade and laid back propping herself on her elbows.

Her feet were dangling over the edge, but once Devon's hands touched her ankles and made their way up the inside of her legs, they could have been floating. His hands were warm on her stockings as he left a trail of tingling heat in their wake. The cool air abraded her thighs when Devon flipped her skirts up, revealing her to his view. Now the only part of her body that was covered was her midsection. The rest was on display for Devon's pleasure. Her hair was a riot, hanging around her shoulders. When Ella lost the pins, she didn't know. On Devon's touch at her core, she ceased caring. She would expire from the feel if he had his way. She was sure. The intimate touch set aflame feelings that kept building, and building, but when Devon knelt and replaced his hand with his mouth, she all but flew off her perch from surprise. As he laved her with his tongue, the feelings built up from the past four years demanded release.

How could she feel such pleasure and wanting, but at the same time, feel an overpowering need to cry? As Devon brought her closer to the abyss, tears welled and threatened to flow forth. Her hands grasped at Devon's shirtsleeves while they trembled with the need for contact. She heard herself moaning and coaxing Devon on, but wasn't aware she was consciously involved. Ella was no longer herself, as all thought ceased. A large warm hand reached up and cradled her right breast rolling the nipple with an expert touch between his fingers. A dagger of white-hot need ripped through her and made her lean into him for more.

She realized at some point that she had weaved her fingers in his hair at her apex. Looking down on the scene gave another aspect to her sensations. As his ministrations increased, she felt the pressure in her hands holding him to her, or was she holding herself to the spot? Faster it built until she thought she might expire. The feeling so overwhelming, she would have stopped him, had she been able to speak at will. Instead, Ella gripped Devon's shoulders and held on, lest she fly off into the heavens. Desire exploded within her as he brought her to release. The all-encompassing sensation brought with it four years of loss, pain, and wanting. As the tears streamed down her cheeks, she was thankful for the darkness of the larder. Devon breathed just as heavily as she did, resting his head in the folds of the dress now bunched at her waist, his arms around her.

Ella couldn't help reaching down and running her hand over his face and into his hair. She loved the weight of him, the sturdiness of his arms around her, grounding her. His brow was damp, but smooth to her touch. Each strand of hair was soft and the curls wound around her fingers. Ella's heart clenched, making her chest tight. Four years ago, she did not allow herself such behavior for fear of being lost in it. The intimacy of this one act was almost more than what they had just done. Ella was in certain danger.

After a moment, she realized the exchange had been one sided. "Devon, aren't you going to take your pleasure?" she asked, preparing for him to move at any moment and finish the job.

"If I did that, I would have to move and I am quite happy where I am," he stated, snuggling in further.

"I'm not strongly versed in the ways of men and women, but isn't the point to bring you to completion?" she asked, sure that it was her job to make sure he was satisfied.

"This was not about me," was his only answer.

"But--" Ella tried to protest.

"Ella, be quiet. You are ruining the moment," he said with a smile in his voice belaying the command as an order. "Four years ago, you gave yourself to me, without any expectation on your part. I am returning the favor."

Ella decided not to push the matter. She liked him lounging on her body thus, but by persisting, it would break the spell. She decided just to try to take in as much as she could to help get her through the lonely nights once he left.

After several minutes, the cool dampness of the larder began to seep into her bones and reality of where they were weighed on her embarrassment. Devon must have felt her body tense, because without saying a word, he rose and helped put her back to rights. The moon had risen in the sky and sent some slight rays into the darkness, so Ella could see the look of satisfaction on Devon's face. Then, his expression changed to one of concern. Did he see the tear streaks on her face? If he did, he reorganized his thoughts and allowed her privacy.

"Now, what was it you wanted me to do with the cinnamon?" he asked with a devilish smirk. Ella cleared the emotion from her throat and resumed giving him orders. Once they finished organizing what they could in the darkness, she led him into the kitchen and back into reality.

"Thank you," Ella said, knowing her gesture was sincere on many levels. In the brighter light of the kitchen, embarrassment crept in.

"You are welcome. I believe I am becoming a fan of chores like organizing the larder. You have made me a convert," he intoned with a good bit of humor. "Now, it is late and I must leave you to your bed. You, my love, must rise with the dawn. I look forward to seeing you again in the next few days." He walked up to Ella and kissed her on the temple, remaining there long enough to make the gesture something wholly not innocent. With that, he made his way to the door and the night beyond, leaving Ella and her frayed, raw nerves, to deal with themselves. If she only had a few days to steel herself against that, she knew she held the losing hand and was already trying to remember why she cared.

CHAPTER 8

$\mathcal{F}$rom behind the tapestry drape in the outer room, Ella heard what she knew was going to be the end of her peaceful, normal day. She had not seen or heard from Devon for three days. Their last meeting had played prominently in her dreams of late, keeping her up and wound tight.

Unaware of her emotional turmoil, life went on as usual. She had been short on bread yesterday and rose early to make extra. The bell had nigh stopped ringing over the door, as the villagers could smell the bread. Penny had been forced to remain out front, while Maddie sat at the table close to Penny playing and taking in the hustle and bustle, leaving Ella to her thoughts as she worked on the dough in the back. She was glad to have the peace. At the sound of Devon's voice, her traitorous body however, felt differently as her stomach gave a decided flip-flop and her heart began pounding in her chest.

"Good morning, Penny," Devon's voice vibrated over her nerves, like water to a man in the desert.

"Good morning, my Lord. My Lord. did you as well hear we have fresh bread today?" Penny greeted the new comers.

"Why no, Penny, should we have?" Clive asked. Ella snuck to the doorway to listen. What the devil did they want? How could she just get them out? Not that she was surprised, she had been expecting them.

"Well," Penny giggled, "I just thought since everyone else has come to buy bread today that you may have heard and decided to partake."

"Actually," Devon interrupted, "my aunts are visiting and we thought it a good day to bring them shopping. They are more accustomed to the Capitol and its diversions."

Aunts? Devon didn't have any aunts.

"Hi," a bright little voice chimed in.

Damn, Ella had forgotten Maddie was in the front room. Her first instinct was to rush out and put Maddie behind her skirts, but she decided to wait. If he were truly interested in his daughter, she might be able to summarize as much.

"Well, good morning, Mistress Maddie." Clive answered. By the rustle of cloth, she could just see him bowing and her loving it.

"Hi," Ella had to work with her as to how a lady would greet someone she thought.

"Good morning, my lady. Has it been a fair morning thus far?" Devon's deep voice seemed filled with humor. In spite of herself, Ella smiled. He too bowed if her hearing was correct.

"Good morning. Mommy made bread. See."

"Ah, I see, and you no doubt are the lucky person to get the first slice? That was my favorite job in the kitchen. Is that honey?"

"Yes, my favorite. Try some."

"Oh, well, I–" Devon's words stopped, and Penny cut in, in a fluster.

"Oh, Maddie, you should never stick your finger in a Lord's mouth. That just isn't done, I would think."

"See, it's good." Maddie said with all seriousness, ignoring Penny's pleas to stop. Then Ella heard Devon smacking his lips together in a very loud way and the whole company laughing.

"Yes, My Lady. I believe that is the best honey I have ever tasted. I am thinking that your dainty finger added to the sweetness however. Honey could never truly be that sweet without a little help." Everyone laughed. Ella wished she were out there to see Maddie beaming. Her heart beat faster if that was possible. Damn the man for being so foolish to entertain a child.

"Who's that?" Maddie asked in a loud whisper.

"Those are Lord Renwick's aunts. They are visiting. Would you like me to introduce you?" Clive answered.

Ella had forgotten about the aunts until Maddie brought them up. Without thinking, she swept through the curtain, and locked eyes with LePrin. It was all she could do to hold back the wail that caught in her throat. Her feet were held to the floorboards by sheer force of will, for they wanted to fly into her arms and weep like she had as a young girl. LePrin's embrace always made things seem more manageable. Her mother's death, her father's cruel words, even those nights when there was not enough food, LePrin would find a way. To Ella, LePrin was the one person who kept her alive during those dark days. She had wept for days when the decision had been made to leave without her. The one person she allowed herself to admit to missing. She was the only servant to her family and took on the role of mother on top of cook, housekeeper, etc. She had cried silently, again in the carriage as it drove them toward Scotland, but she had known LePrin's place was with Devon at The Tate. She knew he would see to her care and not turn her out. Tears sprang to her burning eyes threatening to flow free. She had wanted for so long to share Maddie's life with her, ask her questions about mothering. She longed to be enfolded into LePrin's embrace, but realized she was not an ally now, but an asset to Devon and his plan to win her over. Ella bit back the emotion and buried it as best she could. There would be time, but not now.

Standing next to her Devon's head housekeeper, Flick. They too had become very close in the short time Ella resided at The Tate. Flick had been Devon's nursemaid and remained employed by the family, but when Devon took the title, he promoted her to head housekeeper. Flick tried, but was unable to handle the duties well, due to her kind nature. Once Ella was moved into the Tate by order of His Lordship, Ella helped establish Flick and weed out some troublesome employees for her, while Flick helped Ella learn things about her soon to be husband that she would need to understand him, and begin to fall in love. She owed Flick a debt of gratitude for making her feel like she had some control for once in her life. Both women looked surprised, but not surprised enough. While Clive introduced the women as Lady LePrin and Lady Flick, Ella sought out Devon's face. It was unreadable. He looked at her as one would look at a competitor across a whist table. He was giving away nothing, and that scared her.

"My Ladies, welcome to our tiny village. Will you be staying long?" Ella found her voice making it sound steady, and not giving away her frayed emotions. Damn Devon for his machinations. First by making her heady with his love making, now bringing those in her past that would impact his side the most, she now understood how so many had lost to him at the tables. He plays to win.

"Well, my aunts have no obligations to tear them away anytime in the near future. They have always doted on me." Devon answered with a wicked smile. Sending shivers down her spine and heat rising to her face. From his expression, he knew.

Dratted man.

"Penny, would you take Maddie to the back and wash her up."

"No, please," LePrin all but pleaded. It was enough to bring tears back to Ella's eyes. Devon again stepped in with an explanation.

"I apologize for my aunt, but you see, she lost a loved one not too long ago. Miss Maddie holds a strong liking to that person. I am sure she brings back fond memories for them."

Penny hovered waiting for instruction. "Just bring a wet cloth in to clean the honey off, please. Thank you, Penny."

"She looks just like–" Flick began to say, but was stopped by Clive, who all but shoved a fresh roll into her mouth.

"Don't you just enjoy bread when it is still warm?" He asked.

"So, my Lord, what is it I can get for your party today?" Ella knew she had no choice but to play along.

"Well, I am in need of another bag of those peppermints. In fact, make it two bags." Devon played along. Both moved away from the group over to the large glass canister containing the bright pink and green candies.

"Just what is it you are playing at?" Ella hissed, as she drove the scoop into the candies. The smell of peppermint so strong it stung her eyes.

"You will soon learn, my Lady, I don't play for what I am not determined to win," he said with a bland aristocratic look on his face. "How can I possibly win a bet when I am not allowed to prove the terms?"

"So, you mean to use the only two women I care for against me? That is gentlemanly behavior for certain," she spat.

Ella all but felt the blood drain from her face. He truly meant to go through with the bet. He wanted to prove he would make the perfect father and husband. From behind Devon, the ladies and Maddie were talking and laughing. He was going to use LePrin against her. She took a deep breath and closed her eyes to quiet her thoughts and emotions. She couldn't blame LePrin. Devon had seen to her care when Ella left, and she did leave her behind.

"I am not a wolf about to gobble you whole, Ella. I simply want to prove I am not your father." His voice was so close she could feel his warm, honey tinged breath on her face. When she opened her eyes, he had moved in close, taking her space away and replacing it with his existence. At that moment, she was feeling very much like a tiny little morsel of food for a hungry wolf. He had even separated her from her pack as it were.

"Hmm, you might not be a wolf, sir, but there are many more dangerous creatures lurking about, aren't there? I will not let you have her. She belongs with her mother. I will not allow two women who are obligated to you for your charity to sway my decisions." Ella tried to keep her voice down, but it was costing her a great deal of her patience. She had no reason for the rising panic and fear, save her need to protect Maddie at all cost. It had nothing to do with her fear of being left alone in this world.

"I was hoping to gain the pot at the end of this round, but we shall see. Let's just play out this hand, before we call, shall we?"

"Are these lemon tarts?" Asked LePrin in surprise.

Ella gave what she hoped was one last withering stare in Devon's direction and turned to the woman she never thought she would see again. She wanted to touch her to make sure she was there, but with Penny standing by and many villagers still bustling about outside, she couldn't. "Yes, those are lemon tarts. They were the specialty of the woman who taught me to cook many years ago. They are still my favorite, though not as good as hers."

"I would like two dozen," Clive intoned. "If the ladies are wont of something they shall get it." Ella had noticed Flick standing back watching Devon and Maddie. Devon had put the mints in his pocket and Maddie had found her way to his side. She was busy pilfering his pocket for a few mints. Devon stood trying to appear unaware of the little pick pocket. Flick watched with eyes full of emotion. She must see the boy he was in his child. Ella knew she could see him whenever she looked at her daughter.

"Well, my Lords, my Ladies, thank you for patronizing my bakery. I hope you will see it to your liking and visit again before you leave." If she could just get them out. She didn't know why, but knew it had to be now.

"I have a wonderful notion," Flick, who had remained silent thus far, spoke up. Ella got the impression she hadn't agreed to whatever Devon wanted, until now. "I would love to have the opportunity to get to know Miss Maddie better and I am sure you do not need a young child hanging about with all the work you must have every day. I believe it would be advantageous to all if we were to have Maddie brought to the Manor house every day for the extent of our stay. We can have a grand time together and you then, would be able to get your work completed. I am sure Lord Breakerton could send someone to fetch her and return her every day."

The room had gone silent. Penny's eyes were huge as Ella scanned the room. Panic thick with fear filled her throat. Was Devon attempting to steal her? Would he do such a thing? If he got her back to England, she wouldn't have any legal recourse. Her breathing began to pick up. Just as she would have grabbed Maddie and fled from the room, and the country LePrin put her hand on her arm.

"Child, I promise you will not lose her. She will be returned to you every evening. I can imagine how precious she is to you. I too had a child in my life that reminded me of someone I cared deeply about. You have my promise. Is that not enough?" Ella looked into eyes she had thought lost to her forever. She looked at Devon and his unreadable expression had been replaced by one of misery. Did he realize her fear? Did he care that she didn't trust him? But, she did trust him. She knew deep down he wouldn't just take Maddie. She wasn't sure where her certainty came from, but it was there none-the-less.

"All right," she said in a quiet voice, "I will have Eric bring her in the mornings, and I will arrive to pick her up when I close the bakery. That will give you most of the day. Is that sufficient?" Ella's voice was quiet and resigned. She knew she was about to lose something, and hoped it wasn't herself. Devon had won this hand.

"Yes, that is perfect! What do you think of that Maddie? Would you like to come visit us at the manor house while we are staying there?" Asked Flick who had been holding the child's hand.

"Do you have cakes? And milk?" she asked. "I like cakes and milk."

"Of course, we will have cakes and milk. As much as you would like," answered Clive.

"So will you come?" Asked Flick.

"Yup," answered Maddie, and then went to steal just a few more mints before their departure.

As the odd group filed out, Devon brushed by Ella and placed something in her hand. Once they left, she saw it was a scrap of paper with the words 'thank you' written with charcoal. If winning wasn't enough, he had to stack the deck for the next hand.

Wasn't success supposed to feel good? Yes, it was, so why did he feel like a true blackguard. As he watched Ella in the bakery, he could read her thoughts. They played across her face and in the depths of her eyes. He knew the moment she realized she couldn't control the situation and she would have to concede. He should feel a profound relief. After all, this was an important hand to have won.

Unfortunately, once she gave her verbal consent and the party made to leave, all Devon wanted to do was apologize. His guilt, if that was truly what this ailment was, didn't subside. He spent most of the night tossing and turning with visions of Ella's face filled with defeat swimming in his head.

In the glaring morning light, he was able to gird his loins and acknowledge it was a necessary action to reach his ultimate purpose. Having gained at least a small sense of rightness, he rose from his bed and made to get dressed. One aspect of country life that didn't change from England to Scotland was attending church. Not an activity he normally partook in, but Clive felt the need to attend as the highest ranking nobility in the community.

Once Devon had tended the fire into a comfortable blaze, he walked to the bell pull and rang for his man. As he looked through his choices of wardrobe, he thought about how changed his best friend had been from the man he knew in London. Perhaps Scotland was the place to go for change and new beginnings. A sharp knock on the door put an end to his thoughts as he called for his man to enter. He sat at the dressing table as the valet began giving him a close shave.

Late yesterday afternoon, an official invitation to Sunday luncheon had been sent to Ella. Until the response came accepting the invitation, Devon wasn't sure she would follow through. He had half expected to hear she had fled with Maddie. He still didn't understand how one mother could be so protective, yet another could abandon her only child on a whim.

As the valet finished his ministration, Devon thought about the church service awaiting him. One asset to attending the local sermon would be the chance to see Ella and Maddie in a more social situation. The thought lifted his spirits by a small margin. Once down the stairs, Devon and Clive assisted the elderly women into the carriage and they were off. The day was splendid, one of the warmest mornings yet. The sun glinting off the meadows made them shimmer with fresh greens and heather purples. The women hadn't stopped talking about Ella and Maddie since they left the bakery, and it seemed they were not wont to stop now. Clive sat back enjoying the scenery with a look of contentment on his face. Devon was happy for his friend, but felt it unfair to feel as though he no longer fit in his own skin. He hoped Clive's newfound sense of ease was short lived. His friend deserved nothing less than an unwilling countess such as he was presently dealing.

At the small church, Devon, ranking just below in title than Clive, was shown to the front pew along with Clive and the aunts. Devon, to his chagrin, had noted Ella and Maddie were seated, not in the back of the church, but more in the latter half of the middle. She had acknowledged him and had given a slight bow of her head. A small concession. He smiled at her, but knew it didn't reach his eyes. It rankled him that his countess ranking higher than all those seated in front of her was relegated to the pews of the commoners. Devon knew why she was there, but the possessive beast within wanted to howl with frustration.

Not to mention he had decided his time in the church would be best spent watching the sun play off her perfect complexion and her shimmering golden tresses. Now, he pouted. He would have to sit pretending to pay attention to the sermon while wondering if she was watching him. Could nothing go right?

The sermon, while long winded, wasn't as much of a trial as Devon had expected. A few times during the sermon, he heard Maddie's little giggle reach his ears and despite his foul mood, he found himself smiling. As all of them filed out of the church into the bright sunlight, Devon searched for a glimpse of Ella and Maddie. To his frustration, the vicar wanting to discuss some local concerns with Lord Breakerton waylaid Clive and him. Clive began discussing possible solutions while Devon looked over the crowd, not listening a wit.

He caught sight of her at last. She stood in a circle of women older than her by ten years at least. She looked warm and fresh in a sky blue confection with a matching pelisse. It lacked the usual decorations and trappings of similar dresses he was used to seeing in London, but as he kept reminding himself, she was the town baker, not his countess. She still outshined every woman milling about. Her group seemed to be women who would be a bit above the station of baker, but nonetheless they appeared to be deferring to Ella over whatever topic was being discussed.

"Oh, my Lord, we are so happy to have such important men visit our little church." The vicar's wife had somehow separated him from Clive, and was in the process of gaining his attentions, which did not want to be gained.

"Well, Lord Breakerton has spoken so highly of the entire area, I just had to see for myself." He answered, giving her his most disarming smile. At the same time, he caught Ella's departure from her group of women. She had moved closer to a group of women nearer to her age.

"We are surprisingly happy with his lordship. He is doing a wonderful job."

Devon listened to the woman sing Clive's praises with half an ear. Ella's voice carried on the breeze and he wanted to take this opportunity to hear what was important to her.

"Mister Langly and I were invited to the manor for dinner not two months ago. I have to say, Lord Breakerton is as charming as he is handsome," one of the women was commenting.

"Yes, he is, but his friend seems very favorable as well. His dark looks are quite romantic. That is the type of man I would be tossing my cap at if I were a widow."

Devon felt a blush wash over him. He had always hated being the topic of conversation among women. He hoped Ella hadn't noticed his unease, because she would know he had been listening. The vicar's wife, however, noticed nothing as she continued talking, having switched topics to the history of the church and its buildings.

"I am sure I don't give a care about either of his lordships. I have been invited because his aunts have taken to Maddie and have a wish to spend time with her," he heard Ella say with conviction. "And you are wise to encourage such a connection," one of the women insisted, "for I have heard of young ladies of no more pedigree getting sponsored by Grande Dames of the Ton. And with Maddie's father having been an officer, well, a continued connection with those women could only be to her benefit." The group of women all voiced their agreement. His plan was working at least in the effort not to stain her reputation in the community.

"Do you not think our church a wonderful place for a wedding?" The vicar's wife asked, though Devon, having not heard the rest of her speech wasn't sure how to answer.

"I beg your pardon?" He asked with a sorrowful look on his face

"Our church, the fact that all our marriages have led to happy unions. Wouldn't you agree that Lord Breakerton would be wise to say his vows here when he chooses a bride?"

"Ah, yes, I would think his lordship wouldn't think of any other," Devon answered. "It was very nice to have made your acquaintance, ma'am. It appears my aunts are ready to depart. Have a wonderful day." Devon bowed and made his way toward the aunts who had found Maddie, or she them. They were being afforded a grand show as Maddie was twirling and singing a happy children's tune. He wanted to scoop her up and do whatever it took to extract that lilting giggle from her. Instead, he approached the small group and watched with amusement.

Clive appeared next to him with Ella following. "Ah, here you are. It is time to go. My Lord, My ladies." Ella dropped a curtsy. "I am looking forward to attending luncheon this afternoon. Thank you again for being so generous." She scooped up a wriggling Maddie and headed along the path down the hill toward the village with all the other towns people.

Devon's party made their way toward their carriage. Devon had much to do before Ella and Maddie attended this afternoon. He had a few surprises to get ready.

"Are you sure you don't mind? I mean, I will replace it, but I wouldn't want to take it if it were important to your–"

"Devon, I said I don't mind. Being from a family of women, I am sure if I need to, I can procure a dollhouse and all its trappings with little to no effort on my part. Truth be told, I would much rather be in need of an entire army of men," Clive answered with a cynical tone as he watched Devon place the last of the delicate furniture into the tiny rooms. Devon was thrilled when on a tour of the manor he had spied the dollhouse and its pieces in the nursery. He hoped Maddie liked it. When they moved home, he planned to buy out as many toy makers as he could. He sighed. This would do for now.

"You look rather domestic you know," Clive commented sipping his brandy. "I never thought I would see you reduced to a doting father as my poor brothers-in-law. I guess no man is immune," Clive joked.

"Nonsense." Devon felt the need to defend himself even though he agreed with Clive's estimation. "I am merely trying to find something to occupy her. If I don't, I fear I may be paying for your next refurbishing project."

Clive chuckled. Devon rose and collected his glass on the table next to the wing chair. Ella was due to arrive soon. Clive had sent a carriage to bring them to the manor and it had been gone for half an hour already. He wasn't sure how she would behave at the manor. True, the entire party knew of the game, but the fact was there were still servants about. He had decided to wait and see how she wanted to play.

As if conjured by his thoughts, the butler appeared to announce their arrival. Clive instructed the butler to see them to the parlor and they would join them in a moment. All of a sudden, Devon felt very unsure of himself. The last time a butler had announced her, his life had been altered. He dearly hoped it would again, but in his favor. He gave one last look at the dollhouse sitting on the floor waiting for a little girl to play with it and both men quit the library heading for the brighter atmosphere of the parlor in the east wing.

♥♥♥

Ella was more nervous than she had been in years. She knew Maddie felt like a true lady being driven in a fancy carriage with beautiful horses to the grand manor house. She was only three, but every girl was born with a heart filled with dreams of fairy tales. She couldn't give into the excitement, she thought with sadness. She was of two minds. Part of her wanted Devon to prove he could be a great father and husband. It would be useless for her to try to ignore that part of herself. That's why she left to begin with. She knew she could fall in love with him. Unfortunately, life had become more complicated. She couldn't allow herself to fall in love with him until she knew his feelings. She would not live in a loveless marriage. She had spent most of her life living in a loveless family. If he loved her, that would be different. She knew he cared for Maddie and had decided she would find a way for Devon and Maddie to know each other, but as for Devon and herself, she just didn't trust it.

Next, was the fact that she was being blackmailed for an unknown reason. The blackmailers were getting more threatening and bolder in their demands. The fact she was missing a meeting with them to attend this luncheon could mean real danger. She was hoping she might be able to get away in time to make it. It was her plan to find them, and to find why she was being blackmailed. She wasn't sure she wanted the truth, but she did want the threats to stop.

Once the carriage had deposited them at the door, they were escorted into the house and along a bright hallway lined with windows letting in the late afternoon sun. It felt warm and inviting. To the right at the far end they were ushered into a warm inviting room. Sitting on the sofa were LePrin and Flick busy working on embroidery. When they were announced, the women looked up smiling.

"Thank you, you may leave us. Would you please inform the gentlemen that our guests have arrived?" Asked LePrin.

"Yes, Ma'am," and he retired.

Before Ella could cross the room, LePrin rose and enveloped Ella into a fierce embrace.

"This was the only thing I wanted to do when I saw you alive," she said with emotion.

"I missed you. I am sorry I left as I did. I just–" Ella broke off not knowing how to tell LePrin why she left without admitting to things she didn't want to admit.

LePrin grasped her face in her hands and looked into her eyes. Ella saw her secret reflected in the woman's eyes. She wouldn't have to explain after all. She would always be grateful to Devon for bringing LePrin back into her life.

"She is beautiful. You have done well, as I knew you would," LePrin said to break the spell. She could tell she was trying very hard to hide her French accent. She was doing a commendable job.

"She is a handful. I now know what you and mother went through with me."

"Oh, don't blame yourself, child," Flick intoned. "Devon all but expired his share of nursemaids. I seem to be the only one to brave it through. I see so much of him in this beautiful child." Maddie had crawled up next to Flick and was busy unwinding a bright yellow ball of floss. Ella made her way to the chair in the circle of furniture and LePrin retook her seat, now next to Maddie, under a pile of yellow floss.

They had almost no time to start a conversation when the two men joined them. The large bright room closed in around her. Devon's eyes locked onto hers, sending heat through her. Both men made their way to the seating and made themselves comfortable. Devon folded himself with easy grace into a stuffed chair next to Ella.

"I am glad you could join our little group. I trust the carriage was adequate," Clive stated. She knew he knew the answer, but it was an admirable effort to start the conversation.

"It was lovely. My old mare is indebted to you for allowing her to remain at home resting." Everyone laughed, then fell silent. Ella knew they were waiting for her to set the tone.

"So, Lord Renwick, are you enjoying your stay?" She asked, unsure how to continue.

"I am actually finding Scotland much more to my liking than I thought. It is very restful."

Again, silence. The ladies started a conversation about the locals, and about how much they had been enjoying their stay to fill the vast quiet. Ella allowed them to lead the conversation as she sat back to listen. It also allowed Devon the same and he chose to take the time to lay a penetrating stare on her. Then, he leaned in toward her.

"If it is possible, I would like to take a walk in the garden after luncheon with you just to talk."

Ella raised a brow in speculation. It seemed when he got her alone, his conversations took on a very physical air. At the thought, desire lanced through her sharp and hot. Damn her body's reaction, it always betrayed her. It would not help her to give into a dalliance right now. That decided, she said, "That would be fine." *Wonderful, now her mind was even betting against her.*

Both turned to join in the conversation, when Maddie slid off the sofa and made her way with her bundle of floss to Devon's chair. The adults watched as she then unloaded her burden into his lap, and followed it as she climbed into his lap to show him her prize. Ella watched with rapt attention as Devon sat frozen, not sure what to do. He did give into the part when Maddie used the floss to make a rather messy hat on top of his head. He made her giggle by making a funny face, shaking his head to make the floss fall off onto Maddie's head. Her desire that was still sharp, mingled with a warmth, which scared her more than the desire.

The group was interrupted by the announcement of luncheon that would be served on the terrace. The day was warm and sunny with only a gentle breeze to stir the crisp white linens covering the table. The meal passed with ease and more talk of London and the goings on in the capital. Maddie even managed to pass the meal with little to no food on the surrounding area. Once the meal was finished, the party retired to the library for more conversation. Ella had held back to walk with LePrin, gaining as many precious minutes with her as she could, when she heard Maddie squeal with delight.

As she entered the library, which she decided would house her whole bakery and living quarters, she saw the cause. A miniature dollhouse stood on the circular rug in front of the fire, now out. It was full of furniture and a family of small dolls waiting to be arranged. Devon stood looking very proud of himself for making his daughter trill with delight. The uneasy warmth grew. Ella was in trouble. The gentlemen settled down with glasses of brandy and the women sat listening to Ella talk about her new life and the bakery. Soon, the older women both began to doze. She didn't fall for it for one minute, but played along. Clive took off his jacket, rolled up his shirtsleeves, and got onto the floor to play and distract Maddie. Before she knew what he was about, Devon's deep voice washed over her shoulder tickling her ear.

"Shall we take that walk now?"

She couldn't answer, only nod her agreement. He placed his hand hot and possessive on the small of her back, a bit lower than was acceptable, and turned her to the door. Without speaking, they made their way back to the hallway and out a side door into the brightness of the day.

"So where to?" She asked.

"Nowhere in particular. I just wanted a few moments alone with you. Why don't we head towards the folly?"

"Lead the way," she answered without looking into his eyes. They walked on across the lawn and through the large trimmed hedges that gave off the fresh smell of pine. The smell of pine permeated the air. Ella broke the silence.

"How did LePrin and Flick come to be your aunts?" She asked.

"I have a fondness for elder servant women, what can I say." He smiled.

Ella forged ahead without reacting to his goad. "I just assumed you would turn LePrin out once we left, but I didn't see any way for us to take her with us, as our circumstances were not solid."

"And, you thought that was what your father would do, so that is what I would have done?" He asked with hurt in his voice.

"I guess, yes," she admitted. "I suppose I shouldn't have thought the worst. You never did anything that led me to think you were like him."

Devon seemed to take that and be settled. "Once you left and we thought you were right and truly dead, LePrin mourned for months. She could not be left alone. Once she regained herself, I gave her employ at The Tate. She fit in well and Flick saw her as a confidante. Reynolds also fancied her, and I couldn't bring myself to separate them."

"LePrin and Reynolds? Are you certain? Does he treat her well?" Ella asked, concern for her friend overwhelming her.

"Reynolds treats her like a fragile flower. He dotes on her constantly. She barely has to lift a finger," Devon assured her, but then changed the subject. "As I listened to you talk about your new life, I couldn't help hear the pride in your voice. You like being a baker?" He asked with genuine curiosity and surprise.

"Well, the hours are atrocious, but do I like making my own way? The answer is yes. I make the decisions and there is no one to tell me what I am doing is wrong. It is a good feeling."

"You know, it is possible to depend on someone and not be frightened they would ridicule you."

She turned then and looked up at him. Was he saying he would never ridicule her? "I think it is human nature for a man to always question a woman's decision." They had made their way to the folly that she hadn't realized was overgrown with vines, affording its occupants with complete privacy. He was calculating. She would give him that.

"Two people can have differing views on a topic without ridicule. I have seen it." He helped her sit on the bench, then propped his booted foot on the seat next to her and rested his arm on his raised knee leaning down to face her. "If the two people see each other as equals it can work. Just like two business partners."

"Do you truly feel that marriage is a business venture?" She asked all innocently. She gave him her best card face hoping not to give away the importance of his answer. He studied her face. She knew he guessed his answer couldn't be so simple as a yes or no. After several moments, he attempted to answer.

"Well, I think that any time two individuals are joined in a common goal, that yes, they must treat each other as a partner. I daresay the benefits far outweigh most business ventures. Unfortunately, I can't answer past that, because I have never spent much time considering what a marriage would entail, until now. I am terribly out of my element here. You lived in a home with both parents for some time, what say you?" He had answered her question in such a way that he didn't answer it at all. Blast!

Birds chirped as they jumped among the vines of their haven. The air seemed heavy and warm, more like a summer day than spring. He waited. She knew she couldn't answer him using her own parents, because she would never want what they had. She would not accept anything but a love match. Instead, she spoke of the one example she had. The baker and his wife who took her in when she needed it most.

"I do know something of how a true marriage can work. It was not a Ton marriage. The two people were a team as you said. They worked together every day listening to each other, but it was more than that. You couldn't see it or even explain it, but it was how they looked at each other. How they spoke to one another even when they were disagreeing. I think it was very rare, and possibly unattainable."

He shifted and turned to walk to the other side of the gazebo, leaving a cool breeze in his wake and making her shiver.

"You are talking of a love match?" he asked with his back turned to her. She couldn't read anything in his words.

"Yes, I think that's what it was. It was subtle. Not gloating or intoxicating, but it was there."

"Is that what you want, a love match?" Again, he gave no tell.

If she said yes, she would be giving away too much. Yet, if he didn't love her, that one answer could end this and she would be left alone. The thought further chilled her to the bone and sent a sad shiver to her heart.

"You didn't ask me what I wanted. You asked me what I thought a true marriage was. I explained the only one I have been privy to."

Devon didn't answer right away. He didn't even move. She could tell he had tensed waiting for her answer. She almost expected him to turn and leave her sitting in the gazebo alone. Instead, he turned to face her. "I can't be what you want unless you speak plainly and tell me what that is. If I don't know what your criteria are, how can I meet them?"

"Devon, I don't have criteria. I have no expectations for a husband, because I never wanted one. I saw how a husband could treat his wife like a prisoner. She has no power of her own. Once she agrees to become a man's wife, she gives up her freedoms."

He made his way back to her seat, and sat down next to her. He didn't touch her, but his eyes all but reached out and pulled her in. He studied her face, trying to read her, she knew.

"Women hold more power than they know. It just depends on the woman and how strong she is. You claim you don't have criteria, but the one thing I can promise you is that we will be a partnership. I don't want to own you, Ella. You are my wife. I feel responsible for shielding you from life's hardships. I don't want to control you." He reached up and tucked an errant lock of hair behind her ear. "I know you would not accept anything but a true partnership."

She didn't know what to say. He hadn't spoken of love, but what he did speak of called to her like a siren's song. She wanted to be protected right now to the tips of her toes. Protected from the blackmailers and from him. She just wanted to sink into his arms and never leave. As if he could read her mind, he reached for her, drawing her into him. His embrace was warm and strong. She looked up into a face no longer void of emotion. What she saw, she didn't understand however. She didn't have time to study it further, because he lowered his head to hers and took her lips.

It was not a hungry, greedy kiss this time. This kiss was slow and bone melting. His lips were soft as velvet, but firm. He took only from her what she was willing to give, and heaven help her, the longer he kissed, the more she was willing to give him. She leaned into his chest needing to be closer still. One of her hands wound around his nape and delved into the silkiness that was his hair. He groaned into her mouth, sending shock waves straight to her belly on the vibrations of his voice.

Devon pulled back and she was greedy for more, but held her urge to pull him back to her. She searched the hard plains of his face. They were still unreadable; except for the great effort, she knew it took him to end their embrace.

"We should get you back. Most in the town will be watching to see what transpires."

She cleared away the huskiness in her throat. "Yes, you are right. I am the talk of the town."

He stood and proffered a hand for her. She accepted the chance and allowed him to lead her out of their hiding place and back to the house. Once inside, they headed for the library only to find Clive and Maddie curled up together on the floor sound asleep. Flick and LePrin were absent from the room. Devon went to find a footman to call for the carriage.

Once the carriage had pulled around, he gently picked Maddie up, kicking Clive with more gusto than necessary as he did so. She liked watching the camaraderie the two men had. Her father never, to her memory, had any friends. Acquaintances yes, but none he would have called friend. She thanked a groggy Clive for a wonderful afternoon and followed Devon out to the waiting carriage. The footman helped Ella into the conveyance and Devon placed Maddie on her mother's lap. He then took the soft lap throw and covered his sleeping daughter.

"Well, I am sure we will see you tomorrow when you come to pick up Maddie. I know my *aunts* are looking forward to spending the day with her."

"Yes, once I have finished cleaning the kitchen and preparing for the next day, I will arrive."

"Until tomorrow." He bowed and stepped back allowing the carriage to turn down the drive and out of sight.

Devon watched the carriage disappear. He would stop it and bring it back if he could. He wasn't sure if his estimation of their talk was correct, but could she want a love match? Moreover, could he give it to her? He would take care of her. He would treat her as an equal just as he promised. He would make love to her every day, more if he could manage it, but he couldn't be sure about love. She said that was not her goal, but was she holding something back? He walked through the front door and into the library unseeing or even hearing the footmen closing the doors behind him. Clive had managed to pick himself off the floor and had procured two brandies. He was in the process of lighting the fire.

"Were you able to learn anything new?" He asked Devon.

"Nothing about the blackmailers. She still doesn't trust me enough."

"So you learned something of the personal nature?" He asked, turning to waggle his eyebrows at his friend.

"I learned that women can speak in circles and probably tongues as well if the need arises."

Clive chuckled. "See, all you had to do was ask and I would have told you that. I had that knowledge when I was eight." Clive loved to impart his vast knowledge of the female being on him.

"Yes, well, whether you offered it or no, it still only stands to make me more adrift. I think she wants a love match."

Again, Clive chuckled. "And the problem with that would be?" he asked.

"The problem with that is I don't know if that is possible," Devon commented. "She doesn't trust me, so even if I tried to convince her I loved her, she wouldn't believe it." Devon sat on the sofa and placed his still booted feet on the small stool. He laid his head back and looked up at the old smoke stained beams.

"She won't believe unless it is true."

"Thank you for the help," Devon stated dryly. Clive finished stirring the fire and walked to his usual seat across from the sofa. He too propped his feet up and took his book from the side table. They fell into a comfortable silence. Clive was lost in his book and Devon in his thoughts.

About an hour had passed when they heard a commotion in the hall. Before either man could rise, the butler came in followed by Ella carrying Maddie. The expression on her face was anything but comforting.

"I need your help."

CHAPTER 9

Fear, cold and sharp sliced through him. He couldn't see Maddie under the carriage blanket draped over her. At that moment, he understood what being a parent, a true parent, meant. He looked in Ella's eyes as he crossed the floor in three strides. He saw none of the emotions caged in him reflecting in Ella's eyes. That put him at ease on that account.

"What has happened?" He asked with a forced calm. "Is she ill?" He relieved Ella of her burden, folding the child into his arms and moving the blanket to see for himself.

"Maddie is fine. She was a bit shaken, but I calmed her enough and she fell asleep on the ride back here. It is the bakery. Someone vandalized the front window." Her anguish was audible in the tremor of her voice.

Devon felt the rush of relief as strong as the terror of only minutes ago. Maddie was safe. As the thought took shape in his rattled brain, she murmured in her sleep and snuggled deeper into his chest. Devon held her a bit tighter. After he gained equilibrium once again, he stepped next to Ella, wrapped his free arm around her, and led her to the fire. She sat with her shoulders sagging. She kept rubbing her head and Clive had the presence of mind to have the butler get some tea and have a room prepared for his new houseguests.

"How badly is the window damaged?" Devon asked, able to steer the conversation into the correct direction.

"It's— It's shattered. The blackguards hurled a rock through it." Her other hand rose to rub the other temple. Devon noted the slight shake. She was at her wit's end, he could tell.

"Did anyone see anything? You said there was more than one. Did you see them in the act?"

"No, I didn't see them. When I got home, the deed was done," Ella said looking confused by his question.

"You said 'blackguards' as more than one, so I assume you knew there was at least two."

"Oh, ah I don't know why I said that. It's just that, well I would think cowards need friends to help them," she said with true distaste. Devon knew she thought it was the blackmailers, but now was not the time to make her admit her turmoil.

"You are in the middle of the village. The window faces the street. Surely someone saw the blighter or blighters." Devon could feel his anger rising. What would she do if he were not here? Where would she have gone for help and would there have been anyone to help her? He began to pace in front of the fire and Ella while he still cradled a sleeping Maddie. Clive had finished giving orders and was returning with a tray holding glasses. He set it on the table and handed Ella the first glass, then placed one in Devon's hand, taking the last for himself.

"Here, this will help. It will burn like hell, but after that, all will be well." Clive said with a crooked smile as only he could.

Ella smiled weakly at his use of improper language, and then threw back the entire swallow. To her credit, she coughed only once then cleared her throat. "Thank you," she said and put the glass back on the tray. As if she was all of a sudden aware of her surroundings, she looked up and saw Maddie cuddled up asleep. "Oh, she must be heavy, here let me–"

"No, she's fine. Sit," Devon said in a tone not meant to be questioned. He wasn't giving Maddie up just yet. In his arms, she was safe. He still hadn't been able to quell the fear when he thought her harmed. He was beginning to think it would never leave him. "So, no one saw anything?"

"I don't think so. When we got there, no one was about. The window was smashed in and the huge rock lay in the middle of my floor." She took a deep shaking breath. "It was Sunday. Most villagers don't venture out after the afternoon. I would doubt they were in fear of being caught." She covered her face with her hands, and as Devon stood watching, her shoulders began to shake. She was crying. Before he could turn to find a safe place for Maddie, Clive was there taking the limp warm lump of dark curls. Devon knelt and rested his elbows on Ella's knees. Damn, he had never had to console a woman. What was the protocol?

"It will be fine. I will make it so." Devon pulled her hands from her face to reveal shining eyes with tear tracks streaking her face. "I promise I will fix this. I told you when we first made our deal that I wouldn't leave you in the lurch and I won't."

He waited for that to sink in. He had made no promises of taking care of her. None of his responsibility. He wanted her to understand what he said. If this were the life she would choose instead of him, damn it, she would be the happiest baker in all of Scotland. When he was sure she understood, he continued as he wiped a tear away from her nose. "I will see you and Maddie to your room, and then Clive and I will take some men and materials to the village and cover the window for now. You will have another window as soon as I can dispatch the order. I will find out who did this and have a discussion about how to treat what doesn't belong to oneself. All will be well."

"Oh, well, I am sure it was just some village boys playing a prank. That is it I am sure," she stammered. That only helped to solidify her blackmailers as the culprits.

"Well, then I will have a talk with their parents. Right now, you need to rest. I promise it will be business as usual on the morrow. Your front room might not be as bright as it would be, but I am sure your business won't suffer for it." He would rebuild the entire building if it would make her stop crying.

He rose and tugged her out of the chair. She nodded vacantly and allowed him to lead her toward the door. Clive had followed ready to hand his bundle back over to Devon. He melted a bit more, when Maddie again, snuggled in close and started sucking her thumb. He didn't think he would ever have enough of the feeling of her in his arms. As he made his way behind the butler leading them to the second floor, he couldn't help but realize this was his first true act as the head of a family.

He had a family.

The idea took light and continued to warm him, while at the same time, a slow burning fury began to swell directed toward the men who were attempting to hurt either of them. Regardless of how Ella decided to live, she would always be his wife and Maddie always his daughter. As much as Ella would like to think it, she didn't have a decision to make because he would never again let her do anything without his help or protection.

His thoughts were so all consuming, he hadn't realized they had made their way to the end of the second floor east wing, and the butler was standing next to an open door. As Devon walked past the man, he acknowledged him. "Thank you, Hector, you have done some quick work."

"Anything for Mrs. R.— Lord Renwick," responded the butler. Devon made eye contact and the butler nodded once with eyes that softened. He then stepped back and headed down the hall. *So much for keeping our secret from everyone.* He got the feeling, however, that not a soul would find out any gossip from the butler.

"All right, here we are. The fire is a warm blaze, and I see that Clive has a night rail from one of his sisters laid out for you." He watched Ella wander into the room allowing the fatigue to win out. He crossed to the large bed and put Maddie on the soft mattress. He glanced at Ella and saw she was beginning to undress, unaware of her surroundings or guests. He left her in her own thoughts as he began undressing Maddie.

Once divested of her coat, dress, stockings, and half boots with only her slip left, Devon decided she was not a child, but a china doll all creamy porcelain and fragile pieces. Her little feet fit in the palm of his hand. He took a minute to count her toes. He wasn't sure why, but he was terribly proud to find she had five perfectly formed toes on each foot. Only when she shivered and curled into a ball, did he cover her, hiding her within the bulk of the bedding. Ella sat staring at the fire. He knew she wouldn't sleep for a while yet, but he also knew he had to get down to Clive who had been calling for their horses and some workmen.

"You need to sleep." He knelt next to the chair so she wouldn't have to crane her neck to see him. "Would you like a room made up for you?" He wasn't sure if she would want to sleep in the same bed with Maddie. He was sure his mother would have refused such an inconvenience.

"No, Maddie would wake not knowing where she was. Besides, we share our bed at the bakery. She has never slept without Penny or me. I will be fine. Will you please come and tell me if you find anything?" She asked with tired, but beseeching eyes.

"Well, I think it can wait until morning–" Devon started to say he wouldn't want to wake her.

"I need to know. Please promise you won't wait until tomorrow. Promise." Her eyes were every bit as demanding as her voice was weak.

"I promise." He bent over and tenderly kissed her forehead, holding it longer than necessary. He rose and turned to the door. He wanted to pick her up in his arms and hold her as he had Maddie. Instead, he left the room, shut the door, and made his way with determined strides back down to ride out with Clive.

Once he made the front hall, it was as if it was the middle of the day instead of the waning evening. No less than twelve servants and workmen bustled about. A maid slid past him with a quick bob heading toward Ella's room with the forgotten tea tray, and Clive emerged from the library with his head groundskeeper. "Ah there you are. I had just sent a maid with the tea to fetch you. Is she going to be all right?" Clive asked as he fiddled with his riding gloves.

"Yes, she's fatigued and I think she is beginning to realize she is involved in something she can no longer control, if she ever could." Devon allowed his valet who had appeared from nowhere to help him into his coat and hat. "Let's get down there. I am certain we will find a note or something."

"Yes, but the question is did she find it first? While you were gone, I spoke to the driver and he said she rummaged through the glass on the floor with a lantern even when he insisted she get back into the carriage. I would be willing to double down that she found a note and has it with her," Clive replied as they made their way to the waiting horses. The night had turned cool and crisp. It wasn't until the horses rode out through the gates with the thundering of hooves, the rumbling of a wagon, and more men on horseback behind them that Devon's head cleared.

"I concur, my devious little wife isn't about to give up all her cards just yet, but I am ready to be finished with this particular game. If there is nothing at the bakery, I will make sure I find the note in her clothes when we return. I'm not sure who I am looking more forward to punishing, the blackmailers, or my wife," Devon quipped, trying to make light the situation to prevent drowning in pure frustration. He also realized how desperate Ella must be to have come to him for help. She would never give up her control over a situation unless she was sure she was in danger. The thought sobered him even more.

"I am sure that both will have their merits and be rewarding in their own respect," Clive answered, understanding the need for a bit of joviality.

Three hours later, Devon stood staring down at his sleeping wife draped inelegantly with his sleeping daughter. The damage to the large window was catastrophic, but there had been no other damage. His and Clive's suspicions had been on the mark, however. Lying in the center of the hand-hewn floor of the front room was the offending rock that caused the destruction. Upon closer inspection, he found the torn piece of paper caught under the heavy field stone. The torn piece found its match now being held in Devon's hand, retrieved from his wife's reticule next to her pistol. It was very clear in the directions. As long as Ella continued to produce funds, she and her daughter would not be harmed, but once she was unable to provide, things were going to get very bad. Eric was able to confirm further that Ella had been dealing with some braggarts for some time, but he had been sworn to secrecy from telling Penny anything. He was a young man, but of a solid mind and agreed this foolishness was going too far. Devon felt he had an ally in the young man. The blackmailers had some information about Ella's past and were bent on putting her in harm's way. Devon was certain this had little to do with the money they were demanding, and feared that was only holding them at bay.

As Clive's men swept the glass and cleared the shards from within the pane, they had left them to their work, taking the opportunity to search the kitchen and apartment above stairs for any other signs.

Maddie murmured in her sleep. Devon, remembering the ragged doll in his other hand laid it under the child's arm watching as she clutched it to her and sighed with satisfaction snuggling closer to her mother. Devon walked around the large bed to the window filled with what was left of the moonlight. Looking out, he thought of the place his family had been living, without him. To most of the Haute Ton, it would be nothing but a hovel. Devon, on the other hand, saw a small home filled with love and laughter. It was warm and tidy with those things that he assumed would be found in a home. It wasn't large, only one room. It could have fit in his formal dining room at The Tate with room to spare. The one bed tucked under the eaves was covered not with French silk brocade, but homespun blankets made thick to keep out the winter chill.

How did he feel to know his daughter had grown up in such conditions? He knew how his father would have felt, most of his so-called friends as well. They would think it disgusting and lowly. An owl swooped low to pick a fat little mole from the dark garden below. Devon watched it for only a moment until he shrugged to no one and turned back to the bed.

He didn't care for the word of others— never had. He had grown up, as a child of noble birth should. It was lonely, boring, and at times, scary. His father had withheld love from Devon to teach him what? That you could survive without it, as his father had chosen to do. No, his daughter had spent the beginning of her life where she should have been. How could anyone argue when looking at them in the bed all wound together like a great knot. His only regret was that he was on the outside looking in. What would it be like to wake every morning with Ella draped over his chest and Maddie cuddled up close to her mother? Well, perhaps not every morning, he thought, bringing a half smile to his face. He brought his hand up to rub his whiskered jaw. It was then he remembered the paper in his hand.

When he had first been able to find it, he wanted to wake her from her slumber and shake her for her stubborn ways. As a gentleman, he had taken the high road and instead paced in front of the fire railing in silence at his predicament. He had to protect her. It wasn't just his responsibility anymore. She was his and he wasn't about to allow such scurrilous behavior. No educated man would be able to stomach such poor scribing on purpose, unstable man take what was his. He cursed Ella for putting him in such a position. If he confronted her and tried to force her hand, she would bolt. Of that, he had no doubt. She was scared, that was apparent, but not enough to give over control to him a mere mortal man. No, he was going to have to be devious and dishonest with his wife in order to get to the bottom of this. Careful, so not to disturb her things, he put the note back where he found it.

Well, he thought as he left to start scheming, at least he would have many years to make amends. With luck, he would be making amends because of his conscience and not because he was caught.

"You need to learn, old boy, when you tell them you will do something, whatever you do, don't go back on your word." Clive sat at the breakfast table working on his second plate piled high with food. It wasn't that his friend was throwing his first mistake of the day at him; it was that he was getting advice from a professional bachelor.

"I didn't tell her I would speak to her when we got back, exactly," Devon answered in a bit of a pout. "I told her if we found any proof of the culprit, I would wake her."

"Let me warn you now. They don't speak the King's English. They speak in tongues as you have said before. We think we understand. However, when in fact, we are just being led like lap dogs into danger. You have had the exceedingly rare luxury of only having to suffer a mistress and they by the nature of things tend to be a tad more hushed in their annoyances." He laughed and went back to his poached eggs with ham.

"Well, I'm not sure I could have woken her. They were both so asleep, neither roused when I went in to search the room." He thought of Ella asleep like an angel only hours earlier and then Ella only moments ago when she stormed into the breakfast room ranting about being late. She proceeded to scowl at Devon and accuse him of keeping information from her. He had to assure her he hadn't found anything in the bakery she didn't already know was there. He had decided keeping as close to the truth as possible was his best tack. That way he could more easily follow his own tale. She had stormed out without eating, making sure she had secured his promise to have Maddie returned to the bakery by 5 o'clock.

"Then perhaps you should have said you tried to wake her," Clive offered.

"Then I would have lied," Devon pointed out.

"Survival, my boy, is a nasty business, but one we must endure if we are to commune happily with the gentler of our species. Having been raised with all older sisters, I learned young to know when it is safer to lie than to tell the truth. By the time they find out you were not telling the complete truth, they have calmed a bit."

Clive seemed to feel no man could win against an angry woman.

Devon had to agree with respect to Ella. He turned back to his now cold eggs, trying to decide how to fix this latest setback.

The crisp morning air whipped at Ella while the damp knee high grass lashed at her skirts. Her damp dress would dry once she got to working in the heat of the kitchen. She was glad for the fresh air. Perhaps it would cool her temper and her tenuous emotions. She couldn't believe how rude she had just been. She knew the cause, of course, but had she begun to lose all her manners?

When she had woken in the guest room with sunlight streaming in warming her face, she knew at once, she was late. She couldn't remember the last time she awoke after daybreak. When she was over the shock of her own laziness, she remembered last night. Had Devon come back yet? Looking around the room, her eyes fell on a satchel sitting on the dressing stool and then at Maddie cuddled up with her doll. Yes, he came back and he had been in the room. Even thinking about it in the cool morning air sent a shiver of something delicious down Ella's spine.

She got out of bed and began dressing when she remembered the note she had shoved in her pocket. She chastised herself for being too shaken to think of hiding it better. It was still there, but she had no way of knowing if he had seen it. Would he have found anything to lead him to it? By the time she left the room, she was unsettled to the point of distraction.

Once in the breakfast room, she hadn't been put at ease. Both men sat busy plying themselves with their food as if it was any other day. She didn't trust them for one moment. When she quizzed them about last night, they assured her no other damage had been done to the building or her belongings, for which, she was grateful. Devon had also told her to expect workers today with a new window. She wanted to decline, knowing the cost of the window, not to mention the added price for getting it so soon, but at this point, she couldn't afford to replace it. The blackmailers were going to drain her funds if

CLAIR BRETT

they had their way. She needed to put an end to this, but she still didn't have any more information than before. She did however, have another date tonight. She would have just enough time to get Penny and Maddie settled to make it. She had decided she would double back after and follow them. It was dangerous, but she needed to make some progress.

So caught up in her thoughts, Ella was surprised to see the bakery in front of her as she crested the small hill in the field. She hadn't realized her stride equaled her internal machinations. It was a good thing because she was at least an hour and a half behind her normal routine. She saw long strings of white smoke dancing from the chimney. Penny must not have laid about like a lack-a-bed. She had returned from visiting her family.

The heat from the oven warmed Ella's cool cheeks causing them to sting from the windburn. "Penny? Penny, where are you?" She called, unable to see into the dark room from being outside.

"Ah, there you are." Penny's voice came from beside her in the pantry. "His Lordship sent a boy with news of the window to my parent's house last night. Said you were staying at the manor so ye would be a mite late." She continued to work her way around the pantry and out into the kitchen. Ella could see her friend. Her eyes were filled with concern.

"Yes, well, we are fine. Maddie was still sleeping when I left. I wasn't aware His Lordship would have known where to find you or to think to alert you."

"Well, it was of no consequence, I was more than ready to return. My fither had a list a yard long of potential suitors. I told 'im I was not interested in any of them. That I only want to be with Eric, but he says Eric doesn't have enough money to settle. I tried to remind him that he didn't have enough money for a dowry, so it could be a fair swap."

"Penny, I am sorry your father is so difficult. You know I understand." Ella said. She must have had a tone of something in her voice, because Penny stopped what she was doing and looked up. She had begun kneading the bread. It always helped to think of certain things

130

when kneading bread, it made the task more fulfilling. She took Ella by the hand and sat her at the large workbench opposite her bread dough.

"You need some tea."

"No, Penny truly, I am fine. You have done a splendid job getting things started on time this morning, but I can't let you do everything."

"Nonsense, I am doing fine. You are chilled from your walk, and you need a few moments to settle in before I start in with my plight." Penny placed the cup and saucer in front of her and poured steaming hot tea into it. The smell, mixed with the rising bread and baking pastries, was heaven to her tired soul. She allowed Penny her doting.

"So, what was it like having a knight on a white horse come to your rescue?" Penny asked as she rounded the table and began kneading again.

Ella laughed out loud. She would not call either Clive or Devon knights in shining armor, but she had to admit, once she entered the library last night, she hadn't had to worry about one detail until she left this morning. "Well, I wouldn't go as far as to call them that, but it was a relief to have someone to go to. It is reassuring to have such an involved Lord in our area."

"I wasn't talking about Lord Breakerton." Penny pointed out, with a gleam in her eye. "I was talking about Lord Renwick. He is champion material if I ever saw it."

Laughing again, Ella took a sip of her tea. "Lord Renwick was very helpful as well. I am sure he is acting the part of the perfect English gentleman." She hoped it was dark enough in the dim kitchen to hide her blush.

"Well, if you ask me, no Lord, English or Scottish would take you in and play nursemaid to a child that isn't his for no reason." Ella went still. She needed to get Penny off this train of thought. She didn't realize how close to the truth she was.

"Have you looked in the front room? I am sure it will not be easy doing business today with it so dark."

"Yes, it is very dark. I expect we will have to leave the door propped open." Ella watched as Penny, with practiced skill, shaped then placed the loaves of bread aside to rise.

"Well, I was told to expect some workers today to replace the window. I would imagine they would have to be coming from Edinburgh, so I would think it will be well into the day before we have to suffer that, but it will be good to get it taken care of so quickly."

"Mmhmm," responded Penny, "as I said, His Lordship is awfully generous with his time and funds. I wonder? Does he go around the countryside helping poor widowed bakers? It must be an interesting hobby."

Ella could feel a headache coming on. This was not going to be a day that played out to her favor. Of that, she was sure, but for now, the tea was hot and sweet, and she felt cared for. At least she thought that was lightness in her heart.

Devon quit the breakfast room having finished his cold eggs and ham. He was thankful Ella's snit hadn't curdled the cream in his coffee at least. He needed to find a maid to go look after Maddie. He decided looking in the wing where she still lay sleeping would be a good place to start. With purposeful steps, he walked down the hallway. His feet, slowed, then stopped in front of the bedroom door. He cursed his ridiculous emotions. He wanted to peek in on her, but assumed she would still be sleeping. He crept up to the door and stood in silence, not moving. That was when he heard the first faint sound. Then, another more distinct. Maddie was crying.

Without another thought of a maid, Devon opened the door, careful not to make any noise to scare her. What he saw melted his heart. Sitting in the middle of the huge bed was the three-year-old, legs crossed, clutching the old rag doll he had grabbed the night before. Her hair was a wild mass of curls sticking out at odd angles. As she turned to look at him, he saw the tear stains running down her bright red cheeks.

"Mommy?" she hiccupped.

"Good morning," he said brightly, not sure if he should walk into the room. He didn't want to make her fearful. "Mommy left to go to the bakery. You were still asleep."

She didn't answer, but looked him up and down assessing him. Devon bit back a smile. She looked so like her mother when she did that. She relaxed a bit.

"May I come in and sit with you?" He asked, still not wanting to scare her and not sure what to do. It crossed his mind that Clive would have her laughing and running the halls by now.

She nodded her approval and even sidled over on the bed to give him more room. His heart lurched thinking she might fall off the other side. When she didn't, his heart went back to its normal rhythm. He perched with one hip and knee on the mattress. He leaned his back against the large post at the bottom of the bed. They continued to size each other up.

She broke eye contact and began fussing with her doll's dress. He waited, but she didn't make any move to do anything.

"So, my Lady, what is it you would like to do today?" He asked, hoping she wouldn't say to go back to the bakery. He wanted to spend time with her. The realization shook him. She only shrugged her shoulders without looking up.

"Who is your friend? She is beautiful." Devon knew whenever trying to woo a young lady, you couldn't go wrong with talking about those things she found pleasure in. He hoped it would work on a three year old. She eyed him for only a moment, when he saw her face brighten.

"Lady Mary. She's a princess," she said and turned the doll, presenting her by stretching the rag arms so far Devon feared she would rip them. If Lady Mary was a princess, her attire was not her best. It was too large, and the lace was torn around the hem. It also had what Devon assumed was a honey stain on the sleeve. He bent at the waist in a bow.

"Glad to meet you, your Highness. I didn't realize we were so honored." He bent, and took the dirty cloth hand, placing a kiss on the back. He looked up and knew he had done as he should. Maddie was fair to beaming. "Well, what do you think Lady Mary would like to do today, while visiting this grand manor?" He asked. He hoped his question would aid him further, but wasn't prepared for Maddie to crawl out from around the large pile of blankets, and plop onto his knee. She rested her back and head to his frame, and sat for a moment.

"Lady Mary doesn't know. What is there to do?" She asked almost shyly.

"I am not sure myself. I guess we could take Lady Mary to get some breakfast. That might be a good start. Then, after she breaks her fast, we could go for a stroll, or we could take her for a ride."

"Ride?"

"Yes, Lord Breakerton has many fine horses. Lady Mary would be a proud princess indeed to ride on such a fine mount," Devon proclaimed. He was surprised at how he slipped into the role. He quite liked it as well.

"Lady Mary can't ride." Maddie said with a good bit of disappointment.

"That is of no consequence. I would suggest, if I may, that Lady Mary ride with you, and so we aren't separated, you may ride on my horse with me. How does that sound?"

"Wonderful!" She squealed and jumped off the bed headed for the door in nothing but her slip.

"Hold," he said, and she stopped and turned with an uncertain look on her face. "If I may, Lady Maddie, I will fetch a maid to assist you in preparing for your day. While you are doing that, I will go into the kitchen and make sure all is prepared for her Highness." She smiled and nodded happily. "Come, let us find you a maid." He stepped off the bed and walked to meet her at the doorway. He was unprepared, however, for her to reach up and wrap her tiny fingers around his much larger one. He smiled as they left to find some help.

More than an hour later, Devon had managed to change into his riding suit and find Clive doing the same. He didn't quite trust his instincts in the out of doors. Within the confines of the manor, he felt certain he wouldn't botch the situation, but he needed reinforcements in this venue. Maddie had gobbled down her eggs and toast and guzzled a glass of milk in record time. He could tell she was excited, until they reached the stables and she saw the size of the two huge horses awaiting them. She froze in her tracks more than twenty paces from the gate. He looked at Clive who was distracted by lint on his coat that had just been brushed. Devon considered calling his friend on his tell by asking if he needed to get glasses for his valet.

"Maddie? Are you scared of the horses?" Devon had crouched down so she might look him in the eye. It was then he remembered how everything had once seemed over-sized to him as a child. "They are big, aren't they?" She nodded. "The one on the right is Bane. He is Lord Breakerton's horse. He is very serious, but gentle. The one on the left will be our horse. Would you like to know his name?" Again, she nodded, never taking her eyes off the beasts. "His name is Caesar. He isn't as serious as Bane, but he loves to have his nose petted. Would you like to pet his nose?"

"I won't be able to reach it," she said in a small voice.

"How about if I carry you into the pen. That way, you won't feel quite so small and you will be able to meet Caesar properly, eye to eye."

With the seriousness of her mother across her face, she thought for a moment, and then nodded once. "That would probably be best. That way Lady Mary won't be frightened of them."

"That is true. I hadn't thought Lady Mary might be frightened. Very wise thinking." He reached out and pulled her into his arms as he stood. They made their way into the pen and dispensed with the needed introductions. Once Maddie had been snorted on and nuzzled by both grays, she declared them acceptable to Princess Mary.

Clive took her while Devon mounted, then reached down and pulled her and the doll in front of him. He made certain she was seated with his arms wrapped around her, all of a sudden made aware of just how high one sat in the saddle. Visions of Maddie slipping and falling ran through his mind. He sighed and chastised himself. If he continued thinking as such, he would be in his grave well before he could get her through her first season. That thought sent a new set of unknown feelings of possessiveness soaring through him. He shook his head clear. When he glanced at Clive, he was sure he saw him chuckling.

Damn, fool.

Out through the gates the pair of horses strolled into the warm spring day. Clive promised a gentle ride. Just enough to get some air and give her a grand adventure to go back and tell her mother. He knew it was unfair to use Maddie to get to Ella, but she was thwarting him at most every turn. If she was going to count cards, so could he.

The ride was a resounding success. The visiting royalty had flopped about in Maddie's arms enjoying the countryside. Maddie seemed to have enjoyed her jaunt as well. Devon had even made her giggle a time or two. By the time the party strolled into the stable yard, it was time for luncheon. Maddie had been asleep for about thirty minutes. He had first noted the lack of chatter coming from the dark curly head bobbing in front of him. He was further made certain she had given up the battle when those dark curls fell back and she snuggled into his chest. He was glad she felt so comfortable as to fall asleep with him in charge. On the other hand, it could just be that a three year old would sleep when they needed to.

In truth, he wasn't sure he would be so trusting.

Clive came around the side and reached up to take the limp bundle. She never stirred. Devon dismounted and handed the reins off to a stable boy. He then turned to relieve Clive and he juggled Maddie until her head rested on his shoulder. All in all, he was pleased with his first real day as a father. His own father left riding lessons and any other lessons to someone more equipped to deal with him. He wouldn't be that kind of father, regardless of his social station. He had already lost three years with Maddie. he wouldn't lose anymore without a fight.

The two men walked up the sloping lawn to the side door. Devon glanced over at Clive askew. He was sure his friend would be the first to tell him if he was doing something wrong, after all, Clive knew his history. The hallway was dark and cool as their boots clicked in rhythm making their way to the south parlor where the ladies were chatting.

"Oh, look at her. Such a love. Did she enjoy her ride?" Asked LePrin when the men entered and Devon laid Maddie out on a nearby chaise draping her with a blanket. He was not aware that children slept so much.

"Yes, she didn't stop talking," Devon said.

"That is until she fell asleep," Clive chimed in.

"She must have been exhausted. Nelly told us how she woke up not knowing where her mother was and with the events of last night, the poor little thing," Flick observed. "Why, what must she be thinking of all this? Her little mind must be boggled."

"Once she knew where her mother was, and that she would see her later today, she was fine," Devon assured the concerned women. "I do think a quiet afternoon is probably in order. Should I put her to bed, or will she be fine there?" He asked, unsure what the proper thing would be to do.

"We both have dealt with a sleeping child a few times in our lives. I believe if you leave her where she is, we can quite easily watch a three year old sleep," LePrin assured him.

"After luncheon, once she awakens and eats, we can go for a stroll in the garden with her. I am sure she can find something to entertain out there." Before Devon could raise his concern of them keeping up with her, Flick added, "We will bring Nelly with us to help."

Clive then jumped into the conversation to give a rundown of how Princess Mary fared on her tour of the kingdom. As he was finishing, the butler came carrying a tray filled with cold meats, cheeses and fruit. The gentlemen remained with the ladies until after they ate, then both left. Devon had to deal with some correspondence from London, and Clive, some visiting in the area to see if he could come across any information proving helpful in ferreting out the blackmailers. Their plan was already set for this evening. Ella was meeting with the blackmailers and they were determined to get a good look at them.

♥♥♥

A loud crash and scream made Ella drop a whole platter of rolls she had been planning to put out to sell in the morning. To her consternation, the crash and the scream were caused by the cat Penny had befriended. The meddlesome creature was forever knocking things over.

"Damn it! One of us is going to have to go," Ella snapped at the cat while she bent to pick up the rolls, which would now take her an extra batch of dough in the morning to replace. She had taken the time this afternoon to make them, hoping to save herself time tomorrow. She also was able to keep herself busy. "Why can't you go out and catch mice like other cats?" she asked the feline who was now making amends by prancing around her, rubbing her sleek body along Ella's ankles and purring loudly.

She knew if not for everything on her mind, she would find the act endearing, but today, it was just more frustrating. She couldn't even get a cat to listen to her and do as she asked. She finished picking up the rolls and put them in the barrel she had by the door for food waste for the pigs down the road. The farmer always seemed to send a juicy roast her way during slaughter time since she helped to fatten them up.

After the morning baking, Ella had sent Penny into the main room to help customers. Ella was in no mood to paste a sunny smile on her face and greet people. In addition, she was sick of Penny jumping from playing nursemaid to her and talking about her own sad situation. If Ella could, she would just give Penny the money for a bride's price to give to Eric's father. If things worked out and Devon got his way, perhaps she would just leave the bakery to Penny. Then Eric's father would have no reason to argue the match.

Ella froze in her tracks. If things worked out? If things worked in Devon's favor, she would be leaving Scotland and heading into a life as his Viscountess. She didn't want that–did she? Ella felt light-headed. The notion didn't seem as foul as she had thought earlier. In fact.

No, it was just her nerves working their magic. Nothing could make her want to go back to London and have a man rule over her for the rest of her life. It was just the stress of everything. That is all it was was, just nerves.

Resuming her march across the kitchen, she attempted to shake the chills prickling down her back and arms. Her body betraying her adamant refusal of the notion. She finished cleaning and double-checked the stew bubbling on the fire. She had explained to Penny that she had a meeting and would be leaving soon after Maddie returned. Penny was more than capable. She kept Maddie when Ella went on her trips to Edinburgh.

She wondered about Maddie as she made her way upstairs to change. She hoped Maddie had a good day. She found herself thinking about what they might be doing. Her and Devon. Were they getting on well? Did he claim to want to spend time with her, and then pawn her off on Flick and LePrin? That is what her father would have done, but he wouldn't have claimed a desire to spend time with her. A voice resonated through her mind, *I am not your father. I never will be like your father.* Devon had been thoroughly insulted when she compared him to her father. She remembered the time Devon had caught her father threatening her while they were at The Tate. Her father never raised his voice to her again after that. She knew Devon spoke with him in private after, but she never asked what was said. No one had ever been in a position to stand up for her before. Never.

Once she had dressed and re-pined her hair, she switched her rather soft slippers for sturdy boots. They were at least one size too big, but they worked well in the fields. She crossed to the small table and took up the pouch there. It was heavy and the coins clinked as she opened it to recount the amount again. She didn't dare meet her blackmailers without the money, even if she didn't want to pay them. They broke her window. They should be paying her.

She heard the bell sound over the front door, and heard Maddie's bright voice carrying through the rafters. "Hi Penny! Where is Mommy?"

"Well, did ye 'ave fun today, Poppet?" She heard Penny ask. Ella didn't hear the reply because she turned and hurried down the stairs to the back of the building, making her way into the front room, only to be brought up short. Devon stood tall and regal in the room.

"My Lord, I had expected a footman to escort Maddie home. You needn't have bothered with such a thing," she said, surprise in her voice.

"Mommy!" Maddie squealed and ran to be picked up and hugged.

"I missed you! Did you enjoy yourself?" Ella waited as Maddie seemed to think about her answer.

"Well, I woke up and you were gone," she said with all seriousness. Ella hadn't even thought of Maddie being out of sorts. She should have. She scolded herself.

"I am sorry, sweeting. You must have been scared." She could feel Devon's eyes on her.

"I was, but then he was there. He made Princess Mary laugh and me. Then, we went for a ride on Caesar. We went almost to Edinburgh! I fell asleep, then I played in the garden. Can I go back?" She stopped to take a breath at last, hope in her eyes.

Ella glanced up at Devon and almost laughed. She looked so like him. They both stood with identical pleading looks. The difference was Maddie knew hers. Devon, she figured, was unaware of the look he held on his face. If they were in public together much, people would know the truth. Still, it warmed her heart to see father and daughter want more time together.

"Well, I think tomorrow we had planned on having you go after breakfast. Would you like that?"

"Yes, very much! Did you hear Lord R.? I can come visit tomorrow!" She ran up to him and gave him a big hug, which to Ella's further surprise, he bent to accept.

"I think that is wonderful. Will Princess Mary be joining us?" He asked with true interest.

"She might be too tired after today. I will see in the morning," she stated like a true mother.

"I understand. She is welcome of course. Shall I have the horses ready in the morning?"

"Yes," she stated and turned to her mother.

"Why don't you take Princess Mary up and put her to bed, then come back down for dinner."

Maddie beamed again at Devon, waved, and disappeared. Penny took her cue and left as well. Ella busied herself covering bread loaves for the night. The dratted man seemed to fill any room he was in.

"Thank you. I had a wonderful time with her today."

"You are welcome. It appears she too enjoyed herself." She needed to gain control or she would be begging him to take her into the storage room. If the new window didn't open the shop to the world outside, she wouldn't be adverse to him leaning her against the counter— wonderful, as if she needed to have that image just now. A shiver ran down to the pit of her stomach.

"I was hoping you and I might have some time together. Remember our agreement?" He asked.

"Oh, well, actually, I was just getting ready to go visit a sick woman on the other side of the moor. I take her bread when there is left over. It will have to be another time."

"Tomorrow then?" It was a question that for all purposes was no question at all. She eyed him before she answered.

"Tomorrow would be fine. Would you care to join us for dinner? We eat early because we have to rise so early."

"Perfect. I find all this fresh air increases my appetite. I will leave you to your visit then." He bowed and looked as though he would have kissed her, but he too noted the new glass opening them to the whole of the village. She watched as he lumbered through the door and onto the street. His horse stood waiting. He mounted and headed north toward the manor. Now she would have to wait until she was sure he was gone before she left.

She locked the front door and took a moment to admire the new window Devon had installed. She marveled at the speed of which a man with money could get things done. Shrugging, she made her way back into the kitchen and to the back door. Penny had Maddie well in hand, so she slipped out without disturbing them. She would get some answers tonight. Of that, she was sure.

CHAPTER 10

From her position in the bushes to the west of the clearing, Ella watched for her blackmailers. She still managed to get there early enough to see where her blackmailers were coming from. As she waited, a low eerie mist rolled across the field as if it were chasing the light as it dipped below the horizon. A chill went down her back.

She needed to get her mind off all things dark and dangerous. She conceded that she was not as brave as she would like to be. Her mind went to seeing Devon and Maddie together. They were getting on famously. Ella felt a pang of envy. Maddie not only enjoyed her father's company, but he had enjoyed hers as well. What she would have given for just one day of harmony between her and her father.

Not to mention the fact that Ella was realizing more and more that she wanted to spend time with Devon as Maddie had. She would never begrudge her daughter a thing, but she so wanted to be part of the scene.

The noise of horses to the north brought her out of her reverie. To her left, set back next to the trees was a small cabin crouched in the shadows. The noise stopped behind it, but then male voices could be heard. She couldn't make out the words, but whoever they were, they were not getting on well. After a moment, two men much older than she was came around the front of the cabin.

Both wore plain clothes that were in disrepair. They were of average build, but the one to her left, hugging the shadows with the cabin, was taller and thinner by a bit. Their hair was balding and not well brushed. Where the taller man had a bushy gray-black beard, the other only kept a mustache that was as unkempt as his partner's beard. She thought about how her mother had hated men with mustaches. She would all but cringe when she saw one, a very strange memory to have in the middle of the woods in such a situation. She mentally shrugged. It was obvious Ella was trying to calm her nerves by thinking of her mother.

Even from her distance, she could see the men were related. The angles on their faces were too similar not to be. Then it hit her. She had seen these men before, spoken with them. They were the same men that night in the Buckshead Inn when she was serving. She had met her blackmailers, and never knew. A chill slid down her back and her stomach wretched. How could she have not realized? However, she knew there would have been no way for her to know that night. They didn't give anything away.

She would have liked to wait a bit longer to listen to their argument, but since she was alone and no one knew what she was about, it was not prudent to anger them further by appearing late. Taking a steadying breath and holding her head high, she rose from her crouch and stepped into the clearing. Both men turned in her direction. Their expressions were so sinister that she wanted to turn and run. they were so sinister. Instead, she lifted her chin a notch and continued deeper into the clearing.

Devon sat crouched to the south of the little cottage, hidden by a large group of blown down trees. Thankfully, he had not been late. After leaving the bakery, he proceeded to where he hoped to intercept Clive on his way here. He would have liked to hear what news he was able to dig up on his tenant visits. He must have been held up. Devon abandoned hope of meeting Clive and headed to the meeting spot. He hoped his friend would appear, as he wasn't sure if he would need assistance. Now, he watched as two ruffians arrived on horseback and made their way to the clearing. His suspicions were correct. These two were not of good breeding. They were dressed poorly with the look of bitter anger on their drawn features.

How could Ella have been so foolhardy to agree to meet in such a secluded place alone? Once she was back, safe in London, he would have to have a talk with his independent wife about when it is prudent to allow a man to handle a situation.

A noise to his right gained his attention. The darkness had taken over, but the denseness of the forest was still darker, leaving him to search the shadows. Clive came, none too late, bending low to remain unseen.

"Where have you been?" Devon hissed low at his friend.

"Sorry," Clive whispered with a slight grimace letting Devon know he hadn't meant to be tardy. "My last stop was the Vicar's house."

"Well, what did you find out?" Devon asked still whispering but instilling his restraint.

"It will take too long and now really isn't the time. Later, back at the manor." Clive responded settling more into the blow down of trees that Devon had chosen as their look out spot. Devon wanted to argue. Clive knew something he could tell, but now wasn't the time. Devon ground his teeth. He had no choice, but to sit back, watch and wait.

Just as he stopped glowering at Clive, he turned to see Ella make her entrance. She looked all of the Viscountess that she was. His wife was the bravest woman he knew. Watching the scene unfold, he tried to envision one of his female acquaintances doing the same. Not one would be able to do what Ella could. From the moment she entered his study on the night she proposed they marry, and then fake her death, his life had been forever changed.

Despite his admiration for her tenacity, Devon would prefer her to be safe right now. To their benefit, she kept her distance, so both parties were forced to raise their voices.

"I am here. I assume you gentlemen are the ones attempting to empty my pockets. I don't have much time before I am missed, so let us get this over with." The two men stood, their heads bent together discussing something.

"You are not in charge here, so shut yer mouth! We're gettin' sick of ye choosin' when to follow directions!" The taller man shouted.

"Ye are jus' as uppity as yer mum!"

"My mother? What do you know of my mother?" She shouted back to the shorter man. Devon thought he heard her voice catch.

The taller man laughed. "We didn't think ye knew. We weren't sure that is, but now–"

"Tell me!" Ella hissed.

"I'm not surprised that yer mum never told ye she was a murderin', whore." The shorter of the two beamed. Devon wanted at that moment not to be eavesdropping. He felt unease settle in his stomach. This was going to be very private, and perhaps Ella wouldn't want to share it with him, but he was stuck now. He had to be there in order to protect her. Whatever this was, they would deal with it later, once she was safe. He did look away to afford her that amount of privacy, however small.

Ella stood, unable to breathe. The copse began to sway, or was it her. She couldn't faint. She needed to stay clear-headed. Her mother a murderer? Her mother who was afraid of the wind. They couldn't be speaking of her mother. She was a child of twelve when she passed, but she even remembered the woman being timid and retiring every time her father had visitors. It wasn't possible. And well, as for her mother being a harlot, that was just absurd. She was the most virtuous woman Ella ever knew. In fact, she felt on many occasions that her own behavior would have been looked down upon by her mother for being too overbearing and free minded.

"What's the matter, sweetie, your mum's sins weighing on ye?" teased the shorter one, Ella was beginning to realize he was the angrier of the two which could make him more dangerous.

She wouldn't give them the satisfaction of watching her deny the allegations. "I have no idea what you are talking about. If you can't produce any more in the way of facts than an accusation, I am afraid this meeting is over," she answered back. She could tell her cold tone took them a bit by surprise.

"Ye, want facts, Missy? I'll give ye facts!" she had decided not to anger them, but as usual, she spoke before she thought. The one in charge shook from his rage as he pointed a finger at her. The darkness was overwhelming them, and now, she could see only their forms, not their expressions. "Yer mum killed our brother. How is that by way of a fact? She allowed him to court her. She flirted with him. Led him to thinkin' she wanted more, and then just as he made her his, she killed him." She heard the years of hatred drip from every word. She was beginning to piece together a scenario. One that she wasn't going to be happy with, she was sure.

The taller man continued when the shorter one seemed too over-come with anger to finish the story. Now the darkness had turned the men into outlines and the cottage was gone to her. "After, our Pa wanted justice. He was the oldest son. She was just a female. But, she had convinced her Pa, 'The Lord', she hadn't meant to. Well, her being a 'Lady' made it so. She was married off, and sent away."

Ella heard the snap of a twig at the same moment she felt the arm around her neck. The shorter one was on her. Being just taller than she was, he had the advantage. She felt more than heard his hot, gin filled breath against her ear from the roaring she was hearing in her head as she struggled. "Aren't ye going to say 'ello to yer old uncle?" he hissed.

"No!" The word was ripped from her throat before she knew what was happening. She felt vomit filling her throat, but swallowed hard to clear her head. His grip tightened as he turned to drag her back to the other man. She couldn't let him do it. She could only think of Maddie. She wouldn't allow Maddie to grow up without her mother.

Digging in her heels, she began to fight. He had her by the throat, leaving her arms free. She began throwing her elbows into his ribs with all the force she could muster. She thought she heard a groan and a thud from behind her, but she couldn't be sure. Her captor was grunting and swearing so loudly that she could just be hearing him. Ella connected with a tender spot and he let her go, cursing violently. She didn't wait to try to escape, but it wasn't quick enough.

He grabbed her long hair that had fallen from the struggle and yanked hard. The pain sent bright lights dancing in front of her eyes. She thought she heard it rip from her scalp. The force pulled her back, but it wasn't hard enough to send her to the ground. Instead, Ella turned to face her assailant and was greeted with the back of his hand. Before she recovered, she heard her assailant being overtaken by someone or something. The moonless night did not allow her to see anything but large shapes. She turned to see where her other assailant was, but couldn't spot him. What she did see was a large mound on the ground. Whoever this was, he must have gotten him while she and the shorter one were struggling. Still a bit dizzy from the blow to her face, she tried to make out who was winning. Then she thought about who this might be. She was thankful, but what if it was just a passerby seeing the chance to have a stab at her as well? She took the opportunity, before she had more to deal with and ran as fast as she could into the darkness of the forest. If the stranger killed them, life would get better in quick fashion, but if he didn't— well, she was sure life could get worse. Much worse.

Devon watched as Ella streaked into the woods and out of sight. His fisted hand itched to deliver another blow to the bloody man who dared harm Ella. Had they not slipped away in the darkness and confusion, Devon could have ended this once and for all. Life, however, he was finding, wasn't as tidy as one would hope when his wife was involved.

"Blast!" Clive rounded the cottage panting. "They had horses. At least I know they were not headed in the direction of the village. They headed south."

Devon stood in silence, looking at the spot where Ella had

vanished. His blood boiled with anger for the man who touched her. He was certain at that moment that he would have killed him had he been given the chance, so filled with rage over her potential danger that he could taste it.

"Devon? Did you hear me?" Clive asked, walking closer so Devon could see his disheveled appearance. "I said—"

"Yes, I heard. They went south." Devon interrupted Clive. "Well, was it true?" He continued to ask without removing his eyes from the now empty woods. "Are those men Ella's uncles? Did her mother kill their brother?"

"Well, the generalities of it are I suspect, yes," Clive answered without his customary good humor. "I think the Vicar and his wife may have a more objective version. Let's get the horses and I can fill you in."

Turning, Devon fell in beside Clive as they made their way to the woods and their horses. Neither man spoke. It unsettled him to have Clive so quiet, but it did make the gravity of their situation clearer. Now, how should he proceed? The decisions now would be more complicated. His hand throbbed from the one solid hit he managed to land on Ella's attacker and now his temple began to throb. He would get no sleep this night. He sighed.

Once mounted and heading for the road, Clive filled him in. "The vicar and his wife remember the situation differently. The man in question had an unhealthy interest in the daughter of the Lord, especially being just a farmer's son. He had been removed from the property on more than one occasion because of his unwanted advances." Devon did not like where he knew this story was going. "They remember Ella's mother as a shy, quiet little thing who would never have made advances. After the incident, the boy's family did demand compensation and retribution for their loss, but were turned away because in the Lord's eyes, his daughter had been defiled and abused against her will. It wasn't long after that before Lord Bowen-Thorn was summoned. He had shown interest in her dowry and it was assumed that an early pregnancy would not hinder his enthusiasm. There were threats made and it was decided moving to London would guarantee her safety. Devon, I am afraid their end game is to kill her and Maddie for her mother's sins."

"I am certain of it," Devon replied tightly. He had lost her once because of their parent's bad choices and behavior, he would not risk that a second time.

Everything about Ella's life clicked into place in that instant. Bowen-Thorn had married an already pregnant wife to gain the fortune, which once gone, he would have no need for his wife. Devon assumed the poor woman was so traumatized by her rape that she would not be intimate with her new husband, so he was left with raising a daughter that didn't belong to him and was of lowly birth, with no chance of begetting an heir. It by no means excused his behavior toward Ella, but it did explain it.

"I don't suppose you have a brilliant plan to rid the Scottish countryside of those curs?" Clive quipped as they reached the main road leading back to Aires Meade. "I believe I won't sleep a wink knowing they are wandering about. I am sure we haven't scared them off for long."

Clive's words only substantiated his own thoughts. His need to make sure Ella was safe surged. As the two men rode on, his instincts turned him toward the village instead of the manor. Devon needed only to look at Clive.

"I will not wait up, but do not expect there to be any brandy left in my study upon your arrival."

"Fair enough. Send someone to find Eric and bring him up to snuff with the latest happenings." And he was off.

She had told him she was going to visit an elderly friend. He would not be overstepping his rights to feel the need to see that she made it home. He wanted nothing more than to enter that blasted bakery, yelling at her foolishness for trotting off alone in a secluded wood, to meet with the very blackmailers who are threatening to harm her and her family.

His family!

Unfortunately, the fear of losing her again was strong enough to turn his words sour on his tongue. He was a coward. If he went to White's and told the gentlemen of his acquaintance that he was afraid of losing his wife if he became too overbearing, he would be a laughing stock. Unless those men also loved their wives as much as he was beginning to fear he loved his.

Riding on the dark road, he had nothing to divert his thoughts. They kept going back to the moment he realized that man was going to hurt her. Clive couldn't have stopped him had he tried. If he was trying to keep his control, it died a tragic death when Ella's cry of pain was wrested from her. One minute he was crouched in the forest, the next he was shoving Ella out of the way as he threw the hardest punch he could into his target's jaw.

What if Ella had recognized him? Could she have?

He hadn't thought of it when he went to her rescue, and he would have to admit, he wouldn't have been able to stop himself had it been in the height of the afternoon. Well, if she knew who it was, then he would just have to pay the consequences. Her life was more important than having her next to him every night. He had lived thinking her dead for four years. Neither, choice was the one he wanted, but having the choice, he knew he would choose her alive hating him to her dead. The dim lights of the Inn were approaching to the right. He guessed he would just have to go to the bakery and see her reaction. He preferred being a coward, truth be told, at least where Ella was involved.

Passing the Inn, he heard the loud boisterous voices of the men. He was learning that unlike London, Scotland was in general, a happy place. Perhaps it was more the people than the location, but he didn't think so. He idly wondered what it was about Scotland he hadn't liked before this journey. Around the corner, the bakery stood dark and quiet. There were no candles in the main shop and none shone from the upper floor. Devon turned his horse down an ally and around to the back. As he suspected, a soft glow from the kitchen radiated into the chill of the night.

Devon dismounted, and to his surprise, his mount ambled over to the tree where Devon had been watching the goings on for days at the bakery when not with Maddie or Ella. If his horse knew the routine, perhaps he was a bit too obvious. He followed the horse and tied it. Once done, he turned toward the back door. He decided to knock and see where Ella took the conversation. He would be able to gain knowledge from her reaction— or so he hoped.

He had seen her run from the woods, he knew she headed here, but when no one answered the door right away, fear swelled like the tide. What if she was hurt more than he thought? What if they circled around on a path neither he nor Clive knew? What if she fell? What if...? He rapped again, louder this time. Just as he was about to pound on the door with both fists, it opened.

"Devon, what are you doing here?" Ella asked, surprise evident on her face.

Devon couldn't answer right away. He was too busy calming his scattered nerves. She was all right. She was standing in the doorway, not in a broken heap on the forest floor. He fought the urge to reach out and touch her cheek. As he searched her face for signs of bruises or scrapes, he saw what he thought was relief wash over her features, but as soon as he saw it, it was gone. He bit back a smile.

He bowed. "I kept thinking about you wandering in the woods alone and needed to see for myself that you had returned unharmed."

"Returned?" She asked with nervousness in her voice, perhaps forgetting her earlier story.

"Yes, you did go to visit your elderly friend, did you not?" He asked.

"Oh, yes I did. And as you can see, I returned hale and healthy." Ella said, still not inviting him in.

"I am relieved. I could not have found my bed tonight without knowing you as well had found yours safely." Devon was rewarded with a pretty blush. "May I come in? It seems very foolish to have ridden from the manor just to exchange two sentences. Perhaps we could sit and talk." He watched as she tried to decide. He knew when he had won.

"Fine, just be very quiet. Penny and Maddie are asleep." She stepped back for him to enter. As she did, he noticed it. She wasn't putting any pressure on her left foot.

He made his way to the fire and made to warm his hands. He watched from the corner of his eye and as he thought, she had been injured. She was able to make two steps before it gave out. He reached out and caught her before she hit the floor. Her pain visible in her face, which now in the light, was beginning to show the swelling and bruising from where she was backhanded.

"Good God, woman, what happened?" He said, his concern clear in his voice.

"I— I twisted it on a root. It was dark when I came back from— from my visit. I didn't see it until it was too late," she explained.

Devon scooped her up and sat with her on his lap on the low bench close by. "Does it hurt to move?"

"Not over much, mostly just when I put pressure on it."

Her body warm and alive felt so good that Devon was having trouble following the thread of the conversation. He wanted to sit with her by the fire, curled in each other's arms forever. She smelled of wood smoke and wind, and of Ella. He inhaled to take in as much as possible. His arms tightened around her and he inhaled again. Her quiet cough brought him back to his senses.

He cleared his throat, "Sorry, you smell so damned good, I forgot your injury. Now, I need to look at it, to see that it isn't broken."

He stood with her still in his arms. She wasn't protesting, he noticed, and counted that in his favor. He set her in the rocking chair and he sat on the low foot stool in front. Gingerly, he took her sore leg and laid it across his own. She still wore her kid boots. He untied and then unlaced the offending boot. Ella made no protest until he pulled the shoe off. She whimpered a muffled sound and he saw her eyes fill with tears.

"I know that hurt, but we needed to get it off. I will be very gentle, but you need to tell me if it hurts." She nodded, but said nothing. She was too busy biting down on her lower lip. Most women of his acquaintance would have swooned already and be demanding a physician. Ella sat stock still allowing his ministrations. He started at her knee and worked his way down her leg feeling for anything out of the ordinary. Once at her ankle, he felt her tense and then jerk when he poked the area, but he didn't feel any broken bones.

"I don't think it's broken. Can you move your toes?" He asked. She dutifully wiggled them. "I have never spent much time admiring a woman's toes, but I think I may have to start. You have very sensual toes, Mrs. R.," he quipped.

She made to pull her foot free to no avail. "Toes are not meant to be sensual, I am sure," she argued.

"No? Well, what purpose do they have? I have oft thought that pieces of the human body with no apparent use must have been added purely for my pleasure."

"Hmm," was her reply. He didn't give her the opportunity to make eye contact and see if he was joking. He continued to examine her dainty foot. It was true, he had never much cared one way or the other about a woman's foot, but Ella's were soft, delicate, finely boned, and absolutely arousing, when not swollen to twice its size, he thought. He cleared his head from the sensual fog he had fallen in.

"Well, I don't believe it is broken, but it definitely is one nasty sprain. How did you ever get home after you fell?" He asked.

"Well, it didn't start hurting until after I returned and sat by the fire," she said trying again to pull her leg free. Devon lifted her leg so he could rise, and then placed it on the footrest.

"Would you like for me to go fetch the doctor?"

"No, if it is only a sprain, there is nothing he can do."

"Well, you will have to be off that leg for at least a few days if not more." She opened her mouth to argue. He raised a hand to silence her. "It matters not what you say. You will not be able to put any weight on it for at least that long."

"Wretched! Just Wretched! How am I supposed to work? I can't knead bread and run a bakery while sitting." The frustration of it all caused her to begin trembling. Devon knew the feeling of wanting to act, but not being able to.

"I thought you said your girl Penny could run the bakery?"

"She can, if she knows ahead of time. It takes two people to make all the bread needed in one day. If it is only me, or only her, then we make one batch at night and then one again in the morning. Now, is not enough time to make the one ahead." She slumped, defeated. Devon knew it was the knowledge that the blackmailers had caused this problem.

"I will help Penny in the morning." It was a good solution, or so he thought.

Her snort of laughter was followed by "what?" That led him to believe she didn't agree.

"I will come and assist Penny with the baking in the morning and every other if you would like."

"No, absolutely not," was her strangled response.

"Why?"

"Because, you are— well you are Viscount Renwick."

"And my title has bearing because—?"

"Because, an English Lord does not knead bread dough in a bakery."

"Neither does an English Viscountess." He arched one brow challenging her to argue.

"You don't know how to make bread," she countered.

"True, but Penny will know and I will just follow her direction. You forget I spent most of my boyhood hiding in the kitchens to avoid my father and his mistresses. You don't think cook didn't put me to work? No one loitered in her kitchen long before they had a spoon in their hand." He raised his left brow to follow with the right.

"What if someone sees you?"

"How many customers do you have before the bread is made?"

She scoffed at his sarcastic tone, but didn't protest any longer. Devon was filled to bursting. Perhaps he could show her his worth at last. He was always told by the servants a true relationship was one where the two people shared a burden and helped each other. This was one way he could share her burden. If she could rise before the sun and make bread every morning for four years, surely he could do it for a few days.

"Fine, I will explain to Penny that you insisted on helping. She won't ask for reasons even if she would like to."

"Good, it is settled. Now, if you truly are to rest, you will have to be at the manor."

"Whoa! I did not agree to be at the manor. I am comfortable right here."

"True, but at the manor there are servants who can tend to you. Here, you will have to rely on Penny or me. That would take precious time away from getting the baking finished. We can have Penny explain that you left for another shopping trip if you like."

"What about the servants? They would know I was not on a shopping trip."

"Amazingly, I have found Breakerton's servants to be exceedingly loyal. I am sure all he will need is to say the word."

"I still think it best if I stay here."

"Coward." He wasn't sure what possessed him to say it, but he couldn't help poke fun at her for her apparent fear of being alone and at his mercy. It had the desired effect, however.

"Fine, I will go stay at the manor, but only until it is so I might walk on it," she said, settling more into the rocking chair. "And I am not, nor will I ever be a coward."

Devon laid his hand over his heart and bowed his head. "My deepest apologies. I was mistaken, my Lady." He was heartened by the fact she didn't argue about her title. Every other time he had used it, she had. A good sign indeed. "Now, to bind that leg for the journey." Devon rose from the bench and moved around the warm cozy space looking for something to use as a splint, and linen to use as a binding. Ella sat rocking, giving suggestions and directions. The domesticity of it was not lost on him.

If he hadn't gone tonight, would they be here now, or would she be in mortal danger with no hope for rescue? A cold chill spoiled the moment for him. If this wasn't resolved soon this very menial and domestic act might be lost forever. He found the items and crouched at Ella's feet to bind her leg. He was as gentle as he could be, but he knew the pain was still great. He had arrived ready to throttle her for putting herself in danger, but then seeing her injured and in need of help softened his resolve. Soon enough, he would have to confront her about what was going on. For now, however, Devon was going to soak up every moment he had with her.

When he was finished, he stood, swept her up into his arms, and sat in the rocking chair with her in his lap. She only wiggled in complaint for a moment, then seemed to think better of it and rested her head on his shoulder. He drew his arms around her and just basked in the feel of her warmth, her life. Until a month ago, he thought this an impossibility. He refused to lose it again. Once in a lifetime was all a man could take.

In that instant, he understood his father. He knew why the man had never divorced and remarried. He loved her, and the thought of losing another love was too much to bear. It made sense now. With Ella in his arms, her soft breath warming his ear, everything in the universe made sense. Unwilling to let her go, he gave himself a few more minutes before Ella broke free to leave a note for Penny about what happened. Then they made their way outside to his mount and made for the manor. He would be returning early and would explain things to Penny then.

After settling Ella in, what he now thought of as her room, he managed to make his way to his own chamber. A fire had been lit and upon closing the door, his valet emerged from the changing room.

"His Lordship said you would be late, but in need of assistance upon your return, my Lord." His valet produced his silk changing robe from thin air and waited for Devon.

"Thank you." Was all Devon could manage before the valet helped him out of his coat and boots. "I will be needing to rise by half three. Will you see that I am roused from my bed?"

The man looked at him then at the clock on the mantel. "But, sir, that is but three hours from now," he stated in shock.

A strained laugh rumbled from Devon. "So it is. I had best get myself to bed then." At that, Devon crossed the room and crawled into bed. He was glad this night was over.

♥♥♥

At four o'clock the next morning, Devon rode out toward the bakery. The sun had yet to rise and Devon was certain no living creature could survive on only three hours of sleep. He let a yawn overtake his thoughts. His valet had all but swooned when he said he would be in shirtsleeves with no cravat or waistcoat. His attire felt very liberating. If he ever had the opportunity to remain in the country, this was how he would dress. Shifting in the saddle, his horse gave protest by shaking his head and snorting.

"Oh, what are you complaining about," Devon grumbled. "You weren't kept up with dreams of faceless men grabbing at your wife."

The horse blew its reply, unimpressed it seemed. The three hours allotted to him had not been three hours of mindless slumber, but a collection of nightmarish scenes with Ella being grabbed by garish figures. Devon would run after them trying to grab her back, and just when she was lost to him, he would wake in a cold sweat. So, in defense of his sleep, he might be in better spirits had they been hours of slumber.

The sun hadn't risen when Devon rode through the village. He thought of Ella warm and fast asleep. He had checked on her before he left. The maid he had insisted stay with her was curled up in a chair next to Ella, snoring. Careful not to wake her, he went around the bed. Even if he had not been exhausted, he would have wanted to join his wife. She lay snuggled into the blankets with the glow of warmth on her cheeks. Her chest rose and fell from slow rhythmic breaths. He marveled at the fact that like his daughter, he seemed to be awake watching while she slept. He was certain the view would never grow tiresome.

He turned down the alley, which at this time of the morning, was as dark as the main thoroughfare. When was the last time Ella hadn't needed to be awake before the vary farmers who rose with the sun?

Once she was back at home, he would make sure no one bothered her until well toward noon.

A warm glow, much like last night danced from the small window in the kitchen door. Devon settled his mount and entered the kitchen. Penny was busy grabbing bowls and measuring utensils, humming as she worked. As the door closed, she looked up, concern evident on her face.

"Oh, my Lord," she curtsied, "I hadn't expected you so early."

He hadn't wanted to discomfit Ella's help. He supposed it was a strange thing to see a Viscount in the kitchen in his shirtsleeves, ready to work. He chuckled to himself.

"Please, call me Devon— at least while I am taking direction from you," he tried sounding comforting. By the look on her face, his comforting needed practice. Instead of trying again just yet, he instead moved to grab an apron and settle himself at the bench where Penny had been piling things. "I do not envy you having to rise at such an ungodly hour every morning. I would not have been here had I not made sure my valet roused me. I am sure, however, that he returned to bed and is happily dozing as we speak."

She giggled. "I bet ye have the right of that, Devon." She tried out his name seeming to relax if only just. "How is Ella? When I woke and saw she hadn't found her bed, I was beside meself. It was only by chance I found your note before I ran out to find help to find her."

"She is resting. Her ankle is quite sprained, I am afraid. She could put no weight on it last night. I suspect it will be more so today."

"I tried to tell her not to head out on such a fool's errand," she said as she measured flour into the bowls.

Devon decided to test the waters. He wanted to learn about his wife and perhaps this was the person to teach him. "Well, when she mentioned that she was leaving to visit a friend..." he started but was interrupted.

"Now, —Devon." She was settling into calling him by name. "I may be of low birth, but I am not ignorant. Eric told me the way of things as he kens them. I ken you went to see her safe last night. I am still unsure of why, but I know she trusts you. So, do I. Here," She shoved the immense bowl in his direction. "Stir this until it makes into a ball."

Devon did as he was told. They worked for a time not talking. He realized how difficult bread making could be. He was amazed that Penny or Ella had the strength to mix, and then knead the large ball of dough.

"Where is Maddie? Still asleep?" Devon realized he was looking forward to her thick black curls to come bouncing down the stairs.

"As soon as I read your note, I kenned Ella would want Maddie with her, so when Eric came with the cream, I sent her to the manor."

He felt the disappointment in the pit of his stomach. He all of a sudden wished to be back at the manor, even with Clive's rude servants. However, his familial needs would have to wait, so he changed the subject before he became unsocial. "When did you come to live with Ella?" Devon asked as they shaped the dough that had already risen once into loaves.

"I met her three years ago. My Da was trying to marry me to an awful lout. I wanted none of it and fled. Ella found me in the field to the east of town. She brought me here and told me I could stay."

"I thought you have been visiting your family? Are you now on good terms?" He asked to make conversation.

"Tis better. My Da now sees a worth in what I am doing," was all she offered. They again fell into a companionable silence. Once the dough was all shaped and rising on the large workbench, Penny dismissed him. "Well, I can finish what is left here. Thank you for the assistance."

Devon was skeptical. He knew customers would soon be arriving, and the bread wasn't even in the oven yet. He thought about Ella and Maddie at the manor. "You must need someone to look after the loaves as they are baking."

"Nay, they will have to rise for some time, and then it is just a matter of putting them in the oven. This I have handled many times alone. It was just the mixing and kneading I would have been unable to do. Should I plan on making a batch later today, so I won't have to make two alone on the morrow?"

"No, I will be here in the morning as I was today. There is no reason you should have to do double the work. Why, if Ella ever decides to leave the bakery—"

"Oh, she has already told me when she is finished, I would become the baker. That is why she is training me. I am happy to just wait until she is ready."

Her statement took him aback. Ella was already thinking of leaving the bakery? Where had she planned on going? If she wasn't set on remaining the baker, she might be more easily persuaded to go back to London. "Well, then I will see you in the morning. Will the same time be sufficient?"

"Oh yes, and thank you."

"I don't mind. It is a good physical task—"

"I didn't just mean helping with the baking. I meant taking care of Ella. She needs to be taken care of instead of being the one carrying the entire burden."

Devon left very satisfied with the day. He now had Penny on his side, but he didn't bother telling Penny that taking care of Ella was like cuddling a full grown tiger. It might be necessary, but you are taking your life into your own hands.

The sun had been peeking through the thick curtain for some time before Ella chose to acknowledge it. The maid had left a while ago thinking her still asleep. She had been awake when Devon came in earlier. After four years, it was just natural for her to wake up so early. She watched him from the slits in her eyelids. He hadn't made a move to touch her, but just knowing he was watching her sleep did amazing things to her body. It was still humming as she shifted beneath the wealth of soft fluffy counterpane.

She froze. The pain in her ankle started around her foot and shot up her leg like a lightning bolt. She cried out with the pain.

Damn, she had almost forgotten last night: Devon holding her in the chair, falling in the dark, the blackmailers, her dark family secret. She wasn't sure what time it was, but she was sure Devon would be almost finished at the bakery. Sadness welled within her. Her father, or her stepfather as she should now call him, had often said life was a cruel gamble. If only she could have kept her feelings for Devon unknown to herself. Now, she would have to leave. She couldn't see the reproach in his eyes when he found out what she was.

She was such a coward and not a good one at that, unlike what she had told him last night. A good coward would have been able to hide their true feelings out of fear of being hurt. But, no, she had to begin to believe in something she hadn't realized she wanted so badly. She laughed at her foolishness. She needed to get up. Being in bed when Devon came home would not be wise. She knew what they would both be thinking about. Neither would mention it, but it would be there nonetheless. Gingerly, sliding her legs around, careful not to wiggle her ankle, she dangled her feet over the edge. Her ankle throbbed. The bell pull was just out of her reach, so she managed to hop the few steps to grab it. Today would be a trial many ways.

CHAPTER 11

$\mathcal{T}$he sun all but blinded Devon on his ride home. It felt warm and fresh on his face. After the darkness of the kitchen, it was a stark contrast. It wasn't lost on him that Ella spent every day in that kitchen and then most of her afternoons in the shop. He had never spent much time thinking about those outside of his employ, or to his disappointment, his lower servants. He reveled in the out of doors. The fresh air and unrestraint of it was enthralling. To have whole days go by and not have spent at least a few hours outside was painful to consider. He shook off the offending feeling, but promised himself to make sure all his staff had more time to themselves. At the moment, finding Ella and Maddie were his priority. He wanted to speak with Ella about how capable Penny was and how well run and organized her business appeared to be. Those were things he knew she would care to hear. He pushed his horse into a trot.

The door to the library swung open with only the slightest creak. He heard Clive's booted steps draw closer. He had hoped to be left alone for a bit longer. He was in no temper to be civil. He gulped the dregs of his brandy before Clive spoke.

"Ah, here you are. We were ready to call out the dogs." Clive's voice bounced around the large oak walls with joviality. "I told you we would find him in here. One can always find a beast in a dark den."

Turning, he realized Clive was not alone. Maddie was bouncing with restrained excitement while sitting in the crook of his arm. A good thing he swallowed the retort he was about to hurl.

Upon arriving at the Manor, he had raced like a green schoolboy to Ella's room, only to be told she didn't wish to have any visitors and that she planned to take a tray for her meals alone. His high spirits had plunged. So, he made his way to his room, bathed, shaved, and dressed. Once all the flour was removed, he sought Maddie's attention only to be told she had gone on a walk with a maid. He then decided he shouldn't want any approval or attention from women, and stalked to the library where he had been ever since.

"Good evening, Lord Breakerton. What is it I can do for you?" He asked, trying to sound jovial as well and knowing it fell short.

"Yes, well Lady Maddie wanted to hunt for beasts I told her I knew of a place which housed a most monstrous beast," he said tickling her under the chin to make her scrunch up and giggle. "And, as you can see, my Lady, we have found one."

"That's not a beast," proclaimed Maddie.

"Ah, what a brave soul you are. Why his scowls are enough to send shivers down my spine." She giggled again, but then surprised Devon by reaching out from her perch toward him.

"We have been chasing dragons in the courtyard and I believe Lady Maddie is in need of a rest. I knew you were here and desired something to do, so here you go." He dipped down and placed her in his lap. She settled herself and folded her legs into a ball. What was Clive thinking? He didn't know the least little thing to do with a tired child.

His friend must have anticipated his concern. "Here, I received the post from London this morning. I am sure you haven't had the time to read it. While her Ladyship rests, you can read." Devon opened his mouth to say something, but Clive was already at the door. "You're welcome." And the large door shut with only a slight creak.

Looking down at the fragile child in his arms, he felt big, clumsy, and not very Lord-like. Before he could begin to panic, however, Maddie snuggled in and began to snore almost at once. The silence of the huge library was broken by the sleeping sounds of a bundle of skirts and curly dark locks. If this was what being a father meant, he wanted this over any other thing this world had to offer.

After a few moments, he juggled her into a position so he could read the newssheet. His earlier grievances not forgotten, but less important, almost petty. Ella is hurting, and tired. She also has much to think about. He would sneak in later in the evening to see that she was settled for the night. He had been angry because no one had considered he might have things to share today. Not a feeling he was used to. Instead, he wasn't thinking of what his loved ones needed. When had he become so selfish? He rustled the newssheet to refocus on the article. Maddie slept undisturbed.

A half hour passed in quiet perfection. He was a father, being a father. This was not as hard as he thought. A warm sensation spread. It wasn't that of love or contentment, but more damp now, than warm in his lap. Realizing too late, Devon gave a shout and burst from the chair dangling Maddie out in front of him. She had been sleeping very well and relieved herself all over his trousers.

The door swung open and Clive burst into the room, followed by three servants who no doubt thought their services would be needed for some disaster. The noise at that moment and the feeling of being hung in midair, no doubt, was what woke Maddie. She gave a scream to match her father's.

Devon watched helplessly as his best friend and his servants saw the large damp stain across his thighs while holding a screaming child. Too late, he tried to cradle Maddie to him to calm her. She was reaching for the calm, smiling Clive. He had no choice, but to relinquish the child. He knew he had botched the moment. He wanted to say something to make Maddie not be scared of him, but he drew a blank. Clive whispered something to her and she turned to view him from under her ringlets. She was cautious, but not scared.

"Doesn't he look funny with that big spot on his pants?" Clive asked. She nodded and sheepishly smiled. "Why doesn't Kate take you up to change? How does that sound?" She nodded, but still looked at Devon.

Before the maid in question left with her, Maddie reached out to Devon, and when he bent toward her, she blessed him with a shy kiss on his cheek. Then she was gone, and Devon was left standing in the very masculine library, with wet breeches, a wet cheek, and a melted heart.

Ella was successful at playing coward. When she first managed to rise from her bed, only after ringing for assistance, she settled into a hot bath. She knew what work it was for a household to prepare such a luxury and tried to decline. She was informed 'His Lordship' left instructions. That proved how weak she had become, because tender feelings assailed her. Seeing him was inevitable, but if she could manage to prolong it a bit, she would be able to steel herself. If she were to entertain his comforting in her current state, she would be lost.

Now, sitting alone she felt more balanced, but no less affected. The pain in her ankle had lessened, but by no means enough to fend for herself. Desperately wanting to know how the bakery was, she had agreed to join the men for dinner. Clive was a libertine and rake, but she felt certain his presence would ease the situation.

A gentle knock on the door heralded the footmen the maid had promised would carry her down to the dining room.

"Come in," She called out. She looked up. Her heart pounded, and her stomach sank. Filling the doorway in what she would consider country formal was no footman, but Devon. The planes of his face hard in the candle light. His bottle green waistcoat shimmered from under his jacket. She thought it matched the evening dress Clive sent for her to wear, no doubt one of his sister's. He just stood there not speaking. His gaze discomfited her more than she would have liked.

"Good evening, my Lord," she offered when it became apparent he wasn't going to speak first.

"Your ankle must be worse than I first thought," he said without moving from the doorway.

"Actually, I was just thinking it was much improved from this morning. I am still unable to make it to the dining room, but was able to hobble quite easily to my dressing table."

"I only assumed the worst when I was informed you were not receiving company upon my return." He then entered the room, crossing it in three strides, stopping in front of her. If his gaze was difficult to endure from the length of the room, Ella all but squirmed from his close inspection.

She cleared her throat to break the tension. It had been a very long while since being in such an elegant gown and it didn't feel comfortable. *This is why a woman should not have to endure a man. Drat him, what was he thinking?*

"Have the dinner plans changed? I was expecting two footmen to escort me to dinner."

"Yes, I was informed." His dry tone didn't do anything to mask his annoyance. "I will not have a footman, innocently or otherwise, laying a hand on my wife. If you need to be carried to dinner, it shall be I who does the carrying."

At that, he bent and scooped her with ease into the cradle of his arms. He smelled of sandalwood soap, and a hint of brandy. She felt his large arm braced across her shoulders and the pressure of his other one settling into her thighs and bottom. The first made her feel safe and protected. The second had her nerves on high alert. This was not helping to keep her mind straight.

Without a word, he strode from the room and down the hallway. To her relief, she noted the sharp planes of his face were set with a harshness that would scare someone else. She saw it for what it was. Desire. They were both in the worst of circumstances. He being shackled to and attracted to the kind of woman he should not. Even without him knowing the true lowliness of her birth, he was doing a disservice to his rank by connecting with her. And her falling in love with the one man who could take from her all she had worked so hard to gain. She knew most would see it as a winning situation for her, but only she understood the pain of loving someone who did not reciprocate.

Each step on the staircase drove his lower arms further into the crease just under her buttocks. The crispness of her linen shift rasped her sensitive skin. Knowing he was the cause of the friction made it even more sensual. If she were naked—

Well, that isn't going to help her cause any. It was imperative they both remained clothed, either in reality or in her mind. She needed to be set down, post haste. The hallway seemed unending, or Devon was walking as slow as Maddie did when told to go do something. The comparison made her smile, despite her better judgment.

If she dug her good heel into his side, would he move into a canter like good horseflesh? The thought was so absurd, yet so perfect that she was unable to keep the laughter from bubbling out. She covered her mouth to try to trap it, but to no avail.

"What was that?" His voice rumbled through his chest and vibrated the side of her breast. Drat, him again! "Was that a giggle?"

"Yes," she answered, weakly hoping he would leave it.

"What, may I ask, are you finding humorous just now?" He asked with warmth and a bit of easiness in his voice.

"Well I, ah, just remembered something I had heard about horses. It just popped into my head. Silly really." She attempted to sound as much a featherhead as possible. "Oh, here we are. Thank you, my Lord, for seeing me safely to the dining room."

Devon sauntered into the room, and placed her in the seat across the table from him. Fighting a blush, Ella had tried not to make eye contact with anyone until she was settled. It wasn't until then that, she noticed Maddie sitting next to Devon's seat, beaming with pride. Ella didn't know what to say. She always had meals with the child, but that was not the way of the Ton. She never sat at the table with her parents, and she was only allowed to join the party on occasion, until she was well into her teens when her father felt it would benefit him. She knew the highest echelons would not have allowed it. Maddie, however, sat in her seat as if she belonged. Ella did notice she sat much higher in the seat than she would have thought. Bending, she peered under the table. Maddie's legs dangled charmingly from her perch, and a perch it was. She counted no less than three large tomes piled up and lathed to the chair by what looked like two perfectly white cravats.

Sitting up, she looked at the two men waiting, sitting silent. Neither looked innocent, but neither looked contrite.

"Hello Mommy. Feeling better?" Maddie asked unaware of the adults.

"Yes, darling, I am feeling much better. How was your day?" Ella asked, thankful enough to give a nod and mouth a 'thank you' to the two men. She hadn't seen Maddie since she left to meet her black-mailers. She would have loved to have called her over for a hug, but knew her seat of distinction would outweigh a mother's need for a hug.

"Oh, we hunted princes in the garden. Uncle Clive's good at hunting."

"Hunting princes? Did you catch any?" Ella was having a hard time envisioning Lord Breakerton skulking in the garden searching for hidden princes.

"No, maybe tomorrow," she answered undaunted.

"Well, you certainly had a full day," Ella answered.

"Oh, that wasn't the extent of her day." Clive said chuckling.

"Really?" Ella asked.

"We then went hunting for dragons. We found one of those, didn't we, sweeting?" Clive asked Maddie and she turned red but giggled. Devon coughed and shifted. This was going to be good.

"Well, we heard they were found in dark, dank places, such as libraries. We went-a-hunting and sure enough, we found a great dark dragon in his cave. We had also heard the way to take a dragon's fire breath was to douse it with liquid. And, what do you know, it worked.

Ruined his buckskin breeches, but did tame him. He is now being led around like a mere suckling pup."

Ella sat trying to figure out the puzzle. She had followed it until Clive had started speaking of dousing its fire breath. How could they have used liquid to— oh no, she didn't? "You mean, Maddie, she—"

"She did. She had fallen asleep after her exertions in the garden and--well, you can figure out the rest."

Ella burst out laughing. It started as a tingle in her throat, but soon became a complete open mouthed laugh. Devon sat across from her with no hint of anger either toward Maddie for her accident, or Ella for finding the humor in it. At this moment, she couldn't imagine ever thinking she could have been unaffected by him.

"I hope you don't mind, but I just couldn't allow Lady Maddie to dine in the nursery when we were having what would be considered a family dinner." Devon said out of the blue. The reference to family, even though not meant in that way, sobered Ella. She smiled shakily.

"It is I who should apologize. I am afraid Maddie sees it her due to sit and eat with those in attendance. Dinner usually consists of us and Penny, so there is no cause to impose such rules."

"Neither one of us would ever be accused of sticking with conventions such as this." Clive commented around the soup being served. "The only time my sisters and I were forced to eat in the nursery was if mother felt the company would be too mixed."

"And I was never seated with my father. I eventually ate in the kitchen or in the server's dining area. I never ate alone, but I see no reason above avoiding one's children to sequester them to the nursery for all their meals."

Of all the men of the Ton, these were not the two she would have thought to hear eschewing the strictures of society. Well, Clive perhaps, but never Devon. This dinner was doing nothing to help her plan her escape. In truth, was it an escape if you have left your heart behind?

Dinner continued without incident, with Maddie stealing the moment to twist the two men further around her finger. Lord help the young bucks when she came onto the scene. They would not stand a chance. Here were two of the most jaded being handled like that suckling pup Clive had jested about earlier. Once the pudding was finished, a maid came to fetch Maddie for bed. She skipped around the table, gave her mother a big hug and kiss, and trotted off as if her nightly routine was set. Why couldn't it be so easy?

"Well, what say we move this into the billiard room," Clive suggested while he pushed away from the table. Devon followed, but walked around the table and plucked Ella up as if she weighed no more than the pudding. The billiard room lay only a few doors up the hallway to her relief. A very feminine chaise sat next to the fire where a warm glow emanated along with two other stuffed chairs that were soon occupied by Flick and LePrin.

"We knew you would not be able to join the game, and thought after having your leg down for so long you would appreciate a place to raise it," Devon explained as he set balls into the rack. Ella noted the ease of which he manipulated them into place, moving them around to the correct positions. His hands were rather attractive. Her memory of their skillfulness on her skin was as vivid as if he was touching her. Sensual heat filled her veins. She looked away. When a woman cannot look at a man without getting a flash of heat coursing through her, said woman should not be allowed in respectable company.

"Thank you, after being alone for most of the day, I find I am in no hurry to go upstairs to my room," she answered to cover her woolgathering.

Looking for something else to peak her interest, she began watching Clive. He was just as masculine, but her body seemed only to respond to Devon's brand of masculinity. As Clive readied the ques for each of them, she felt the easiness of the company. These men were friends in the truest sense. The thought passed in her mind that Clive saw a need to call attention to her whereabouts when he could have left well enough alone. He knew what our agreement was, and yet he felt the need to break the agreement. She would have to speak with him about his reasons. Was Devon as miserable without her as she was without him? Shifting on the chaise, she pulled herself out of her fanciful thoughts. They were preposterous considering she was planning an escape.

Ella sat watching the men, commenting on a good play and enjoying the conversation from the women who she had grown to love in London. The time passed well, like old friends. Ella had yet to ask about the bakery, but wasn't sure how much Clive knew. She decided to wait until Devon carried her back to her room to drill him for information.

After three rather long games, Clive cried off, claiming *prince hunting* was more tiring than anyone knew. Devon once again claimed her in his arms. It awed her to know he could lift her and carry her as if she weighed no more than a billiard ball. She might as well be a doll filled with feathers. She bade farewell to the ladies and promised to join them for breakfast in the morning. The ride back up the stairs, combined with his unexpected kindnesses throughout dinner, was wearing on her reserve. If she were a smart woman, she would thank him and not keep him in her room talking about the bakery or anything else.

"Where should I let you down?" He asked as he entered her chamber.

"Just at the dressing table. I will need to be there for the maid to help me prepare for bed." The last word hung in the room like smoke from the fire. It swirled and danced. Taunted.

"There is no reason to call a maid. Allow me." He stepped toward her.

"No!" She all but yelled. "I mean, that's not necessary. The maid will be here as soon as I ring the bell. There is no need for you to trouble yourself."

"Well, not that undressing a woman has ever been on my list of things that troubled me, I am certain I am able to unbutton a row for you." Not allowing her to argue, he unbuttoned her long row of pearls running down the back of her dress. Ella thought with the pang of a jealous wife, how he became so adept at undressing women.

"I assumed you would want to know about the bakery. Why

haven't you asked?" He asked conversationally, which in Ella's mind did nothing to cool the sensuality of the moment.

"I wasn't sure what Clive knew and didn't want to say something you would rather he not know."

This was the first time in their troubled past that she was awake when he unclothed her. The first time they were together, she went to him naked, and the last time they had sex, she fell asleep clothed and awoke naked. The storage room couldn't be counted, because he neither undressed her nor found his own pleasure.

This time— Whoa, this time?

She was lost. She knew it before the words came to her mind, he wasn't leaving tonight. He never intended to, but she now realized she never intended him to leave either. She should be very angry with herself, but as the cool air swept over her back, he slid the fabric from her shoulders and ran a light touch along her skin. She couldn't find the anger through her rising haze of desire.

CHAPTER 12

*W*hich tingled the fine hairs on her neck more, she wasn't sure, either the cool air or those tantalizing fingers. Her head rolled to the side giving him more access to the tender skin. She was no longer thinking, but only feeling. Rational thought be gone! Tonight was about just being. Being his. His wife, his Viscountess, his lover, whatever he wanted. If she could shut her mind out and just feel, she would. His scent swirled around her. The fire light flickered against her closed eyelids. Hearing her own heartbeat, her body responded to its urgent tattoo.

Could a person expire from sensing so completely? A delicious pang built within her core. She opened her eyes and her vision was filled with his handsome face looking at her in the mirror of the dressing table. Her arm felt heavy as she raised a hand to cup his rough cheek. Devon closed his eyes at her touch and watching the scene through the lens of the mirror made it more sensual somehow. She slid her hand behind his neck and pulled his mouth to hers. She could feel his restraint in allowing her the lead. As she worked his lips with her own, she could taste the port wine left from the billiards room. She licked across his mouth and was rewarded when her tongue dipped into his warm mouth without resistance. She knew when his resolve ended, because he took a quick nibble of its tip, making her jump and smile.

He pushed the silken material off her arms and down to her waist. Without breaking the kiss, which was getting more urgent by the minute, he wrapped one arm around her waist and lifted her. With his other hand, he removed the fabric from underneath, and she felt it flow down her legs to lay pooled on the floor, discarded. What she hadn't realized was he had made haste with her shift pushing it above her buttocks. He broke the kiss only long enough to be rid of that offending piece of cloth as well. It was sent to join the gown. Her chair felt cool on her bare thighs.

Pulling away, both were panting. His eyes devoured her. She had always believed her true power came only with her independence, but seeing the rigid planes on his face and the hard set of his mouth, she felt powerful. At this moment, she was his existence. It was a heady feeling.

His thigh rubbed against her bare leg, the fabric rough on her tender skin. She reached out, running her palm up the outer part. Solid. Pure male strength. She stopped at his hip and reversed her path. She then, returned up again at reaching his knee. This time, she turned her path inward with a hesitant hand, rubbing her palm over his erection.

He groaned and his head fell back. Encouraged, she applied more pressure. He liked her touching him, she thought, encouraged. As a widow, she had become privy to many conversations that at the time had made her ears red with a blush, but now she was curious. Would Devon, a Lord of the Realm, enjoy such things? She didn't know the answer, but intended to find out. His placard proved troublesome, but Ella was able to maneuver the buttons out of their hold and his penis sprang forth from its confines. Without hesitation, Ella wrapped her fingers around it. It was hot. Again, Devon groaned his approval. With caution, she began to stroke it. First, slow, and then from Devon's encouraging sounds, faster. Once satisfied at least that part of what she had been told was correct, she bent her head and moistened the tip with her tongue. She was rewarded with his sharp intake of breath.

The last step she had been told was to take him fully in her mouth and use it to do the stroking. She felt him go still. She stopped, not daring to move. If he didn't like it, she should pull away. Disappointed, she made to sit up. A hand cupped the back of her head and splayed into her hair sending pins scattering to the floor. She sensed more than felt the gentle pull back to her ministrations. She took him deeper into her mouth and glided back up. She repeated this several times. He tasted good. Just as she was settling into a rhythm, his hands settled on her shoulders and withdrew her. She looked up to see Devon watching her. She must have had the question in her eyes, because he answered.

"If you don't care to see me lose control like a schoolboy, I suggest we retire to your bed." His voice was deep, throaty with desire, his breathing deep, and heavy. He finished what she had started by removing what was left of his clothing. His jacket, thankfully still sat in the library discarded earlier during their games. His shirt and cravat were dealt with. Once naked, he bent, sweeping her into his arms. He was halfway to the bed when he stopped and pierced her with a determined stare.

"Where did you learn that little trick?" He asked. With a tad bit too much nonchalance to his voice.

"As a widow, you might be surprised what women will talk about in front of you. I wasn't sure you would enjoy it, but was curious." She was too embarrassed to look him in the eye, so watched her finger make little circles in his chest hair.

"You should invite these women for tea more often," he said as he laid her naked form on the bed. He kissed her on the tip of her nose. "As for your curiosity, consider yourself free to quench it whenever you feel the need. I am yours to do as you please."

Her heart sang, and then dropped. There wouldn't be many more times she would be able to quench her curiosity. She was already lost. If she remained, she might never recover losing him again. She sighed to herself and put the idea out of her mind. No point in thinking too much. She would enjoy this moment right now.

"My turn," he said to pull her out of her woolgathering.

Before she could question what he meant, he laid her on the bed and made certain to prop her sore ankle on a pile of pillows, and then settled himself between her thighs. She noted he hadn't taken off her stockings for fear of hurting her ankle she assumed. The green ribbon at her thigh looked strangely sensual, even to her. Devon took a moment to trace around the one on the left and smiled a devilish smile that sent chills throughout Ella. Running a finger up the inner part of the stocking, he stopped just below her bare skin. Bending, he licked a line just above the fabric.

She moaned with pleasure. The sound ignited the flame kindling within. He laved a path up her thigh to his destination. At first contact, Ella thought she might lift off the bed. His mouth was hot and his tongue— whatever he was doing, she didn't want him to stop. Moving to join him, she rewarded his diligence with more sensual moans and sighs. When she was sure she would expire from pleasure, he made his way up her body tasting as he went. Finding her lips, he fed from their sweetness. She reveled in the taste of him and the feel of his mouth devouring hers.

"You taste like one of your confections," he drawled, resting on his elbows at either side of her head. She felt shielded by the world. They were in their own private world in the enclosure of his arms. His stare was so stark and all consuming she would have looked away, but could not allow it. If there were a moment frozen in time, she would be happy with this one.

"I need you now," he said to her with little restrained control in his voice. Without a word, Ella wrapped her uninjured leg around his waist and tugged him into her.

With an unhurried motion, he settled over her, resting his erection at her center. Her slow moan was enough encouragement as inch by inch he filled her. Pausing, he ran a hand from her hip around to her buttocks and up her thigh to the sensitive skin behind her knee. The sensation made her giggle out loud. Was she supposed to giggle? She looked to find him smiling wickedly.

"Whatever are you smiling like a fool for?" She asked.

"You giggled. I like that noise. If I do that again will you giggle?" He asked as he, with the lightest of touches, retraced his path to extract an equally enthusiastic giggle from her. She swatted at his hand, but without much real interest in his stopping. She was having fun. Who would have thought?

Unable to wait any longer, Devon started a slow rhythm. Before long, the gentle long strokes became more frantic, more demanding. Ella could feel herself climbing, but just as she would have expired, she exploded, fracturing into a million stars. At the same, time Devon as well came to his pleasure. He collapsed, careful to rest most of his weight next to her she noted. Both were sweat glistened and panting. As to fend off a chill, he bent and pulled the blanket around their bodies. Pulling her more into him, he settled into the mattress and held her fast as she fell asleep in her husband's arms.

Again, Devon watched the sun just peak above the horizon on his way to the bakery. Sleep tugged at his eyes, and his body yearned to be curled up with Ella in her bed. He had awoken sometime in the night. His wife was draped over him like a silken throw. Her uninjured leg wound up and over his hip and her dainty foot was wedged heel first between his legs. Her arm rested across his chest, with her fingers woven into his hair. One breast sat at his ribcage. The long flowing hair he loved, wrapped around his neck and face. He was hard just thinking about her. The urge to roll her over and take her again had been a hard one to quell, but he knew he was lost to the clock. Soon, the maids would be about. Taking care not to wake her, he gathered his clothes and left for his own room, only to be greeted by his valet who had been instructed to wake him.

Now, the cool crispness of the morning bit at his cheeks. He reveled in the feel. All too soon, he would be holed up in the hot bakery until luncheon. As soon as Devon dismounted, the faithful mount lumbered to the patch of grass under the tree. If he didn't bother to tie him to the tree, Devon was sure the beast would be right there when he was finished. Not wanting to chance it, he followed and tied the reins around the trunk.

Penny must have been out early. The door was not latched, sending a thin ray of light onto the ground. The door only made noise when he closed it behind him. The warmth from the large stone oven permeated the room.

The girl looked up. "Mornin', Devon," she chirped. The use of his Christian name made him chuckle. He knew he should feel uncomfortable, but he was in Scotland after all. Who would ever know? He understood why his friend felt so at ease here. If not for being the sole person responsible for his holdings, he might think about running away and living out his days here.

"Good morning to you, Penny. Where should I begin?" He asked as he plucked an apron from the peg by the door and tied it around his waist. Yesterday, the only section of his body not covered in flour was where the apron had been.

"I 'ave been measuring the dry ingredients, and the yeast cake is bloomin' over there." She pointed to the pot of steaming water by the fireplace. "You can measure the milk and put it to scald."

Devon walked to the storeroom and found the buckets of milk left by a local farmer. He used the cups he was shown the day before and measured the correct amount into a nearby pot. He returned the remaining milk to the coolness of the storage room. Sitting on a stool, he stirred the milk to keep it from burning on the bottom. Penny bustled around the room humming a familiar tune as she did so. This was only the second day of his employ. However, he was going to miss the atmosphere. It reminded him of his childhood. The only fond memories. Penny went to stir the coals in the stone oven. He could hear the crackle and a pop. Penny jumped at the sound.

"Oh, I wish it would stop that," Penny complained. She bustled back to the stack of wood.

"Here, you stir, I will get the wood."

179

"I am perfectly capable—"

Devon cut her off, "You are very much like your employer." She smiled a shy smile. "You might as well use me to the best of my ability while I am here. I am more suited for lugging wood and you for stirring milk."

He could tell she considered arguing, but took the wooden spoon and sat.

He walked past the stone oven and another loud pop rang out. He didn't remember hearing those pops yesterday. "Does that happen often?" He asked while piling sticks of wood onto his arm.

"Nay, not that I have ever heard. It crackles, but I 'ave never heard those pops."

The fire was too hot for him to get a clear look inside. He piled the wood at the base of the oven and added a few of the bigger pieces. Once those burned down to coals, they would be ready to place the loaves in for baking. It was an old method, but an efficient one.

Work continued with Penny entertaining Devon with stories of the locals, the lore, and his favorite, Ella. He was sure his wife didn't know it, but she had a friend in Penny like most people wished for. Lord help the person who would say a word against Ella. Devon was satisfied when he hadn't heard of any men involved with her.

"Ella is a very beautiful woman. Have there not been any gentlemen interested in her?" He asked with a casual tone, he hoped, while kneading the last of the first batch of bread.

"Aye, they were thick in the air early on. Not as much now that they know she won't play the pretty to them."

"Why is that, do you think?"

"Oh, tis' easy. She loved her husband," she answered.

"How can you be sure? Many marriages are not love matches." He questioned, hoping he wouldn't have to probe more and feeling torn at the thought of Ella loving him four years ago.

"True, but I catch her sometimes, looking at Maddie. She loves her, but I can tell she's thinking of him." She took a breath, Devon thought, so she could continue, but she thought better of it and put her hands to shaping the bread.

Eric appeared soon after the first batch had been placed in the oven. Penny filled two bowls with steaming porridge. One for Eric and one for him. He had never been much for porridge, but didn't care to be rude. Along with the bowl of cereal, she set out a jar of fresh honey, apple butter, and several jams. Eric retrieved one of the buckets of milk and proceeded to mix the fresh milk into the hot bowl with a generous portion of honey and currant jam.

His porridge had only ever consisted of a bit of butter, and well, that was it. Devon chose honey and milk, but he preferred blackberry jam. It was the best porridge he had ever had. His cook will think such a peasant meal beneath her, but she would learn. They sat eating and chatting. Devon filled Eric in as best he could with Penny listening on. He did get the idea Penny knew more than she told. He suspected she knew exactly how to extricate information from poor Eric. The boy was so lovesick he fairly stank of it. The only question was who stank more, him or Eric.

The smell of fresh cooked bread wafted in the air. Penny rose to take the first batch out and stoke the fire before the next batch went in. She insisted the men rest and talk. Devon wasn't sure why Eric couldn't keep the thread of any conversation with her in his view. The bread out, she began adding the wood Devon had collected earlier. Again, you could hear the wood crackle as it caught. She stuck the poker in to move the fire around. The air helped to ignite the wood. Crackle, crackle. It was a good sound.

Pop! They looked toward the oven. That sound was louder than before.

"What was that?" Eric asked.

"Not sure. It's done it several times. That was the loudest," Penny answered.

"When we are out a huntin', we sometimes get light stones in our fire rings. Ye know stone that can't take the heat of the fire. They pop like that when they break. We once had one fly out of the fire altogether." Eric shrugged at his thought, and went back to eating.

The hair on Devon's neck prickled. He remembered the door this morning, and the fact it made no sound until he latched it. "Penny, did you go outside this morning for anything?"

Penny didn't turn to him as she was busy piling more wood into the fire. "Nay, Eric brought the milk last eve, and I had everything else ready."

"Penny, I want you to walk away from the oven." Devon tried to sound as calm as possible. Penny didn't seem to notice anything, but Eric froze with his spoon half way to his mouth.

"Whatever for? If I don't get this hot enough to burn down, the bread will be tough for sitting too long."

Pop!

"Penny--"

Pop, Pop, Pop!

Devon didn't bother. He left the table, picked Penny up around the waist, and headed for the door. Eric never questioned just hurried out behind him. Before Penny could get her feet on the ground, she was spitting and complaining. Devon didn't have a chance to explain his suspicions.

Bang!

"Go get the inn keeper! Bring buckets. I am afraid we will need them!" Devon commanded as he turned and ran for the door. "Penny, grab my horse, move him into the field!" He didn't turn back to make sure she was doing it.

Smoke rolled from the kitchen door. It filled his throat and eyes, making both burn. Through the thickness, he could see flames dancing from the side of the oven where a good sized hole had appeared. There were, however, no signs the flames had spread. He raced to grab the pot of water near the stove to drown the flames. More black smoke rolled off the now wet coals.

Once, he was sure the fire was out, he began to look on the floor in the murky darkness for the culprit. Within moments of walking straight from where the hole lay ripped from the oven, he found what he was looking for. A 'light' rock as Eric called it, but not a small one. This was meant to do major damage. As he looked at the rock, he realized it was still so hot it was beginning to set the floor on fire.

Devon grabbed the only thing left by the fireplace. The smell of curdled milk burned his nose, but it did the trick.

"Hello!" He heard from the direction of the door.

"In here, Eric. There is no fire." He could hear Eric and several others shuffle through the smoke, which was now leaving through all means necessary.

"What in blazes happened here?" He heard the Innkeeper.

"This happened," Devon answered motioning to the rock. "Can you send someone to get Lord Breakerton? He needs to see this."

"Aye," The Innkeeper turned and bellowed, "Boy, gGo get the laird. Tell 'im tis bloody hell important!"

"How would a rock get into an oven?" The Innkeeper asked, looking over Devon's shoulder.

"Not by itself. That's for sure," Devon answered dryly.

CHAPTER 13

"*E*lla – Ella, say something."

Say something? He wanted her to say something?

Ella sat in the small orangery, the scent of the blossoms filling the air. The moment she had seen Devon, she knew something was wrong. Her oven, her very livelihood was destroyed. What does one say on such an occasion?

You win?

She looked down at her hands with white knuckles clasped in her lap. If she only had time to think, she could plan her next move, but he was waiting; waiting for her to say something, anything. A strong independent woman should rally. Right now, she was just trying not to fall apart in front of him. She would have to save rallying for another time.

"You said no one was hurt. That is a good thing for sure." She fell silent again. She knew that was what she should say so she said it.

After a few moments of him waiting for more, he forged ahead. "There was very little damage from the smoke above stairs. The building is well built. Clive has people there airing it out and cleaning."

"That's fine." She knew he wanted more, but she was empty. After all the work, all the dealings with the blackmailers, she was empty, not to mention her coffers. She had spent all she could allow herself. Penniless she was not, but closer than she would like to admit. She looked up to see Devon's beautiful eyes searching her face. She had hoped to leave the bakery to Penny when she took her leave, but that was not to be. "Thank you for taking such good care of things," she said breaking their connection. "I guess I now have some thinking to do." She felt removed from the scene. All the colors had dimmed and the room kind of fell away. She had nothing left to give of herself. She had failed, just as her father said.

"What is there to think about? You and Maddie will come back to London with me. You should not have to worry about such things," Devon said moving to inspect an orange blossom hanging low near his shoulder.

A fear settled in her chest. She had assumed the blackmailers had been at work, but what if it had been a more sinister devil? "Why would you think that? It is just a broken oven. One good mason and his apprentice can have it in working order in a fortnight." She knew that was the truth, but the cost would be immense. She watched him digest her words. What would be his next move? She hated to think that he was behind this, but her long taught beliefs were too strong. She felt her heart shatter in a million pieces. She had started to hope, no actually believe that perhaps she was meant to find her happiness at last, and that it was with Devon.

"I, I simply thought you might finally be done with all this." He swung his arm around to signify the whole of her existence. "Could I point out, Madame, you have had mishap after mishap since I have been here. How can one run a successful business in that fashion?" He looked at her with determined eyes.

"You are correct, My Lord, I have come upon some hardships as of late, and you are correct that it is not the best business practice to entertain such expensive repairs. I am, however, an independent woman, and can therefore take care of any issues that I must." He was becoming more agitated. She hoped her emotions were not getting the best of her, but what if he was the one. She had her doubts about the blackmailers even being intelligent enough to know how to rig the oven. What if it was he? Was he trying to force her hand? Her emptiness filled so quickly with riotous anger it made her dizzy.

"Why can't you accept assistance when offered? I want to take you away from all of the strife that, you seem to be toiling with. Is your independence worth your apparent safety? In addition that of our daughter? Does that not worry you?" He looked angry now.

The orangery suddenly felt stifling. The trees hung heavy and draped, closing them in. Ella stood not wanting to feel or appear any smaller than she was. She had begun to trust him. She had considered, before she found out who she was, going back with him. Was she only one touch away from forgetting all her promises to herself? She wanted independence. She hadn't wanted to depend on anyone. When you depended on people was when they let you down.

She looked at him, and caught his gaze. She searched his face for a hint of innocence. She wasn't sure what it would look like. All she could see was arrogant male. Oh, she didn't want to believe it. For once, since she had been dealing with the blackmailers, she hoped it was their doing, but until she knew for sure, she couldn't make any decisions.

"Why? Was it really that important for you to win our bet?" She stepped closer to him still hobbling on only one good ankle and turned her head up to study his reaction. It was a mix of confusion and angry frustration.

"What in the devil are you talking about? Why what?" He asked.

Ella stepped away. His scent even over powered that of the blossoms. She made her way around the bench she had been sitting on. Her leg was throbbing, but she used the pain to fuel her resolve. She stepped up to the back of the bench and put both hands on its rim, in part to hold her weight off her ankle and to hide her shaking hands.

"It was you, wasn't it? You couldn't stand the thought of not being able to convince me to leave, so you planted the rock in the oven."

The room began to spin. Devon went still. She was blaming him. The hardheaded, impossible woman actually thought to blame him.

What of the two men who tried to accost you in the woods and want you dead? He wanted to ask. After all, if he were to weigh the danger, he personally would have gone in that direction. A slow hot anger began to build within him. It had to be anger, because the other option was hurt. He couldn't allow himself to be thus affected. Love was enough, but to feel hurt this deeply would surely kill him, no, anger he could deal with.

"Are you suggesting, actually, suggesting that I was so sure you were going to turn me down, that I, after making love to you half the night, rose from your bed hours before I needed to, and raced into the forest to find a stone. I might be obliged to add that said stone would have taken two men to carry and lift into the blasted oven." He took one more step and placed his hands on either side of hers leaning into the bench only a fraction from her face. "That I then carried said stone to the bakery, snuck in, deposited it, left, and made it back in time to appear that I had just arrived? Not to mention putting both Penny and Eric in danger?" The last he ground out on a growl barely containing the beast just under the surface.

"Well, I..." She was uneasy, but he wasn't so blinded by his emotion that he didn't notice she never looked away.

"You, my Lady," he let sarcasm drip from those two words, "have a more lofty idea of your self-worth than I thought, or you have a much lower idea of my character. Either way, I am afraid I can no longer remain in your presence. Good day." He turned never looking back. The glass door of the orangery rang as he strode toward the main house. He needed to ride, but he needed clean clothes. As heavily as he breathed, the smell of black burned bread filled his nostrils again and again. A good hot bath, then a good hard ride, might allow him to be in civil company, but he doubted it. Could she really make love to him as she did last night, and in the light of day, accuse him of such violence?

"You are absolutely sure it wasn't him?" Ella knew how foolish she sounded, but Penny's look of shock proved it. As soon as she saw the hurt in Devon's eyes, she had been aware of what she had done. The last thing she ever wanted to do was hurt him. She couldn't be with him, that she understood, but the thought of him thinking she thought him capable of something so terrible ate at her.

"Aye, I'm certain. If 'e hadn't moved me when 'e did, I might not be here, and after, well if you had seen 'im after, 'e was all business." Penny said with enough passion that you would have thought her smitten. "You ought to be ashamed of yerself for considering such," she stated the next with a good helping of disdain.

"You are correct, of course. I just–" Ella shook her head. "I don't know what I was thinking." They sat having tea. Clive insisted Penny move into the manor instead of having to go back to her parents' home until the bakery could be cleaned. Flick and LePrin had also scolded her about her accusation and took their leave with Maddie and a promise of cake. She hadn't seen or heard from Devon since he left, but it had been time she needed. She knew what would happen if she remained. Regardless if the bakery could be fixed or not, she had to leave. She was in love with Devon. She wasn't denying it, but that didn't mean she had to give in to it. If she stayed, it wouldn't take many more nights like this last one to make her putty in his hands. She would agree to go to London, take on the Ton and all the gossip-mongers, settle in, only then would it be revealed whom she was. By then Devon would not be able to turn her out and she would live the rest of her life loving a man who could not stand the sight of her. Not to mention that after her misguided accusation earlier, he might be happy to see her go. No, Maddie and she would have to leave. Soon.

The long patio stretched the length of the back of the manor. Vines trailed along the low wall separating it from the lawn. It was a very pleasant place. She looked out over the lawn. She loved Scotland. This was where she felt herself. The desire to leave didn't exist, but she also knew Devon would look for her, if he could forgive her rudeness. He would get tired of the search after a while, but she needed to move somewhere he wouldn't look. Perhaps she would settle in well, in Northern England. The landscape was still similar, but he would assume she would remain in Scotland. In her reality, she knew she would travel until she found a place that suited her, so thinking about it was useless.

"Ella?" Penny asked touching her arm to bring her back.

"Oh, sorry, I guess I am just still shaken from the events." She covered her woolgathering.

"Well, tis understandable. I meself will not sleep as well as I would like in that soft bed." She giggled a bit. She had assumed Clive would put her in the servant's quarters, but he had said she was a guest and would be treated as such.

"I trust your room is to your liking?" Ella asked, knowing the answer already.

"Oh, tis beautiful. If I wasn't already in love with me Eric, I would be setting my cap for His Lordship." She giggled again.

The two women finished their tea and talked of plans for when the bakery was open again. Ella excused herself after a half an hour and returned to her room. She had letters to write and packing to do. She was very happy her ankle bothered her only the slightest bit when she was on it for long periods. Sitting at her desk, she took out her ink well, pen, and a scrap of paper. She had been in this position before. All the feelings were the same, but this time, she knew how leaving would feel before she did, and was certain she would be leaving her heart behind.

Devon sat at his writing desk, pen hovering over the paper. The last piece had at least three large drops of ink because he couldn't bring himself to begin. What did he want to say? He had spoken with his father only once about his mother. When he asked what his father wanted most, his father had said he wanted a chance to tell her what she had done to him. It made sense. The last word, as they say. His problem was that his father had been at the point in his life where the anger outweighed the love.

Devon wasn't there. As soon as he began to write, he knew his true feelings would be obvious for the world. She didn't love him.

That was obvious by her accusation. She didn't trust him. He didn't care if both her parents had been coal miners, he loved her, damn it!

The scratch of point to paper filled the room and continued for a good hour and several more sheets of paper. Finally, he sat back and reread his declaration. He sanded the paper, folded it and put his seal on it. He was not sure where his life was about to go, but he would no longer hide behind his father's hurt. If he was truly to live, he had to own his own hurt, joy, or regret. If she still wanted her independence above a life with him, then he would congratulate her for her courage, even though he believed it was her cowardice keeping her from something special.

Crossing the room, Devon pulled the bell pull and collected the other papers from the mason, which included a receipt for work paid for in advance. She wouldn't be able to argue with him and throw his generosity back at him he thought. The last packet of papers was that of Maddie's dowry which had been posted in time for him to leave that as well. He refused not be in her life, but that was a battle for another time. He needed to concentrate on her mother first.

"You rang, my Lord?" His valet stood ready in the doorway. To his credit, he only just glanced at the bag sitting by the chair at the fireplace.

"Yes, I did. I would like you to deliver these to Lady Ella. Make sure they are in this order when you give them to her." He had made sure to put the mason's papers, Maddie's packet, and his letter last. It would give him some time to make away. "I am taking a trip. I will not need your services. I will contact you when I am settled and give you instructions."

"Yes, my Lord," the valet answered dutifully. "Do you have a note for Lord Breakerton or have you already spoken to him?"

"I have not spoken with him. Please, mention to him I was called away and that I will let him know when I am settled and my business is concluded."

"Yes, my Lord," he said, bowed, and left the doorway.

Devon bent to retrieve his bag. He made his way out the side door of the manor and down the long lawn to the stable where he had instructed Eric to ready his horse. He was not surprised when Clive met him, leaning on a post as he entered the barn.

"You're good, but not that good," he commented.

"Drinking this early is not a good sign for a man who lives alone in the hills of Scotland," was all Devon answered as he went to ready his horse since Clive had dismissed Eric, he assumed.

"You know, I think I liked you better with no humor. The dark brooding Lord." Clive pushed himself away from the post and walked to pet the horse's muzzle. "Oh, but wait, if you survive your suicide mission to kill two insane farmers, you will go back to London alone and return to your father's legacy of being the embittered dark brooding Lord, so I guess there is hope for the status quo after all. That is, if you survive."

"You can shut up at any time, you know. How do you know I am not just leaving on some urgent business and will be back in a fortnight?" He looked at Clive and didn't need him to answer. He moved around him getting the saddle and hefted it up onto the horse. "You know, you seem very smug for a man hiding from your father's ghost yourself. Are you here for the solitude or because no one here speaks of how perfect your father was, and that you have large shoes to fill?"

Devon was satisfied in a cruel way to see emotion fill his friend's face, then go back into his easy devil may care smile. "You can't do this alone. You need help. Let me help."

"No."

"Why?" He moved from the muzzle of the horse to standing in front of Devon making him look at him.

"Because," Devon sighed, "she needs someone to look after her. I need to know you are here to watch over her. She trusts you because for some reason, she doesn't fear you like she does me."

Clive laughed and shook his head. "Why is it, my sisters love throwing lovers together? It is truly more work than it is worth." He turned and walked back to his post. "Are you as ignorant, or is it just the state? She trusts me and doesn't fear me because she isn't in love with me." The implication hung in the air. Oh, how Devon wanted to believe it, but right now with her words a sharp knife in his back, it wasn't possible.

"Just promise me you will protect her. I will ride out and spend the night at an inn I passed when I first came. I plan to strike at night only after I have had the opportunity to make a plan. I will attempt to send word when the deed is done." He swung up onto his mount and reached down for his friend's hand.

Only after a moment, Clive reached up and grabbed him at the elbow in a strong embrace. "I understand. I don't agree, but I understand. I will protect her, you have my word."

"Thank you." And with that, left the barn to give Ella her independence. It was independence from her worries of money, her worries of her past and her blackmailers, and potentially from him.

CHAPTER 14

"**D**amn, Damn, Damn!"

"Pardon, my Lady?" The valet asked Ella as he stood stoically in the doorway of her room after delivering Devon's letter.

"Oh, sorry. It wasn't of any import. Thank you. Um, will you be seeing His Lordship soon?"

"I am not sure, my Lady. He has instructed we are to remain here until he sends word. I am sure he will not be gone long."

Ella asked trying to keep the emotion at bay. She had never read words any more romantic, or unworthy in her life. After the way she had treated, Devon she did not deserve the words on the velum. Once he found out the truth about her birth, he would recant every declaration anyway, so it was of no consequence. At least that was what she needed to tell herself in order to make her escape, because if she thought it would be different, it would be impossible to leave. She had gambled her heart and once again lost.

"Of course, I am sure he won't." Ella answered distractedly as she made her way to the desk, moving the thick letter she had just penned to Devon to the back of the secretary. She took up the smaller letter to Clive, the rich velum, feeling smooth between her fingers.

Once she dispatched this letter, there would be no turning back. She had thought it fitting that she once again found herself running from the only man she loved, but it was not to be. The pen clinked the side of the inkbottle as she readied it. It was more fitting she decided that he be the one to leave her. She had all but told him to leave.

Actually, Ella thought with a pang of remorse, she had done exactly that. It was better this way. She would be spared the pain of seeing disgust in his eyes once he found out she was a bastard child, and Maddie would not suffer for her misfortune. She decided to ask Clive to return only the money he wanted to give her. She would not contest the generous dowry for Maddie. She deserved a chance at life. As for the bakery, she would need to leave word with Penny who the beneficiary was that paid to fix the oven. It felt good to know she would still be able to leave Penny with the bakery. Clearing her mind, she put the now dry tip back into the well and then scratched out a quick note to Clive. With luck, by the time he read it, she would be on her way.

Devon settled in to watch the dilapidated farm where Ella's uncles resided. He wasn't sure how much money these men had extorted from his wife, but they by no means spent any to improve their living conditions. The sun was still an hour or two from setting and his hideout was in an optimum position. The Inn was surprisingly close so it took no time to throw his bag on the bed in his rented room and be off again.

There was no movement around the farm. The ill looking horse from the woods stood with his head bent close to what appeared a lean to for the poor beast. Not a man of great patience, Devon ground his teeth. Sitting back against a tree, he began plotting his route around the farm. He had a feeling he would be waiting quite a while.

When Clive made his way back to the library, he was in quite a temper. How the devil could he sit by knowing his best friend might very well be walking into his own death? He had promised to look after Ella and Maddie's welfare. To his mind, the best way to do that would be to make sure Devon was unharmed. Slumping into a chair, he sighed deeply. He was sure love wasn't supposed to be so painful for the onlookers.

A polite cough pulled him from his dark thoughts, "What is it? Devon has stepped out," he commented to Devon's valet.

"Yes, my Lord. I am aware of that. I assume you have spoken with him. He left instructions for me to give his apologies for leaving so unexpectedly."

"No need, my good man. Your esteemed employer dismissed himself. Thank you." Clive dearly wanted to get back to his pouting, and he was about to hit his stride.

"My Lord, there was something else." The valet crossed to his chair. Clive looked down at the envelope the valet extended from his hand. This could not be good news. Clive plucked the offending velum from the servant's hand. If there was a God, he was the humorous sort. He read, anticipating its contents. With a disgusted sound, Clive rose from his chair. His pout would have to wait.

"Thank you. I'll take care of this. Do you know where Lady Ella is?" He asked as he made his way to his desk to pen his own note to Eric. He would have to put Eric on his staff after this farce was cleared up.

"She instructed me to wait an hour before giving it to you. I would not claim to know where she may be, my Lord," he stated. "However, I got the impression she would be leaving the manor today."

"Thank you," Clive said in a tight voice, as he rushed from the room. "Those two bloody well deserve each other. That is clear, and if they can't see it, for my own well-being I will inform them of it as soon as I throw them out of my home on their ears," he grumbled out loud, not caring the gardeners were staring as he stalked to the stable to ready his horse and send a messenger to find Eric.

♥♥♥

The bakery was silent when Ella and Maddie parked the gig in the backyard. Every possible opening stood wide to rid the putrid air within. The kitchen was dark with only the light from the two doorways, but the damage was easy to spot. Ella swallowed a lump in her throat. She wasn't sure if it was brought on by the devastation to her kitchen, or because this would be her last memory of her home. Giving herself a mental shake, she turned to get Maddie to work.

"Come, darling, we are going on a trip. Shall we collect what things we need from upstairs so we might be off?"

"A trip? How fun!" Maddie jumped and clapped her hands together. Her enthusiasm would be contagious if Ella was ready to leave. She fell in behind Maddie as they ascended the stairs and fell further behind making sure to get the knot on her reticule secured to the inside of her skirts. Maddie ran ahead and was well into the center of the room before she made the last step. It was then that she noted the large dark shadow in the corner closest to Maddie. She took a step, but at that moment, a beefy arm came around her waist and held her firm. The greasy voice in her ear sent a cold chill down her spine.

"Ah, dear niece, we've come to aid in yer escape. How fortunate 'tis for us that ye decided to flee like yer cowardly mum. No one'll think te look fer ye until 'tis too late."

She attempted to struggle until she saw the other man grab Maddie and heft her up in his arms. Bile rose and she barely forced it down as she went very still. "Leave the child. This is not about her."

"Oh, but isn't it? She is the last of the line. Last of the heathen offspring of our dear brother's killer she is. It may be more 'bout her than you, deary."

Had Ella not wanted to save her daughter above all else she might have given in to the desire to swoon. These men were going to kill her and Maddie. If it were her last act on this Earth, she would save her daughter. Those were her last thoughts before a sharp pain vibrated from behind her ear and all went black, save for little white stars dancing until those as well were extinguished.

Night had fallen and still no movement within the small dilapidated house. Devon had long since decided its occupants were not there. The question was where were they? If he left to go back to the inn, he might very well miss something, but if he were already too late, then what? He hadn't thought of that. Panic rose quick and hot in his chest. If he were here while they were already acting on their plan, he would never know. He voiced an oath. He had to check on Ella. Just as he began to rise, a noise sent him back into the brush. He watched as Clive rode boldly into the farmyard. His horse shook and pranced hinting at its rider's unease.

"Devon?" Clive called into the woods. He wouldn't be so blatantly obvious if he didn't know something. Dread settled into his bones.

"What happened?" Devon asked making his way out of the woods. "Where is Ella?"

Clive's horse pranced in a circle as Clive strove to bring him about. "She sent a note saying she was leaving the area. I went to try to head her off at the bakery and found this on the worktable. Her gig was hitched to that all but dead beast of hers ready to flee." Devon took the dirty sheet of paper from Clive and read the note.

"It appears they want me to witness the death of my family," Devon bit out coldly.

"I agree. They are going to try to gain some more blunt before they do the deed. Greedy buggers," Clive spat.

"Well, my friend, that will be their demise." He turned and ran to his horse in the wooded area he had been hiding in for so long. Damn it, Ella may not want him, or his help, but she would have to suffer it now, and for the rest of her life. After this, he would never let her out of his sight.

The pain in her head came hard and fast. As did her memory of why. Fear rose by degrees as she tried in vain to open her eyes. She needed to find Maddie. Was her little girl in the room with her? Was she even in a room? The air was thick with mildew and filled with a large rushing sound like a waterfall. Again trying to open her eyes, the sharp pain behind her right ear made her moan. Maybe if she could calm herself, she could press through the pain and be effective.

She lay on the hard pricking surface, obviously hay, slowing her breathing and willing her heart to stop pounding. She had never been so frightened. Many times her father had pushed her or grabbed her arm, and once, soon after her mother died, he had struck her in the face sending her to the ground. Never had he struck her so hard she lost consciousness. Gently, she touched her ear. Her hair was matted and sticky from the thick blood there. She had to find Maddie. Now.

Once able to fight past the shooting pain forcing her eyes to open and take in her surroundings. She was in a room. It was dark with several holes cut in the walls for light. The room was empty save for a few wooden crates and a tall workbench with a stool set to one side. Her neck ached as she stretched to take in the area. As she sat up a wave of nausea took her. That was not a good sign. She sat calming her churning stomach and head. Maddie was not in this room.

Now what? Should she call out to Maddie? If she did, would anyone hear her? The rushing water she heard was coming from the large water wheel outside the building to the right. She must be at a mill. That would explain the pungent earthy smell, but it didn't explain where her daughter was. It would not be very difficult to dispatch a three year old. She would be defenseless against those horrible men. Her heart slammed into her chest with fear. Ella was the only hope her daughter had. No one would think to look for them. She had seen to that. With her letter from Devon and her note to Clive, she had made sure no one would look for her, at least not soon.

She drew her legs to her and noticed her ankles tied together in a loose knot. With slow moves to try to stave off the dizziness, she set to unbinding herself. They had not expected her to gain consciousness. Pulling herself to her knees, she could just see out of the window holes. The view she was afforded was nothing but treetops, which told her she was in the top of the building. Maddie could be anywhere, or nowhere. The bile was swallowed as she made it the rest of the way onto her feet. Another wave of nausea came as the room swayed and dipped in her vision, but she was ready and quelled it. Her ankle throbbed still, but not so much so that she couldn't walk.

Oh, how she wished Devon were here. She knew he would fix things, but he wasn't. She was alone. That is what she had wanted. She had met a man who claimed he wanted her in his life and would care for her. A man who loved his daughter and wanted to be a true father. Ella was yanked from her thoughts by a loud noise outside the door at the other end of the room.

Ella threw herself back down to the floor and the loose bed of straw. Her head spun. She barely covered her now unbound ankles before her uncles entered the room.

"I ken ye're in charge, but 'tis it smart to keep the bairn alive?" The taller one asked following her shorter more dangerous looking uncle into the room. Ella watched the blurry visions through a tiny slit in her eyelids. Her heart soared and her breath caught. Maddie was still alive. She hoped they could not hear her heart pounding.

"Stop naggin' me, ye idiot. Ain't I tryin' to get us what we should've had all along?"

"Well, I ken ye are tryin'--"

"Jus' let me handle things," the short man spat. Ella decided she hadn't missed anything. For the first time, she actually missed her father. He wasn't as loving and caring as she would have liked, but it was better than this. "Me first worry is this lass."

They were standing over her now, looking down at her. Her stomach turned.

"Did ye kill her straight off? I kenned ye was going to wait 'till that fancy gent showed?"

CLAIR BRETT

Stuck frozen, unable to react to his words, they settled around her.

What gent?

Devon?

It had to be. Apparently, if these two could figure out the connection, they hadn't done a bang up job at hiding it. They must be hoping to bargain with Devon for her life. The irony was funny, so much so, Ella had to steel herself not to laugh. There was no way Devon would bargain for her. First, she had left him once and forced him to leave her a second time. Second, he never wanted a wife much less a child. Once Devon found out these were her uncles and where she truly came from, he would more likely thank the heavens for dispatching her so as not to saddle him with the likes of her.

To her chagrin, a single tear escaped and rolled down mixing with the sticky blood surrounding her ear. She was sure Devon would not allow her to be killed, but then would cast her off as any nobleman would do. She loved him and couldn't bear to see it in his eyes. Acting now was imperative.

The men continued arguing over her as to the best way to wake her or to check if she was dead. It was a good chance to see what she could do. From the tight slit in her eyelids, she could just see the men to their waists. The shorter one had a pistol stuffed in his breeches. If she could grab it that would give her one shot. Unfortunately, one shot wouldn't kill two men. The other taller man had a knife in his hand, which meant she would have to wrestle for it. Her chances weren't good, she knew. Her only chance, she decided, was to get the pistol and perhaps try to bargain with them herself. Then she remembered her own lady's pistol in her reticule, if they hadn't taken it from her. She willed herself to feel if the reticule were still sitting at her hip under her skirts. After a bit of concentration, she did feel the pouch and she could feel the heaviness of the pistol. Now, all she had to do was wait for a chance to get to it. It would not be easy or modest because she would have to go up under her skirts for quick access.

Dearly hoping her nausea and dizziness had subsided, she moved

200

with a quickness she didn't know she had. Both men yelped at seeing her spring into action. Her uncle with the knife jumped and she noticed something fly out of his hand and land with a thud in the hay, but it wasn't the knife. She had been able to move, so the shorter man didn't have a chance to defend his weapon. She dove for the pistol that had been thrown from the surprise of her jumping up. The handgrip of the pistol was cold in her palm and heavy. With it steadied on her uncles, she felt a measure of control to see their distress.

"Now, what ye gonna do with that, poppet?" The short uncle asked. "Ye ain't gonna kill us." His voice was filled with taunting.

Ella couldn't take anymore. She got right to the point. "I am sure that is what your brother said to my dear mother before she dispatched him." Understanding dawned on both their faces to her satisfaction. "Now I believe I may be in charge. So, I am asking only once. Where is my daughter?" Walking toward him forcing him back, she pointed the gun at his chest.

"Calm yeself, lass, she's close, tied nice and tight. Me brother here wanted to be done with her, but I had too much compassion for the bairn to allow it." The shorter man began.

"Quiet!" She yelled, not wanting to hear his lies. What should she do next? They wouldn't stand here long allowing her to hold them at gun point. What seemed like an eternity stretched before her. Time slowed. That's when she smelled it. Just a hint at first, but the smoke began to fill her nostrils. Fire. Her uncle had been holding a pipe when she jumped. Where one uncle dropped the pistol the other one threw his lighted pipe.

"Ye can't win. Ye knows it too," again, the shorter man said in his oily tone with an even oilier smile. "Give me the gun." He reached out for her to relinquish her weapon. Only half listening, Ella turned in time to see the room behind her filling with smoke.

The whole wall where the hay had been piled was aflame.

A movement brought her back, in time to see her uncle grab for the weapon. Without thinking, she discharged the weapon. Her uncle realized at the same time as her. She had shot him. Adrenaline surged within her. Not taking chances, she ran for him and shoved. She had backed him up to a window hole. She watched in horror and relief as he disappeared from view.

Turning to see if anything could be done to extinguish the flames, she felt a searing pain in her arm. The knife. In the excitement, she had forgotten her taller uncle and his knife. He was unconcerned about the fire spreading up the wall of the mill, the smoke now filling the air and sending acrid fumes into their lungs.

"Ye killed 'im. Ye killed me brother," he said in astonishment.

"Yes, I did." She could feel the hot blood run down the sleeve of her dress. If she didn't do something soon, she would be too weak to save both herself and Maddie.

Light flooded the clearing as Devon and Clive rode to the mill. The water rushed loudly over the falls and around the large water wheel. The smoke they had spied on the road, rolled from the upper floor. Two of the four walls were fully engulfed. A wagon and horse stood to the left of the building. Devon dismounted and ran to the wagon. In the thin layer of hay, even in the growing darkness, he saw what he feared.

Blood. To make sure, he reached in, rubbing it between his fingers. An absolute panic gripped him coiled with the need for blood himself.

"There doesn't appear to be enough to indicate death," Clive said of the amount of blood they were examining. "It would seem a wound for ease of travel. I am sure your wife didn't go willingly," he added.

"I am aware of that, but what of Maddie?" Devon growled, with frustration. The men began to search the area with urgency.

"Can you see that?" Clive pointed up toward the figures as well. "Is it her?"

"I can't tell." His focus shifted as the single shot rang out. He felt more than heard Ella's name being ripped from his chest.

Both men headed for the double doors of the mill at a dead run. They watched as a body fell from a side window hitting the ground with a thud. It was obvious not to be Ella. The body lay still in the dirt. One uncle. Devon looked up at the window. Nothing.

Wasting no more time, the men rose and headed for the doors. "I'll check the downstairs for Maddie. You go help Ella!" Clive hollered over the din of the fire and rushing water.

Once inside, Devon found the stairs at the far end of the large open room. Smoke now poured from the upper floor making him bend low as he neared the top of the stairs. He would not be able to see anything.

Ella stood stunned. She had killed someone. Her uncle stood waiting for her next move. He wouldn't just let her leave. Fighting her way out was the only option. Before that, she needed information about Maddie.

"Where's my daughter?" She asked with warning in her voice. He held the knife in front of him ready to make another swipe. The fire behind her was spreading and she could feel the almost unbearable heat on her back.

"Ye won't be needing that knowledge. Ye'll be dyin' right here. T'was the plan all along, but we figered to git some blunt before we did," he spat angrily.

"Where is my daughter?" She yelled walking toward him. The smoke now filled the room stinging her eyes. If she didn't move now, she would die in the flames if not by a knife.

As she made another step, she tripped on a crate all but forgotten in her fear. Her momentum thrust her forward, landing with a thud on the floor. She felt her pistol slip from her pocket. Damn. Head swimming, still not cleared from the blow she had suffered, she shook the fog from her brain and rolled to her back in time to see the other man lunge for her. The need to get away filled her, but her legs were entangled in her skirts and had no other option but to brace for the impact. Perhaps he would miss and she would still be able to get Maddie out. Eyes closed tight, she waited for the searing pain, but instead, she heard a grunt. Opening her eyes, Devon knelt over her uncle wresting the knife from his hands. Stunned for only a moment, she watched the two men fight.

"Can you walk?" Devon grunted out while holding the man down.

She shook her head and then answered, "I can." When she realized he couldn't see her.

"Then go! Get out!" He ground out, still struggling with the man.

"No, I won't leave you!" She demanded, surprised he would want to help her much less risk his life after what she had done to him.

"Go, now!" He demanded, just as a beam creaked from above them. She turned seeing the pistol lying on the floor at her feet. She bent to retrieve it.

"Devon," she yelled. When he turned, she slid the pistol on the floor until it hit his boot. Pulling her skirts up as not to trip, she ran from the fire. Tears hotter than the flames covered her face. The stairs were in front of her, somewhere. What if she missed something? What if Maddie were on this level? As she groped her way through the thick smoke, she tried to call for the child.

In the distance, she heard her gun being fired, but she was too far gone with fear to care anymore. With every breath, her lungs felt heavier and burned more. She couldn't leave her daughter. Before she could turn and try to look further for Maddie, she was grabbed from behind and all but dragged to the lower level.

"Maddie? They have her. We need to find her. Please!" Ella begged as fresh air filled her lungs again. "I tried to get them to tell me, but they wouldn't. She may be in the building. We have--"

"She isn't inside," Clive answered from behind her, helping them both away from the flames. "I checked the lower level while Devon went to help you."

Devon came staggering from the engulfed building. When he got to them, he saw the fear on her face. He knew how she felt. They had to find Maddie. He would not let Ella down. He would not let his family down. "We'll find her, I promise," he said as he held her. It was a measure of relief to be holding her to him.

"How? I was unconscious until I woke up in the mill. The last I remember, we were in the bakery."

"They would have brought her with them. They wanted to get money from me, so they would have needed her as well as you," Devon explained.

"We should split up and just start calling for her," Clive suggested. "I'll go toward the road, you go toward the woods."

The three broke up and began calling for the child. With every second, Devon became more filled with fear. He glanced at Ella walking next to him, and his fear came full and wild within him. "You need to sit. You've lost blood and have a head injury."

"No, I need to find Maddie," she demanded, even as she allowed him to turn her back toward the wagon. Clive was in the wagon with the wooden carriage box in the back flung open pulling horse blankets out, but no Maddie. Devon turned more toward the road, then he heard it. Quiet at first, but with more power as he walked closer to the large trees lining the road. Right before his eyes, a very alive and wriggling Maddie appeared, dangling from a tree branch higher up. He could have fallen to the ground with relief. Instead, he moved a log over and was able to lift her restraints off the twig holding her. He felt more than saw Ella stagger for her daughter. He held Ella and she had Maddie in her arms smothering her with kisses as they made their way back to the wagon. The child had been drugged and still seemed to be in and out of consciousness, but calmed in her mother's embrace. With any luck, the drug had prevented her from too much trauma. He was certain, however, that there would be more than one night in the near future where he would be woken in a cold sweat reliving this scene. Ella was sobbing uncontrollably, repeating thank you through the hiccups.

"If I could bring them back to life to kill them again after this, I would," he assured his wife as he tugged them in closer, absorbing the warmth of their living, breathing bodies.

Devon noted Clive sat on the edge of the wagon as white as his cravat. His face said it all. He caught his friend's eyes and without words, expressed his gratitude for everything he had managed to bring back to him.

He pulled his family closer and a calm filled him and roared in his ears. They were safe. He couldn't believe his incredible luck. He knew what it meant not to have this. He would never lose it again. As if to cement the moment, his daughter snuggled in her mother's arms, still very groggy, turned and reached out for Devon to take her, which he did gladly. Once settled, he took the other woman in his life into his embrace as well. If she wanted to remain in Scotland running a bakery, he would gladly live his last days here as long as he could have this forever.

"You came to save me, even after what I accused you of?" Ella said with surprise in her voice.

"It's over. They're dead," he rasped out, his voice hoarse even to his own ears. "You're free. Your blasted uncles will never threaten you again. I told you I would keep you safe."

The look of sadness that washed over her face disquieted him. "You know..." she asked, "you know I am a bastard, and you saved me anyway?"

"You are my Viscountess. That is all that matters. That is all that ever mattered. I just wanted to see you safe," he added, to make sure she understood.

"You knew they were my uncles? What else did you know?"

"I knew you were in trouble from the day I arrived. I found out you were being blackmailed and threatened. With help from Clive, I was able to find out the tragedy that led your father to marry your mother. And— "he brushed his thumb along her chin and up her cheek, "I knew I loved you and would not let you leave as easily as you might have liked."

At his declaration, he felt her go still. Tears glistened in her eyes, threatened and overflowed down her cheek. "Why?"

"Why do I love you?" He asked. She nodded.

"I love you because you challenge me. You make me reconsider those things I thought I understood. I love you because you want to be independent, but you still need to be taken care of. Most of all, I love you because from the moment you appeared on my foyer floor like a rain soaked fairy, I couldn't get you out of my mind." He bent and took her lips to his. The acrid taste of smoke was not even a deterrent to Devon. The feel of her very warm, very alive, supple lips was amazing. He broke contact and studied her face in the gleam of the burning building.

"I was hoping for a declaration in kind, wife," he said bringing her back to the moment, and she smiled a big white smile against the black soot surrounding her face.

"Yes, I love you. I have loved you for four years. I just didn't want to stay with you because you felt a duty to do so. I never thought you could love me."

"Darling, I mourned you once, and it was enough for even a bloody fool like myself to realize when I was given another chance with you, I would need to do it right. It is a duty, love, but it will be a labor of love. I promise you."

Devon only just noticed the flurry of movement with shouts and the sound of horse beats. Clive came to them with a carriage blanket and led them to a carriage that had arrived with Eric in the lead. Devon lifted his daughter and placed her in her mother's lap.

"Go back to the manor and rest. I need to stay and help sort out this mess." When she would have made to argue, Devon showed her a staying hand. "Flick and LePrin will be beside themselves with worry, as will Penny. There is no need for Maddie to remain here and she will want to be with her mother. I said I intended to take care of you and that includes cleaning up unsightly messes."

He only calmed a margin when he saw her acquiesce, sitting back against the squabs. "Go have a hot bath, and have that arm tended. When I get back, we will talk."

"What will we talk of?" She asked quietly.

"We will discuss where we shall be residing, London or Scotland."

"How will this work, what will the Ton—" He put a staying finger on her mouth.

"Darling, is it going to be a daily occurrence that I have to remind you, you will never have to do anything alone again?" He was given a huge smile as his prize.

"I'm not alone, am I?" She asked.

"Never," he said as he stepped down and hailed Eric to be on his way. The sooner he cleaned up this mess, the sooner he would be home with his family. She would never be alone, but neither would he. They would be together in love. Scotland wasn't that bad after all.

HEIRESS BY MIDNIGHT-BOOK 2

EXCERPT

July 12, 1817

"It's about bloody time," grumbled Clive Edward Colcord, Lord of Breakerton. He had traveled the length of the Milton Road looking for a highwayman that he was beginning to think did not exist. Not that he had anything better to do, but he had begun to consider the men who implored him to find the highwayman threatening the area had done so on a lark. His spirits rose knowing he had not been taken for a fool. He could hear the waves beating against the shore, signaling how close he was to the sea. His blood was still boiling from the two gunshots sending his team careening along the moonlit road. It was only just that Clive managed to get a grasp on his walking stick cum saber, but his pistol had been misplaced within the carriage somewhere.

"Step free of the vehicle. I shan't ask again," he heard the impatient braggart demand. Considering the hours Clive was forced to ride the Milton tonight looking for this criminal, he could wait.

The moon still shone brightly, but his foe was crafty and remained in the shadows while the cool briny wind from the ocean stung his face. "Good evening. Wonderfully bright evening, is it not?" Clive quizzed in his usual jovial manner. The reports of this fiend were woefully vacant of tales of violence. He decided to be at his leisure until the situation called for doing otherwise. He was satisfied when his foe stepped further into the shadows. "How might I be of assistance?"

"I am in need of but two things, and as luck would have it, you can assist me with both," the inky figure answered back in an unusual raspy tone sending Clive's nerves on edge.

"I am at your service." Clive started toward the voice in hopes of better seeing the person who was speaking.

"Stop!" The shadow ordered. "That will be far enough. What I need is for you to leave your coin purse on that rock to your right, and then regain your carriage, instruct your driver to turn around and go back from whence you came."

"If you are playing at being a highwayman, might I ask why you did not instruct me to stand and deliver? I am not accustomed to such employment, but was under the impression it was a requirement of your profession," Clive taunted with humor clear in his voice. His would-be assailant seemed to be taken aback momentarily.

"You, sir, seem to have read your share of penny novels. I would have thought them below your station and gender for that matter."

Clive quite liked a quick wit and it seemed even in these circumstances, he could appreciate it. "Well played, lad," he commended with a bow of his head. "It is quite refreshing to meet one who is so industrious and forward thinking in their craft. I am afraid I will be unable to acquiesce, however." He turned to see what he already knew he would. Paul, his driver, had been instructed to make haste in hiding out of sight. He might like the diversion of hunting dastardly deed doers, but it was no reason to put his people in danger. "As you can see, I am afraid my driver fled. I do believe he is unaccustomed to having someone shoot at him. Not to mention, I quite like where my coin purse is and would rather keep it on my person. Also, I have business ahead on this road, not behind." The din of the waves drowned out the usual night sounds, making this encounter seem even more intimate than he would have thought.

Strange, that.

A stunned silence filled the expanse between them except for the sound of the sea and the wisps of salt air mussing his locks. In the silence, he heard the clean sound of a sword leaving its sheath. Clive, never wanting to be left out, did the same, but continued his attempt at conversation. "Shall I bid you farewell then?" He prodded.

"I am afraid you may not," the voice answered with a deadly tinge to the huskiness. The shadow advanced with a slow stride. One had to be impressed by such confidence, Clive decided. The moon glinted off the highly polished steel. "I will ask only once more. Leave your change purse, then turn tail and take your arse to whence you came."

"I don't believe my arse is any of your concern, but thank you," Clive answered. He was enjoying himself quite a bit, which easily waylaid his annoyance from earlier. If nothing else, this highwayman appeared above the pale where intelligence was concerned. "Did you bring that sword for show or were you planning to use it?" He heckled.

Before he could ready himself for the answer, he was forced to jump out of the way, as the blade hummed past his ear. Along with the humming sound, came the smell of--jasmine? He managed to rally and block the next blow with his own sword making his arm tingle from the reverberation of the swords coming to blows. They volleyed back and forth for several moments.

This highwayman had been trained with the blade. Of that, Clive was sure. He himself had studied at Angelo's Fencing Academy. He felt a pang of homesickness for London, and all his chums that spent time at the prestigious academy. However, he doubted any of them would believe he was at this moment fencing for something more than a free pint. Again, the smell of jasmine skittered across his nose filling his senses. That, mixed with the brine of the ocean was a sensual mix. Clive shook his head. When had he gotten so depraved that a sword fight became sexually arousing? As he again blocked and parried, he decided he needed to seek out a mistress as soon as he returned home. Either that or call for one of his sisters to come and sign him into Bedlam. When a man began getting sexually aroused during a sword fight--well, let us just say it conjures up all sorts of complications, not to mention many safety hazards. He made a lunge toward his opponent, just missing the braggart's shoulder.

That was when he saw it. At first, he thought, along with his nostrils, his eyes were beginning to falter, but then the moonlight caught and trailed down a distinctly feminine lock of black, curly hair. It lay along the shoulder Clive almost ran through only moments before, trailing along her arm.

A woman.

The damned highwayman was a woman. It all clicked into place. The smell of jasmine, his physical reaction, and the lack of information the other victims, all men, were willing to give.

Unfortunately, his concentration was broken just enough and his jasmine scented thief lunged and made contact. Pain shot down his arm to his fingers, almost forcing him to drop his blade. The litany of expletives was enough to make him blush, but in the shadows, he could see a satisfied cat-like smirk on his opponent. The only woman as of late who could make his loins react was also the one person who could best him in a sword fight. This was not boding well for him in the least.

"I hope you realize my tailor will be less than impressed. This happens to be an original," he said through gritted teeth. The truth was that she had managed to slice him in the meaty upper arm muscle. He could already feel the hot blood covering his left arm, and it hurt like hell.

"I am willing to consider this a warning. Now, toss over your change purse please, then leave, go back and tell your friends not to come this way unless they care to have a similar fate."

She stood silently waiting. He did his best to remain upright as the pain worsened. He was still digesting the fact she was a woman. Angelo would be so disappointed. He eyed her for the tick of a second hand on a watch.

"I would love to do as you have so convincingly asked. However, I am unable to now reach in my waistcoat to procure said item. I am afraid if you truly want my money you will have to gain it yourself. It's on the right side." Clive added to the effect by popping out his right hip. How much did she want his money and how bold was she?

She was out of the darkness enough for him to see her open her mouth then close it again. He could just imagine how lush her lips were. He saw in her eyes the moment she decided to have a go. She took a moment to pull her neckerchief around her nose to hide her appearance and that beautifully full mouth, and then she advanced. He stood still, not attempting a bit of assistance. Not very gentlemanly, but she had just delivered quite a nasty cut to his arm. When she finally wrenched the purse free, Clive's libido reacted and he was grinning despite the pain in his arm. She looked for only a fleeting moment at him. Her eyes were a deep color. The moon was not bright enough to make out the hue, however.

Quickly, she stood back. "Thank you, sir, for your generosity," she said with a flare Clive appreciated.

He inclined his head. "No, thank you. I have never been robbed by one with such a gentle touch. You may have ruined me for my current affair."

She gaped at him for only a moment, and then she was gone. Just like that. In the darkness, he could hear rustling, and then hoof beats leaving the scene. He scanned the darkness for only a moment until Phillip came to the rescue.

"He got ye, my lord! I could see it from where I was! Are ye gonna die on me?" He heard Phillip ask as he ran to assist.

"No, I am afraid you will be stuck with me for a while longer." He chose not to enlighten Phillip on his newfound knowledge. His arm, however, needed some tending. "I would ask that we find our way home post haste."

"Of course, Milord. Jus' hold on."

Once in the carriage, Clive wrapped his cravat around the throbbing under his coat. She did an admirable job, damn it. He tied a knot to secure his expensive makeshift bandage. Adrenaline surged through him, as he could still smell jasmine. He closed his eyes and still heard her voice. Her voice, a raspy, husky, sultry tremor, should have given away her gender. He laid his head against the squabs. When he left for this little assignment, he was intrigued, but now, he was exhilarated. This would prove to be diverting after all.

"Hold on, Milord, we're almost there!" Clive heard Phillip shout. He must have called out in pain, but he didn't remember. Closing his eyes, he hoped his driver was true to his word and he would soon be able to exit this insufferable vehicle. Visions of his assailant were no longer easy to conjure over the pain and queasiness played in his mind.

He laid his head back on the squabs as his prison on wheels continued down the road. He stretched his good arm out to the corner of the bench. His hand slid over something smooth and cool. Clive laughed, which caused him to wince as his shoulders shook and jarred his wound. His pistol had been on the bench all the while. The thought of what he could have done sobered him instantly. Had he put his hand on the firearm earlier, he might well have shot and killed a woman. He wouldn't now be in so much pain bleeding on his favorite London-made waistcoat, but this mystery woman would be dead. Even though she did steal from him and all but cut him to shreds, there was something more to this woman. His jasmine scented highway woman. The magistrate might have put him to finding and stopping a dangerous highwayman, but he now finding a damsel in distress took precedence. The question was whether she would even want a champion. At the end of the day, would he have what it took to be one?

"Oi, this will be exhilarating." He closed his eyes giving into the darkness that engulfed his thoughts and his pain.

"I do not need a surgeon," a very harassed Clive complained the next morning as his housekeeper, butler, and valet fussed over him. As soon as he arrived home the prior night, they had clucked and fretted. It hurt like hell, but he knew it was not life threatening once they staunched the flow of blood. Cook had immediately brought water and linen to clean him up. The bleeding had stopped and he was able to examine his injury. It was a long gash running horizontally along his inner arm. Had it been but a scratch, he would have been thankful, but his little minx of a thief cut him deeply. Therefore, every time he moved his arm, it would begin gushing anew.

"Aye, ye do," grumbled Mrs. St. Syer. "If'n ye don't get that stitched up ye'll bleed out afore ye can heal. May I show 'im up?" She bustled around the bed plumping pillows and smoothing wrinkles from the coverlet.

Could he ever become free of meddling women? "Very well." There was nothing to do but suffer the attentions.

More than an hour later, Clive lay in bed waiting for his brandy. The effects of laudanum were not to his liking. He needed to keep his wits about him, and after years of practice, brandy did not seem to fog his mind as much. He had managed to send word to the magistrate that he had some information about the thief. Just what he was going to offer of all he knew he had yet to decide. It went without saying he could not let the secret of her gender be known. If word got out, several might take a try at apprehending her. That would lead to nothing Clive wished to consider. In fact, any of the men who knew of her gender were unwilling to admit they had been bested by one of the more genteel persuasion. If he could make it appear he believed it to be a man, he might very well be able to keep those men quiet--at least for the moment.

The fire crackled, which was a touch Mrs. St. Syer insisted on. She claimed he might catch a chill. As it was now moving into the summer months, he doubted it greatly. His valet managed to open the window next to his bed and pull the drapes when she wasn't looking in hopes to cool the room a trifle. Lying in the center of the large four-poster bed, he wondered why the room couldn't hold this much heat in the dead of winter.

It had taken much of his remaining energy, but once he managed to throw the last of his well-meaning assailants out of his room and nibbed the lock, he was able to tear his way out of his nightshirt and dressing gown. The saving grace, however, were the drapes, which once covered the window were now a puddle on the floor, allowing in the blessed Scottish breeze. The caress of the heather filled the room and kissed his chest. Goosebumps bristled along his skin and his nipples hardened. The brandy had soothed the worst of the pain, but he could still feel each pucker where the surgeon had put a stitch. Exhaustion pulled on his eyelids while visions of beautiful black hair, luminescent dark eyes, and full rich burgundy lips, drew him down into brandy-hazed dreams.

For the time being.

About Clair

Author of 7 Historical romances, including the Improper Wives for Proper Lords series, Clair Brett lives in NH with her ever-emptying nest which includes her children when they visit, two cats, a willful boxer/beagle mix, a "mean" pitbull mix, that will lick your to death and run into her kennel when you speak loudly, and one grand dog who one day just moved in. And an ever-harassed husband who takes it all in stride. A lover of all things Regency, Clair was hooked when she first read Jane Austen. She is a firm believer that a reader finds a piece of who they are or learns something about the world with every book they read. She wants her readers to be empowered and to have a refreshed belief in the goodness of people and the power of love after reading her work.

Contact Clair

Website
Https://www.clairbrett.com
Facebook
http://facebook.com/@AuthorClairBrett
Twitter
http://twitter.com/@clairbrett
Pinterest
Https://www.pinterest.com/clairbrett
Instagram
Https://www.instagram.com/clairbrettauthor/
Patreon
Https://www.patreon.com/clairbrett
Goodreads
Https://www.goodreads.com/clairbrett
Bookbub
Https://www.bookbub.com/authors/clair-brett

Join Clair's Newsletter
Https://www.clairbrett.com/newsletter-sign-up

Also Available From Clair

Improper Wives for Proper Lords Series
Dealing with the Viscount
An Heiress by Midnight
Marked for Love
Courtesan's Wicked Desire

English Roses Series
Visions of Pleasure
Ruination of a Rogue

Stand-alone Novels
Winn's Fall